THE IVIES

ALEXA DONNE

CROWN
NEW YORK

Text copyright © 2021 by Alexa Donne
Jacket art copyright © 2021 by Christine Blackburne

All rights reserved. Published in the United States by Crown Books for Young Readers, an imprint of Random House Children's Books, a division of Penguin Random House LLC, New York.

Crown and the colophon are registered trademarks of Penguin Random House LLC.

Visit us on the Web! GetUnderlined.com

Educators and librarians, for a variety of teaching tools, visit us at RHTeachersLibrarians.com

Library of Congress Cataloging-in-Publication Data
Names: Donne, Alexa, author.
Title: The Ivies / Alexa Donne.
Description: New York: Crown Books for Young Readers, 2021. | Audience: Ages 14+. | Audience: Grades 10–12. | Summary: The Ivies, five prep school elites who would kill to get into the colleges of their dreams.
Identifiers: LCCN 2020050625 (print) | LCCN 2020050626 (ebook) | ISBN 978-0-593-30370-2 (hardcover) | ISBN 978-0-593-30371-9 (library binding) | ISBN 978-0-593-30372-6 (ebook)
Subjects: CYAC: Boarding schools—Fiction. | Schools—Fiction. | College choice—Fiction. | Murder—Fiction.
Classification: LCC PZ7.1.D648 Ivi 2021 (print) | LCC PZ7.1.D648 (ebook) | DDC [Fic]—dc23

The text of this book is set in 12-point Arno.
Interior design by Ken Crossland

Printed in the United States of America
10 9 8 7 6 5 4 3 2 1
First Edition

For my mom. Love you best, always.

PROLOGUE

Everyone knows the Ivies: Brown, Columbia, Cornell, Dartmouth, Harvard, UPenn, Princeton, Yale. This consortium of eight schools is considered the most elite in the United States and, in some cases, the world. The only reason it's called the Ivy League is because, eighty years ago, some journalist coined the phrase to refer to an athletic conference. That's it. All of this because of football. There is a far more complex and nuanced history of the Ivy League, but it's not one that matters. Far more important are *the Ivies.* The Ivies at Claflin Academy, that is.

Five girls with the same mission: to get into the Ivy League by any means necessary. Avery Montfort is the mastermind, the mafia don, the sun to her clique of rotating planets.

She found us, decided we were worthy of her company, and assigned us our own Ivy League school to compete for. Avery is Harvard, I'm Penn, Emma Russo is Brown, Sierra Watson is Yale, and Margot Kim is Princeton. Yes, there are only five of us and eight Ivy League schools, but have you ever tried to have a friend group with that many people? Untenable. Five is pretty messy as it is. Also, Avery isn't fond of Dartmouth.

Our fellow students don't know the calculated way in which

we targeted them and took many of them down, though there are definitely rumors. They know us as the Ivies. They point to us at meals, in the halls, whispering and guessing. But every Ivy mission is planned to have total deniability. It's easy to write off ruthless teenage behavior because hyperelite schools like Claflin are built on ultracompetitive cutthroatedness. There were ruthless students before us—they just weren't as well organized.

Avery makes up the rules and controls the List. We've cataloged our competition, our marks, our fellow students whose success we need to disrupt in order to improve our own chances of securing those coveted entrance spots at each university. There are two per school, maybe three—never four.

We disrupt class ranks, club leaderships, summer internships, academic competitions, and musical auditions. We improve our own odds by slightly decreasing the fortunes of others.

Because hyperelite, competitive college admissions is some serious fucking shit.

I learned that the hard way.

CHAPTER ONE

Today, half the seniors at Claflin Academy will die.

On the inside, that is.

A hundred kids will obsessively refresh their emails and portals so a dancing bulldog, or a tiger, or whatever mascot represents all their hopes and dreams for the future can tell them:

Welcome to Harvard, class of 2025!

Or:

We regret to inform you that we must crush all your hopes and dreams. . . .

Or at least that's what we interpret. It's early decision day, and hearts are going to break.

Then heads will roll.

College admissions is always a heady mix of longing, desperation, and rage. Claflin kids are quick to the rage part. *How dare they reject me?! Don't they know who I am?!*

Me? I am nobody. My mother isn't a senator; my dad isn't a

high-priced corporate lawyer. No one in my family has won a Pulitzer or an Oscar. And I'm certainly no prodigious math or music scholar. Nice SAT word, though, right?

I had to take the test three times, but I finally cracked 1400. I lied about my score, of course, pretending my first try had netted a comfortable 1520, and the other two times were to get a perfect score. The Ivies think I landed a 1550 and called it a day—more than good enough for Penn. My real score is my secret shame.

But at least I know I'm not the only kid at Claflin lying about their application. You can't doctor test scores—colleges get them directly from the testing companies. But everything else?

My peers lie about the stuff that colleges don't bother to check. Like the clubs they founded and are president of, awards and honors won, that sort of thing. Last year a Claflin senior, Chelsea Cunningham, copied another girl's résumé down to the letter. She got away with it because the student she copied was accepted to Dartmouth early decision. So when Chelsea's app showed up, Princeton didn't have two applications from two different girls both claiming to be the president of Model UN, *and* a summer intern for the *Boston Globe* newspaper, *and* the recipient of a Scholastic Gold Key Award for Novel Writing. Sloppiness gives colleges a reason to make phone calls to high school counselors. It's how you get caught.

Or, you know, committing a federal crime. When celebrities and CEOs got caught in that huge college admissions scandal a couple years back, I laughed. The prevailing view at Claflin was restrained relief that none of the academy's parents were indicted. Students here had long ago learned far more subtle, and legal, ways to cheat. Really, money is the ultimate cheat—rich kids get all sorts of advantages in the admissions process, no lawbreaking

4

required. Anyway, Chelsea got into Princeton on her fake credentials, and the world keeps turning. She's lucky she wasn't in our graduating class. The Ivies would have turned Chelsea's ass in and gotten her expelled for good measure. Karma is a bitch.

I guess I'm a bitch, too. It's an unfortunate side effect of being an Ivy.

But the Ivies get results. I look across the table at Margot surreptitiously scrolling through the Princeton clubs and organizations page on her phone. She got in three days ago, early action. The elites start sending their ED—early decision—results the second week of December. It's like blackjack: What day will the decisions for your dream school land? The vast majority drop on December 15, though, so Claflin calls it ED day.

"Because no one eats all day," Avery jokes almost every time someone says it. And today, the words *ED day* are slipping past our lips a lot as we all count down the seconds and minutes to 5:00 p.m. ET, when most schools will pull the trigger. Then tonight we'll let loose at Claflin's infamous ED day party. Accepted or rejected, every senior gets drunk off their face.

"ED day is so much worse than I thought it would be." Emma Russo, aka Brown University, shoves her iPhone into her bag so she can't look anymore. I give her a minute before she pulls it out again.

On cue, Avery makes her tasteless eating disorder joke. Normally, I let her barbs slide, because calling her out isn't worth it. She always turns it back around on me, like a jellyfish: you step on her and she stings. Today, though, I'm practically vibrating from nerves and could use a diversion.

"I fucking hate that joke," I snap, stabbing my fork into a piece of grilled chicken before deliberately chewing and swallowing it. I

5

wait for Avery's eyes to flash cold as she delivers an oblique threat, but instead she throws back her head, blond curls swinging in a perfect arc over her shoulder, and laughs.

"I guess it *is* getting a bit old," she concedes.

"Is that all it takes to get you to back down when you're being a bitch? Wow, Olivia, you have a superpower or something." Emma's tone is spun sugar, but it lands like an anvil on the table, though the tension is hardly new. Usually, Emma's the only one among us with the stones to bite back at Avery. They've known each other since first grade, when they met at a fancy-ass private grade school in Wellesley. They wrestle back and forth for queen bee dominance.

Margot Kim and Sierra Watson—Princeton and Yale, respectively—are looking anywhere but at Emma or Avery, refusing to wade into this conflict. I catch Sierra's eye briefly, and we exchange a knowing glance. This has to be about Tyler, Emma's boyfriend and Avery's stepbrother of a year. He's supposed to be off-limits to the Ivies—*Don't shit where you eat,* Aves said, cruder than her WASPy exterior hinted. But Emma started going out with Tyler anyway, and Avery takes every chance she gets to jab the knife under Emma's rib cage and simply . . . wriggle it around. Having a weakness is dangerous where Avery Montfort is concerned.

The confrontation fizzles as we all dive back into our phones. We've fallen into what might be termed companionable silence, though we all know it's more of a détente. I scan the room, taking in my fellow students who are assigned to lunch slot B. It was Sierra's job to ensure that all the Ivies got a class schedule that put us in the same lunch period. That's her hook.

In a school of elites, Avery has a way of attracting the very

6

best to stand by her side. President of the Girls Who Code club, Claflin chapter, Sierra figured out how to hack into the school's administrative system before spring semester freshman year, and it remains her most useful asset as an Ivy. Margot is the school's premier actress, surely Broadway bound; she can charm (i.e., deceive) teachers and students alike. Emma's the social Renaissance woman, in with every conceivable group. As captain of FIRST Robotics, first-chair flute in band, butterfly champion on the swim team, and tech director for the drama club, Emma's got a finger in every pie.

I'm not technologically or socially gifted, but as one of the few scholarship students at Claflin, I offer Avery a bit of social-proofing. How open-minded and gracious of her to hang with me. Although I *am* editor in chief of the *Claflin Ledger*. Well, co-editor. And it's my access as a work-study student in the main office that gave Sierra the edge to hack the scheduling system. I'm just as valuable as anyone else.

I meet eyes with Ethan Kendall, who throws me a wave from four tables over, even though I'm going to see him next period. Hasn't he learned yet that I never acknowledge him outside of journalism class? I can't, because that would mean—

"Olivia Caroline Winters!" Emma scolds me as if she were my mother. Though as my roommate and the neater of the two of us, it's not the first time. "Are you flirting with Canadian Ken?"

This is why I couldn't wave at Ethan even if I wanted to, and the microsmile I let slip was a mistake. I opened myself up as the next social sacrifice, and Emma seized the opportunity. I don't really blame her. Any of us would do the same. No Ivy is exempt from being terrible. These are my best friends, but sometimes I hate them.

"I wasn't flirting," I mumble. "Don't be an asshole." I smack Emma playfully on the shoulder. Unfazed, she merely shrugs and checks her phone again. It sets us all off. We check our phones, too, even though it's only quarter to one and everyone knows that the magic hour is yet to come. Anxiety is contagious.

I steal a glance back at Ethan. His unruly dark hair is an inch too long to be fashionable. Freckles dust his light brown cheeks, his face offset by chunky plastic-framed glasses. He's what defensive suburban moms would call "husky." The opposite of a Ken doll. Emma really is an asshole. But I can't help the way my whole body flushes at the sight of him. He's perfect.

He's also a walking Canadian stereotype, which means he's far too nice for the likes of me. I don't deserve him.

"Hey, babe, budge over." Tyler appears, and Emma does as he says, scooting over in her chair until half her butt hangs off, so he can share her seat. Now, this is the kind of boy who is acceptable for me to be attracted to, according to Ivy standards: tall, with an aquiline nose and chiseled cheekbones, a dimpled smile that can—and does—literally charm the pants off people. Tyler looks like he should be on the CW. If he weren't going to major in engineering at Cornell next year, I'm sure that's precisely where he'd be.

A plate with the largest slice of cake I have ever seen clatters onto the table in front of him, and me, since I'm next to Emma. I can see thin slivers of carrot poking out from the doughy layers, cream cheese frosting standing tall atop it, at least a half inch thick on all sides. My mouth begins to water, but Coach will kill me if I indulge. Even though I'm pretty sure the cream cheese frosting counts as protein, and that's what matters, right?

"That looks like half a cake," Sierra says, licking her lips. She can't have any, either. We're on the crew team together.

"Susan gave me an extra-large slice. A congratulations gift." He grins.

Most of the stations at the dining hall are self-serve, but not dessert. Once upon a time, it was, too, but last year a boy walked out with an entire pie. Dining employees started staffing the station shortly after that.

Avery glares at her newly minted stepbrother, and her nostrils flare. "Does Cornell know they accepted a total douchebag? You don't see Margot rubbing it in."

Margot nearly drops her phone. I know for a fact that she almost wore her Princeton hoodie today, but Sierra talked her out of it.

"Don't hate me because I'm stress-free until April." Tyler flashes Avery a shit-eating grin, then spears a giant forkful of cake into his mouth. "And you should chill, sis. You'll be out of your misery in a few hours. Mommy's legacy is going to get you into Harvard."

"Like your daddy's money got you into Cornell?" Avery simpers.

I see Tyler's jaw flex hard, his eyes suddenly flint. I'll never stop marveling at rich kids getting upset about other people calling them rich. They're so sensitive.

"So, what happens if you lot don't get in?" He points a finger at all of us still in school limbo—everyone except for Margot, basically. "Do we have to change your nicknames? Brown." He nudges Emma. "Yale." Indicates Sierra. "Penn." Pushes his slice of cake toward me. "And brilliant Harvard." He grins across at Avery. "What are your safety schools again?"

"Fuck you, Ty," Aves spits.

"The nicknames are stupid," Margot says. "I might not even go to Princeton."

"What?" Avery is horrified. "Of course you're going to Princeton! You got in!"

"It's not binding." Margot squirms, staring intently at the table. "I might apply to a few more places regular decision. See where I get in."

I try to imagine feeling so nonchalant about getting into my dream school. Harvard. My dream school is *Harvard*, not Penn.

My mom always told me: no one hands anything to a kid from a working-class neighborhood in Maryland. You have to scratch and fight your way to the top, prove you deserve a shot. She was the first in her family to go to college, ended up teaching at a really good school. She got her feet onto the first rung of the ladder so that I could climb. *Dream big, Olivia,* my mom always said. *Keep one foot on the ground, though: dreams are useless without a practical plan of action.*

So here I am at Claflin. If I'm going to prove I am worthy of the top, that means gunning for it. And Harvard is synonymous with the best. It also has, hands down, one of the most highly regarded college newspapers. *Claflin Ledger,* then *Harvard Crimson,* then the *New York Times.* That's what I want. Penn is fine, but have *you* heard of Penn's student paper? I didn't think so. *Harvard Crimson* or bust. It is my best shot at my dream career.

But soon after I transferred to Claflin and fell in with my friends, I learned about Avery's rule and the school quotas. One school per girl. Because friends don't compete with each other for spots. Heck, Avery was so intense about it that none of us have the same academic strengths, hobbies, or interests. Sierra and I are an exception, both being "allowed" to row.

Why all this Machiavellian meddling? Because it's an unspoken rule that every college has a quota. Not official, and no one can say precisely what it is. But we do know what it *isn't.* Harvard isn't going to accept four seniors from Claflin. It's never taken more than three. Yale typically takes two. Princeton, two. And so on. Every student at your school becomes your direct competition, even your friends. So I *wanted* to go to Harvard, but Avery was having none of it. Avery's school is Harvard, and she is a legacy, so I shut up about how it's been my dream school since I was eight.

Deep down, I know why. I'm a coward. I want my friends to like me. Because it's better to have these friends than none.

My first week at Claflin, I was unmoored. Transferring in as a sophomore, already sure social suicide, was bad enough, but I was a scholarship kid to boot. I sat in the back of Honors European History with my head down, willing myself to blend in, maybe disappear, and hoped the teacher wouldn't make me stand up to introduce myself. But before that horror could begin, a girl sitting diagonally in front of me sniggered. "Is it true you have to work in the office as part of your scholarship? How sad."

"Hey, Nora, stop being such a twatwaffle." A vision appeared like a knight in shining armor. Glossy red hair, perfect skin, and designer clothes, she took the seat next to me and extended a hand. "I'm Emma. I like your top. Is that from Brandy Melville? And Doc Martens? Sweet."

It was. And they were. I'd worked all summer shilling popcorn at my local AMC to pay for my Claflin wardrobe. This pair of boots was the most expensive thing I had ever bought, and using my own money was the only way to get what I needed to fit in. My mom thought knockoffs and remainders from T.J. Maxx were fine, but I knew this place was full of sharks. One wrong move and you were chum. I nodded, words of thanks stuck in my throat.

"So, you transferred in from public school, I heard? That's cool. You'll have to tell us all about it at lunch."

And that was how I joined the Ivies. That simple. So I put up with all the rules and social hierarchy—of which I am at the bottom—because I'm flattered by their attention, because I don't want to be tossed out on my ass, and because being their friend has its benefits, starting with helping me get to the top of the academic pecking order. My life at Claflin has inevitably been easier, better, because of the company I keep. The Ivies opened a door, and I stepped through it. So I am Penn.

But the secret quota rules don't start and end with students deferring to each other, which few outside the Ivies do. The school itself enforces who can and can't apply—or at least who gets a real shot at the hyperelites. Enter the superpowered college counselor.

Claflin has seven of them, a ridiculous number given the size of the student body, and we're "randomly" assigned to a counselor in junior year. Everyone knows that if you aren't assigned to Karen "Ivy Whisperer" Bankhead, your chances are automatically halved. Ms. Bankhead has been in the industry nearly thirty years and has all the top elites on lock—a recommendation letter from her is as good as an acceptance. She controls most of the spots at the Ivies, as well as the rest of the T20s (top twenty ranked colleges, according to *U.S. News & World Report*'s list). It is pure coincidence that the richest and most connected Claflin students "randomly" get Bankhead, of course. Avery, Margot, and Sierra got her.

Emma and I were stuck with a new guy, Tipton. Twenty-four, bro-y, and far too gullible, he came to Claflin this year after working at some private school in Georgia. He didn't know the elite-school rules. He didn't know it was his job to limit who applied where.

Which is how I was able to apply single-choice early action to Harvard.

I check my phone. It's 12:55. In approximately four hours, I'll find out whether Avery Montfort is going to kill me.

CHAPTER TWO

I turtle into my fluffy down coat and make my way across the quad to my next class as a crisp wind slams against me. Claflin's campus is stupidly picturesque, with red-bricked Georgian buildings dotting leafy green paths, though in blustery mid-December the trees are brown and bare. I watch my feet shuffle over the gravel path edged with short, strawlike grass, and I nearly plow into a tour group smack-dab in the middle of the quad. Rebecca Ito, super student and Ivy competition ranked fourth behind Avery, Sierra, and Emma, is delivering the Claflin spiel to the throng of eager well-to-dos and their shivering offspring.

"Claflin keeps student numbers low so each student may benefit from the maximum individualized attention and resources. There are only four hundred and forty students across grades nine through twelve, with an average student-to-teacher ratio of eleven to one. Every classroom is outfitted with state-of-the-art technology, and the school focuses on conversation-based learning. Claflin students thrive, inside and outside the classroom. And an impressive average of twenty-seven percent of our senior class is admitted into the Ivy League."

I stop short with a frown and walk around the group, grass

crunching beneath my boots. A couple sporting a Birkin bag and a Rolex between them raise their brows at the Ivies statistic, and the woman thumbs through the Claflin admissions brochure with interest. It's strange to see my friends' model grins staring back at me from the cover. A statistic I don't hear Rebecca parroting to the parents: while only 17 percent of the student body are students of color, notably 60 percent of the students featured on the school website and in the brochures fall under the umbrella of diversity. So Sierra, who is Black, and Margot, a Korean American, get to play cover girls.

That's Claflin Academy in a nutshell: private, elite, and bleeding bullshit from every red-bricked building. Not that I'm not happy to take advantage of the school's desire to appear generous. I attend Claflin on an almost-full-ride scholarship, thanks to my skills at rowing and lower-middle-class "sob story." My mother is an elementary school teacher, which is apparently tragic. Single mom, too. I am shrouded in scandal. Anyway, I look great on paper for the school, and even better at the national championships.

I check my phone one more time before ducking into journalism class, in case the Harvard admissions office has decided to cap off lunch by pulling the trigger. It hasn't.

And for good measure, I tap on the camera and switch to selfie mode. The stubborn cowlick at the back of my head is a lost cause, but the rest of my dark blond beachy waves are on point. I don't bother with more than mascara and blush most days, funneling all my focus into my alarming collection of lip glosses. Today I'm wearing an Anastasia Beverly Hills gloss I couldn't really afford, but when Avery gasped and told me the peachy shimmer was perfect on me, I had to buy it. There is no greater peer pressure than that experienced when shopping with your friends at a Sephora. I expect an angry call from my mom in a few weeks when she sees the credit card charge. She won't care that I chose the least among evils—the relatively cheap lip gloss over the Becca highlighter and Fenty foundation the girls were pressuring me to buy.

I'm the last one inside, about a minute past the bell. The journalism teacher, Ms. Vasquez, looks up from her computer screen, one brow carefully arched, and lets me go without any consequence. She knows it's ED day. We're all distracted.

I scoot past the U-shaped desk in the middle of the room, where six of the staff reporters type away on their laptops, and make my way to the back corner where the Beasts live. The beautiful, hulking desktop towers, each with their own twin thirty-two-inch monitors on their own desk. I pass behind Ethan, who is clacking away on his keyboard, the *Ledger* website back end pulled up on the left-hand screen, his newspaper email on the right.

"Hi, Ethan," I say as I pull back my chair. I aggressively jiggle the mouse for my computer to bring it awake. The InDesign layout for the December special edition pops up on my right-hand screen. Ethan and I are co-editors in chief—he handles the online edition, while I handle the print one. It should have all been mine—the *Ledger* never split editor in chief duties before. But during coronavirus quarantine, when all of Claflin was sent home to complete the semester online, Ethan jumped in to beef up and innovate the digital edition, impressing Ms. Vasquez. So while the outgoing editor in chief normally chooses their replacement, this time around Vasquez thought it only fair to reward Ethan for his digital savvy.

On the one hand, I prefer the print edition. On the other . . . it burns that I have to share the title on my applications.

Still, I enjoy the work. I know the print edition is antiquated and not at all helpful for most future job prospects, but I love creating the layouts on the screen, dragging and dropping heds, decks, pull quotes, and images to create the perfect reading experience. The website content management system is so soulless, comparatively. And you can't hold the finished product in your hand. I keep every issue I've produced in a box underneath my bed, and when I put together my clips for my portfolio, they look so much more professional with the newsprint and the byline right by the headline and subhead copy. Ethan likes to tease me about being a journalistic grandma.

Now he swivels his chair around to face me. "You look like you swallowed a frog, so I'm guessing the decisions aren't out yet?"

"There'd be screaming in the hallways right now if the rest of the Ivies had dropped," I reply as I check the editor's in-box.

I steal a glance at him to see if he's looking at me, but naturally he's not. This is a one-sided crush, I remind myself. Ethan is as unfailingly polite as befits his Canadian pedigree, and even though our competition for editor in chief got pretty ugly— and ultimately led to our split duties—he treats me as his peer. But I know to him I'm nothing but a psychotically competitive boarding-school bitch. He transferred to Claflin in junior year, by which time my reputation as an Ivy preceded me. We make small talk, but he's never bothered to ask me about my background, what I really think of this place, my friends. Why would he? I'm cordial in class and don't acknowledge him at all outside it.

But I can't help wanting him to *want* to know me. He's one of the few people who aren't entangled in Claflin's high-stakes elite college admissions game. He's told me a million times that Canadian universities only require grades and test scores. He's free of the kind of bullshit that infects most of this place. It's refreshing.

"What are you working on?" I initiate the small talk this time.

"Waiting on the same stuff as you, probably," he says. "Bella's review of the new drama club show, Brent's holiday movie wrap-up, and the ED list."

I pull up the spread I have reserved for the early-decision college results for the senior class. **Congratulations, Class of 2021!** the left-hand page reads. The right side is blank, with a three-column box faintly outlined in pink, waiting for me to copy and paste in the final list. Typically, the *Ledger* comes out on the fifteenth of every month, but we always hold the December issue until right before the winter break so we can print a list of the schools everyone got into early.

I drag the layout onto my left-hand screen, which is angled so as not to afford Ethan a complete view. I type carefully.

Harvard, Olivia Winters. My eyes scrape over each letter; I whisper the words, feeling them on my tongue. God, I need this, and I'm dreading it. If I get in and Avery finds out I applied behind her back, she will literally kill me.

"Didn't you apply to Penn?"

I jump a good foot in the air. Twist around to find Ethan leaning over to peer at the screen. I jab aggressively at the backspace key.

"I was just—" I start to hedge, but then Nisha Khan begins screaming.

"I GOT INTO MOTHERFUCKING NORTHWESTERN!"

"Nisha, language!" Ms. Vasquez snaps. Then she breaks into a wide grin. "But congratulations! That's amazing."

We all chime in, congratulating Nisha on the good news. Northwestern is one of the best journalism schools in the country. My stomach turns over, and I feel my lunch inch up my esophagus. It's starting.

This was a mistake. I should have applied early decision to Penn, the way I was supposed to. It's an incredible school, with this independent Writers House thing that would be absolutely perfect for me for journalism. I've been communicating with the recruiter there, like a good girl, and I probably would have gotten in.

But Penn's early-decision program is binding, and Avery and the other Ivies don't understand how stressful it is for me, not knowing if I can afford a school that has a binding admissions decision. Harvard's single-choice early action offers me an out— I don't have to decide right away. If I get in, I can still apply to other schools regular decision and then pick the one with the best financial aid package in April.

Every time money comes up, I can't stand the patronizing side glances, my friends' clueless reassurances that I'll be fine because schools just love to throw money at people like me. It's a ridiculous myth that elite schools are full of the deserving poor on full rides. No, most students who matriculate are pretty damn wealthy. Financially needy students like me basically have to survive an application cage match for a shot at one of a few coveted full-ride spots. Heck, I'd be happy with full tuition; I can take loans for room and board. Why else have I been playing the Ivies' game all these years? To survive.

Sierra and Emma might understand. They're rich, but not

"my parents have their own jet" rich (something both Margot and Avery can boast). Margot wouldn't care, but she'd tell Avery, who would blow a gasket. So I didn't tell any of the Ivies I applied.

"Olivia, are you okay?"

I feel Ethan's warm, broad hand on my shoulder and look up into concerned hazel eyes behind those chunky plastic frames. They make him look like Harry Potter, and I find it so damn attractive.

He's snapped me out of my spiral, and I manage a bright, if false, smile. "Definitely. Nisha's gonna get shit-faced tonight at the ED day party. Will you be there?"

"Well, yeah. It's in my dorm, remember?"

I ignore the heat in my cheeks. "Right! So, when do Canadian university decisions drop? You probably think we're all insane."

"Only a little unhinged." His laugh could melt snow and cause blooms to sprout. "And sometime in early spring. I'm not worried about it."

"Lucky," I say as we get back to work, or at least pretend to. No one's on task today.

Nisha goes out into the hallway to call her parents, and we can hear her screaming and crying for the next ten minutes. When she returns to her open laptop, I see her close a Word doc and go to College Confidential, where she stays for the rest of class. Because I am a glutton for punishment, I do the same, opening two tabs in my browser: one the Harvard SCEA thread on College Confidential, the other the Harvard Applicant Portal. I spend the next thirty minutes refreshing both every three minutes or so, like a normal person.

*　*　*

A spate of LACs—aka liberal arts colleges—drop their decisions during sixth period, which for me is AP Calculus, a class I'm taking even though I despise math and it's my most challenging subject. Can't be seen to have not taken the most challenging classes available to me, though. Sierra's in this one with me, thank god, because she helps me with my work so I don't have to suffer the shame of hiring a tutor. Not that I could afford one, anyway.

I'm trudging through a problem set when Colby, Hamilton, and Williams drop. We have an ecstatic Purple Cow (tragically, yes, that's the Williams mascot) in our class, I get a group text from Margot about a Colby kid in AP Bio, and then Avery replies about a Hamilton in Drama (naturally). So far we're only hearing about acceptances. Guess the kids who aren't getting in aren't crowing too loudly.

Then, with two minutes until the bell is supposed to ring, we hear the hiss of a litany of "shits" from Jason Wang in the front row. Oh well. Premed at WashU is very competitive. Maybe he's lucky and got deferred. The bell rings, and so does his phone. Apparently, his parents were refreshing College Confidential religiously, too. I feel bad for him.

As I hurry from AP Calc to my final and favorite class of the day, AP Brit Lit, the mood in the halls has shifted. Now I can see the rejections as plain as day on so many faces. Eden Hannon's mascara is streaked across her cheeks, and her watermelon lipstick is smudged. I know she applied ED to Northwestern, so she's been rocking the look for over an hour.

Chris Hardin stops me just outside Brit Lit. "Hey, Olivia, have you seen Emma?"

"Uh, no, why?" He smells of weed, so we know how *he's* dealing with the pressures of ED day.

Chris chuckles and says, "I owe her a big thank-you, is all. Catch you later."

I don't want to know what the glint in his eyes means. Are they hooking up? No, Emma wouldn't go for a loser bro like Hardin. Probably buying weed off him or something.

Chris isn't watching where he's going, and his shoulder smacks hard into Seth Feldstein, who merely scowls and keeps going. His jaw is set so tight, I can practically hear his teeth grinding as he passes. That means MIT is out.

Fuck, when are the Ivies dropping? We're expecting Yale and Harvard today, at least. It's like someone's inserted screws underneath my rib cage and is slowly drilling them tighter, tighter. My breath comes in short pants, though maybe it's the rushing through the halls. I drop into my seat at the back of the class, next to Avery, who only had to walk one room over to get here. She's cool as a cucumber. Avery's mom is the heir to a massive pharmaceutical fortune, a triple Harvard legacy, and a devoted donor. I'm fairly certain there's a wing named after the Montforts somewhere on campus.

Thomas Hardy does his best to distract me, and it's the slow-building rage against all men ever that manages to keep my attention for a solid thirty-five-minute stretch. Angel Clare is a dick. And Hardy really liked trees.

My phone is resting on my thigh. I've been compulsively fingering the power button, willing myself not to press it, to illuminate the screen and angle it so I can see it. Finally, I give in. And I see the *M*-emblazoned envelope at the very top of the home screen. I have an email.

I suck in a breath. Steal a glance over at Avery, also looking at her phone. Shit. They send out decisions in waves. I know this.

Acceptances first. Then deferrals. Finally rejections. How long has Avery been looking at her phone? Am I wait-listed or rejected?

"Olivia, what do you think Hardy is trying to say in contrasting Angel and Alec?"

Ms. Kaylor calls on me—her revenge, I'm sure, for looking at my phone. Screw the rules on a day like this! We're all on our phones. But lucky for me, I didn't have to pay attention to answer this one.

"All men let you down, both the obvious devils and the angels in disguise," I say. "Alec is the devil, a rapist, but Angel is almost worse. He promises to love Tess and then betrays her at the first opportunity, because of some purity nonsense. Angel is a coward and a hypocrite."

"Whoa, whoa, *rapist*? Isn't that a bit much?" Tyler twists around in his seat. "It's ambiguous in the text."

"I didn't find it ambiguous at all," I huff. "It was pretty obvious to me."

"What is it, Ty? See a bit of yourself in Alec?" Avery jumps in. She may be a viper, but I like when she spits venom on my behalf.

"Fuck you, Aves."

"Hey!" Ms. Kaylor snaps. "That is unacceptable!" If it were any other pair of students, I'm sure she'd send them to Head-mistress Fitzgerald's office. But the Montforts and St. Clairs mean big money. Instead, she asks Eden to explain the importance of nature motifs in the text. With her attention drawn elsewhere, I go back to my phone. Slip my finger to the phone's underside, press my fingertip to the scanner, and swipe up on the save screen, then down on my notifications bar. The email is from Harvard. Shit.

There's a text from Sierra, too. The preview shows a row of fire emojis.

I decide to check on her. I'd rather prolong the inevitable. Avery's barb at Tyler's expense was the bravado of someone who just got in. I was a fool to think I could ever compete. My email can only contain a deferral or an outright rejection. I need a minute to prepare myself to smile and give Avery a big hug, congratulating her inevitable reign of superiority. She can never know I applied. I tap into the group text.

> 🔥🔥🔥🔥🔥I GOT INTO YALE, BITCHES!!!!

Then Sierra sends a row of dog emojis—Yale's mascot is a comely bulldog. A wave of genuine happiness for her blossoms in my chest. Sierra single-handedly organized the Claflin trip to the Women's March and campaigned for Elizabeth Warren. Plus, she's smart as shit and has worked her ass off, Ivies or no.

Avery squeaks next to me, and Tyler starts to laugh—silently but very clearly at his stepsister's expense. Avery's cheeks are mottled red, and her nostrils flare. For a second, I think it's belated anger at Tyler for his clapback, but then I see the glint of tears in her eyes.

"Aves, what's wrong?" I ask, leaning into the aisle, careful to keep my voice low so Ms. Kaylor doesn't hear.

"They *rejected me*," she hisses. "Those bastards."

Avery. Got rejected. From Harvard.

My stomach plummets as time seems to slow. Whatever Ms. Kaylor is saying now is muffled in my ears. The Queen of Claflin, with valedictorian on lock, *triple legacy*, didn't get in. I'm definitely fucked.

I reach across to touch her arm. "Avery, I'm so sor—" She

doesn't let me finish, jerking away from my fingers. As if Avery is made of stone, cold runs through me.

"I'm fine." She wills her eyes to dry, tosses back her shoulders and her stupidly perfect curls, affecting a flawless, icy demeanor.

The bell rings shrilly, classes done for the day. Avery bolts from her seat. I move slowly, as if through water, practicing breathing exercises I picked up in a yoga class Margot dragged me to last year. Dread is a lead weight in my stomach, my heart is pounding, and I fear I might be sick. I've spent all day in spiraling misery, but that was nothing compared to this. That was anxious waiting, but this is certainty: Avery and I got our emails at the same time. Or maybe I got mine a bit before she did? That means mine is a deferral or a rejection. It is there, in my in-box, right now.

Anxiety pushes at my limbs, and I move quickly toward the school exit. Don't want to keep still. I burst out into the crisp December air and savor the way my blood vessels constrict. Sensory distraction. It's cold, the campus a mix of browns, reds, and grays; we've had one dusting so far this year, but we're still in the stretch where your nose is nipped but nothing as pretty as snow deigns to fall.

Tears prick at my eyes. I haven't even read the rejection and I'm already a mess. I can't bear to open the email while I'm exposed in the quad, and I'm due in the admin office, anyway, for my work-study shift. It's a favor they throw at all the scholarship kids, an after-school job that earns us spending money to cover extras, like Cougar Points for the convenience store, and school trips. I can't miss my shift. I need every penny.

My phone is still in my pocket when I arrive at Austen Hall, breathless, waving at Cathy, the administrative assistant who mostly looks the other way while I use my job time to study. She's a good egg, but at the moment she's casting a tight smile at the pair from the parent tour I ran into earlier.

"I hope I answered all your questions! Have a wonderful day! Bye!"

Birkin bag and Rolex turn to leave, though I can tell they had more questions. Probably about how their precious angel will handle things like remembering to do their homework and laundry. *Laundry service for freshmen comes on Mondays,* I have memorized, and it flows off the tongue so easily. *I'm sure they'll have no trouble managing their own academics,* less so, when what I want to say is, *They'll figure it the fuck out—they're fifteen, not five!* I duck my head as they pass so they can't rope me into a Q and A. Cathy's shoulders decline a good two inches as she greets me.

"Thank goodness you're here. We're already receiving the calls, and Headmistress Fitzgerald has locked herself in her office, not to be disturbed, as usual."

I shrug out of my cold-weather gear and dump my backpack next to the spare desk where I sit. I know the drill after two years of ED days at Claflin. The irate calls from entitled helicopter parents roll in right after the early decisions.

Even without college rejections at hand, the parents routinely call to shout, *I PAY SIXTY-FIVE THOUSAND DOLLARS A YEAR FOR THIS SCHOOL!* through the phone line when they are displeased. I have heard those exact words more than once. I'm often tempted to thank the apoplectic parents profusely for their tuition—their generosity helps in part to pay mine.

But I would never dare be so glib. Not today. The phone rings, shredding already-delicate nerves, and I jump into action. *Yes, we understand you are upset; no, you cannot speak to the headmistress at this time.* Kill them with kindness but remain firm. Promise to take down their details and Headmistress Fitzgerald will give them top priority as soon as possible. With each call, as I try to coax them off the line so I can gain a reprieve, I stare at my phone, lying facedown on the desk in front of me. I had to turn it over so I would stop fingering the power button and compulsively swiping at the email subject line. I missed what Mrs. Feldstein was yelling at me more than once and had to ask her to repeat herself, only making her more upset.

The calls come fast and thick for almost an hour, until finally there's a break. Guess those moms are giving their lawyers a call about suing Claflin, as promised. In the lull, I finally grab my phone. I spy Cathy, still consoling someone in her soft, grandmotherly way. She's a pro at talking people down. When she's not paying attention to me, I slip into the faculty lounge and shut the door.

I tap into Gmail. It's bold and screaming at me, the email from Harvard. I try not to look at the preview text; a part of me still wants to put this off as long as possible. I've already waited this long, right? But my traitorous eyes flick across the screen.

I don't understand the words I see. They make no sense. I read them again.

It is our pleasure to inform you . . .

Holy shit, I got in.

CHAPTER THREE

My first thought is that there must be some mistake. They emailed me instead of Avery. Girls like Avery get in. Girls like me . . .

We scheme to apply behind our friend's back and then we steal her spot.

And immediately the happiness pricking at my insides sours, and I come crashing to the ground. What have I done? How is this even possible?

You have the fifth-highest GPA in your class, two Gold Circle Awards from Columbia Scholastic Press Association. You write for High School Insider at the Los Angeles Times *and attended the Medill-Northwestern Journalism Institute summer program,* I remind myself. I am worthy. More than good enough.

But I didn't really believe it until this moment.

The phone rings, and I scurry back to my desk. The voice on the other end freezes my blood.

"Transfer me to Headmistress Fitzgerald. Now."

Katherine Montfort. Avery's mother. I picture her on the other end of the line, a frosty blonde with a look that could curdle milk.

My Harvard acceptance sticks in my throat. Can she sense it

through the phone? That she should be reaching through the receiver and strangling me?

"Hello?"

"Yes, hi, s-sorry, I—I can't," I stammer. "The headmistress isn't here."

"You sniveling liar, I know she is. Don't you know who I am? I pay sixty-five thousand . . ."

The rest is as expected. The school is a fraud, a failure; she'll report Claflin to the authorities, etc. I hold her off as best I can, marveling that she still hasn't recognized my voice.

I cut her off in the middle of a comment about underrepresented minorities. "Ms. Montfort, the headmistress will call you back as soon as possible. Have a lovely afternoon."

"Hope you've planned your funeral." A Starbucks cup plunks down in front of me. I look up to see my angel of caffeine. Sierra. "Hanging up on Avery's mom is a bold move. She's sued people for less." Sierra perches on the edge of the desk, sipping her drink.

"She said some underqualified minority probably took Avery's spot at Harvard."

"Okay, burn her."

We laugh, as much as one can laugh about pointed racism, and cheers with our coffees. Then Sierra's expression turns grim.

"There are plenty of Katherine Montforts here, and I don't just mean the adults. All the kids at this school think I'm on easy street because I'm Black. Like affirmative action in college admissions isn't there because of centuries of systemic racism and inequities, especially in education and opportunity. Ignorance is easier, though."

"Sierra, no way, we don't—"

She cuts me off. "It's exhausting. 'My precious genius baby

29

didn't get in so it must be affirmative action,' they cry, like I'm not on track to graduate salutatorian with a perfect SAT score and a ton of other shit. Maybe their kids are just mediocre. Or unlucky. Assholes."

Sierra doesn't invite further commentary, so I follow her lead and stay silent. We both drown ourselves in caffeine for a minute.

"What brings you here?" I ask once I've come up for air. "Not that I'm not happy for the company, or the coffee, but usually it's Em who's on office-friend duty."

"I know." Sierra jiggles her knee. "Avery . . . is losing her shit about Harvard. And now her spring semester schedule isn't going to work, so I'm here to fix it. She'll need to demonstrate better class rigor for regular decisions. May I?"

First, I check that Cathy's back is turned so she doesn't see, and then I push back from my desk and vacate my chair for Sierra. She gets to work, fingers flying over the keys as she coaxes the administrative software to do her bidding. Sierra cracked the security years ago and installed a back door for herself on my machine—the easiest way not to get caught—and so it takes only two minutes to switch Avery from Photography II to History of Capitalism, an econ elective. She has to bump Jason Wang out of the class and into another one to make it work, but that's a problem for later.

"Now that's done, and if you don't mind, I'd like to kill some time with you." She drinks more coffee. "I was glad for the errand, to be honest. I couldn't be around her anymore. Every time I smiled, she screamed at me for gloating like a bitch."

Her Yale acceptance comes back to me. I totally blanked on it.

"Oh, dammit, Sierra, I'm sorry." I jump up, give her a hug.

"You deserve to celebrate your own good news. I know it's bad for Aves, but like . . . Yale! This is what you worked for!"

"Thanks." She sighs. "I'm sure you'll get good news from Penn. I heard they're dropping tomorrow." I must make a face, a dead giveaway, because Sierra narrows her eyes, tilts her head. "Liv?"

It pushes up my throat like hot lava, burns my tongue. I'm desperate to tell someone. Sierra and I are teammates. Surely she'll have my back. "I got into Harvard. By accident. Kind of."

I get a parody of a reaction; Sierra's eyes go wide, and an expletive flies from her mouth as she loses her balance and falls off the desk. "How do you *accidentally* apply to Harvard?"

"It was a mistake, I mean. Not the application. I didn't think I'd get in. . . ."

"Well, you goddamn did, didn't you? Fuck." Sierra rubs the bridge of her nose, shakes her head. "You *cannot* tell Avery. Not today. She's already off the rails."

"Is it that bad?" I ask, though I already know the answer.

Sierra throws me a look communicating her distaste. "God, and now I'm in the middle, too. I wish you hadn't told me."

That lights the spark of annoyance in me. "Oh, I'm so sorry for telling you, my *friend*, my good news."

Sierra softens. "I'm sorry. It's just . . . Avery will crack me like an egg."

"You mean *Margot* will crack you like an egg and then tell Avery," I offer. Every dictator has her spymaster. Margot has an uncanny ability to root out secrets. "You're a better actress than I am, anyway. I'm the bigger risk."

Sierra doesn't disagree with me. "We need time to practice. You can say you were deferred at Penn and then apply RD to cover your ass. I'll pretend we never had this conversation. By April, no one will be the wiser."

I let it sink in for a moment that she's essentially saying I cannot go to Harvard, period. Defiance curls in my gut, but then I push it down, like always. That can't be what she means. A friend would never expect me to give up on my dream for, what? Avery's pride? Before I can ask for clarification, my phone screeches, dances across the desk surface. Sierra's chimes from her bag. We both have the same text from Avery:

> Emergency strategy session, my room, NOW!

"I think we're out of time," I say, swallowing thickly. When Avery calls the Ivies to assembly, we don't keep her waiting.

We meet in Avery's dorm room. She has a single, of course, the best money can buy, and she also has a state-of-the-art projection system so we can watch movies—or whatever else—on a giant screen. Avery's room is boarding-school-catalog perfect: lavender Kate Spade carnation comforter piled high with a gaggle of decorative pillows, whimsical vinyl wall decals, a cascade of fairy-light picture clips, and even custom royal-purple curtains. Plus, a Harvard pennant next to a poster of Lexa from *The 100*, Avery's sole basic-bitch piece of décor. We got it at Hot Topic sophomore year. The faculty in residence ignore the contraband espresso maker atop the dresser, as well as the wine fridge in the closet. All Ivies group hangs happen here, the nicest room on the floor.

When Sierra and I arrive, the lights are down and the List is projected onto the wall across from Avery's bed. Margot controls the laptop, creating a new subsection of the Google Docs spread-sheet under the headline **Regular Decision.**

"Good, you're here," Avery greets us. "Have a seat."

We do, on a love seat Avery brought with her to "fill out the room." Margot is in the desk chair, which is springy and ergonomic, not Claflin issue, and Avery takes the bed as we wait for our final member, Emma.

My eyes scan the top part of the List. There are twelve names of our marks—I mean, classmates—whose GPAs, class ranks, clubs and leadership positions, test scores, and finally ED application plans we've meticulously tracked. A few we targeted specifically, a bit of manipulation here and there to increase our own odds. Not a lot, in the grand scheme of things, but enough.

My own name jumps out at me from the **Ivy assigned** column, and my stomach turns, though I remind myself that nothing we've done is *that* bad. Avery always knows what tiny ripples will create the biggest waves, pushing us to the top. I asked her once where she came up with her ideas, and she answered darkly, "Big Pharma is a fascinating business."

Between my office access and Sierra's computer skills, we ensured that the Ivies always got the best teachers and spots in coveted AP classes. I planted a story or two in the *Ledger,* while Margot stirred the rumor mill as needed. Avery "accidentally" passed on incorrect notes when someone missed class for being sick, while Sierra and I were always good for innocently remarking to an RA that we'd seen Rebecca Ito or Diana Klein sneaking in just shy of 5:00 a.m., indicating an off-limits overnight in the boys' dorm. With enough demerits for illegal fraternization, students were docked club hours. Miss too many and there went your president title or lead role in the musical. Crafty stuff.

I never minded when we exposed a plagiarist or cheater, and we were always careful to send in our most charming members, Margot and Emma, to merely plant the idea of suspicion in the teachers' minds so that it never traced back to us. And once, in our coup de grâce, we set off the fire alarm in Whitley the night before a big chemistry exam to give Avery and Margot an edge over, well, all the senior boys.

None of it was good, exactly, but nothing was too terrible, either. It got me into Harvard, after all, didn't it?

Not that I'm telling Avery that.

Emma breezes in five minutes late with kiss-swollen lips that announce precisely the reason for her tardiness. Avery shoots her a Look, then checks that Margot is ready to go as Emma shimmies her tiny body between Sierra and me on the love seat. Margot poises her fingers over the keyboard, ready to type. And we jump right in.

"We have two jobs." Avery holds up two fingers, paces the floor in front of us. "One, find out who took my spot at Harvard. I want to know who got in."

My stomach somersaults, and Sierra darts a glance my way. Lucky for me, Emma starts coughing loudly, drawing Avery's attention. "Do you need a cough drop?"

Emma shakes her head, now clearing her throat gently.

"What happens to the person, or people, who got in?" I ask, fighting to keep the tremor out of my voice.

Avery scoffs, my question beneath her. My mind conjures up all manner of worst-case scenarios, from Avery pulling a Tonya Harding to slipping Nair into someone's shampoo. Once she swapped a girl's fifty-dollar foundation for a nine-dollar bottle of CoverGirl just because the girl bragged about scoring higher on a test than

Avery. She's someone who favors raw, unmitigated revenge. Unconsciously I touch my hair, smooth it down against my skull.

"Two, I need a regular-decision school list," Avery keeps going. "Then we're going to find out who else is left for RD round, and we develop our new List. Mostly for me, but this goes for anyone else who doesn't get in ED."

I swear to god, Avery looks to me for a microsecond. Fire licks at my insides. I have half a mind to tell her, *I got in, you smug bitch,* but no. I have to swallow my pride and let Avery and everyone else believe that I've been deferred at Penn. But I can't play that fiction until tomorrow.

"Ugh, I thought we were done with this shit," Sierra groans. "Can't we enjoy things for once? It's only a few weeks until apps are due, and there's not much we can do. We should leave it."

"That's easy for you to say, since you're going to Yale." Avery throws her a glare. But I notice the way Aves is playing with her fingernails, something she does when she's feeling nervous. Or hurt. This is what we do for each other, the basis of our friendship. Sabotage. If Sierra isn't interested, how does she fit with us?

She doesn't need us anymore. My gut pangs as I contemplate whether our friendship could really mean that little to her.

"Obviously, we'll help." Emma cuts through the tension, as she is wont to do. "You tell us your school list, and we'll figure out who to target. We'll do what we can."

"Yes, Aves. You know we will." Margot opens a new tab and labels it **Avery RD Schools.**

I nod, because this is how I fit. By going along.

Sierra huffs, shoulders slumping in surrender. Of course she won't abandon us now. We're not supposed to question the lasting quality of our friendships until much closer to graduation.

"We'll use the ED day party tonight to gather intel." Avery assesses the group. "The question is how to divide and conquer. Some of you need to figure out who got into Harvard. The others suss out who didn't get in ED and will be throwing themselves into the RD cycle. Get top-choice schools if you can, obviously. Then we can strategize on how to knock back anyone applying to my top schools." Avery scrunches her nose, unsure. There is no plan for how to sabotage the competition this late in the game. We stopped most of our work months ago. Almost everything is locked in by first semester senior year.

My hand shoots up. "I'll ask around about Harvard."

"Me too," Sierra volunteers, just a shade of panic in her voice. She whacks me on the thigh when the others aren't watching. We share a look. *Why have I done this to her?* Volunteering was an impulse, but my logic is sound. Avery can't find out about me if I'm the one telling her about . . . me. Or not. I'll find out who the other one or two people are and throw them under the bus. Easy.

"Good. Then Emma, Margot, and I will compile a list of RD competitors." Avery worries her lip. "For now, let's look out in particular for anyone applying to Yale, Penn, Columbia, Wellesley, and Georgetown."

Margot adds each school to Avery's list in the Google Doc. Sierra and I keep mum about Avery applying to "our" schools regular decision. All bets are off now that Harvard has rejected her. I'm one to talk, anyway.

Not much else needs to be said. Avery has spoken, and we all know the drill. We'll do our reconnaissance at the party, feeding any critical updates into the Google Doc via our phones. It won't be our first intelligence-gathering mission. The CIA should call us. But then, we probably wouldn't pass the lie-detector test.

CHAPTER FOUR

We skip dinner in the dining hall, using the time to get ready. The ED day party is a Claflin institution. After a week of ED results, you drink either to celebrate the school you got into—or to obliterate the sting of rejection. There's also pizza. Sierra sends me a series of texts in the interim. All skull-and-bones and dagger emojis. She's still pissed that I've dragged her into my ruse. Fair. The other person I can't keep this from? My mother.

"Harvard?" She shrieks on the line, nearly puncturing my eardrums. "Olivia, that is incredible! How much are they giving you?" Right down to brass tacks. That's my mom.

"They gapped me by about fifteen thousand," I say. The less-than-silver lining to my dream school acceptance. The Ivies may not get it, but my mom does. She lets out a deep sigh. I concentrate on Emma's *Marie Antoinette* movie poster across the room, let it distract me from my mom's disappointment.

"Sixty thousand is a lot to take in loans. Have you put any more thought into the University of Maryland?"

I want to scream at her, *I got into Harvard! Who cares that I didn't apply to UMD?* But I don't, because I know she's right. This launches us into an hour-long talk about regular-decision strategy

37

and merit aid. She reminds me for the thousandth time that the University of Maryland is a great school, and did I remember to apply by the priority aid deadline? I tell her yes, even though it's a lie. Some things I just can't tell my mom. I want her to be proud of me.

Emma bursts into our room, eyes wild, and when she sees me on the phone, she makes a slashing motion across her neck. I take the hint and wrap things up with my mom. I cross the room to my closet to get out the mint-green A-line dress that will make my eyes pop, when Emma cries out dramatically, "I can't take it anymore!"

I round on her and find that she's thrown herself backward onto her bed, like a tragic princess. "What?"

"I got into Harvard!"

I blink slowly. Shake my head as if to clear it. Because I must have misheard.

"I'm sorry, what?"

"Harvard . . . I got in." Emma bites her lip. "I know you're in charge of finding out who took Avery's spot. It was me. I can't take the guilt anymore. Had to tell you. You'd figure it out eventually."

"But you're Brown," I say. "You applied to Brown."

She shrugs, guilt seeming to have evaporated. "Avery decided on Brown, based on something I told her when I was eleven. Like everyone wasn't a bit in love with Emma Watson, right? And it's not even the best school for STEM, and you know how into FIRST Robotics I've gotten. It's the linchpin of my application. So I changed my mind, and Joe didn't seem to think it was a big deal. . . ."

"Joe?"

Emma hops up, heads over to her dresser to touch up her curls. "Mr. Tipton. College counselor? It's his job to control who applies, so I figured Avery was number one, and I was number two...."

"You know that Rebecca Ito was number two. Which makes *you* number three."

And me four. So, if Emma got in, and so did I . . . does that mean Rebecca did, too? Could I tell Avery that it was Rebecca and Emma who caused her rejection, saving myself? It was reasonable to assume Harvard had accepted only two students this year ED, but not only one. If Rebecca didn't get in, Avery would find me out—

"Liv? Hello?"

I snap back to attention. "I don't know what to do," I say honestly.

"What do you mean? I'm telling you the truth now so you don't have to spend all night looking for, well, me. And I'll tell Avery. We're both big girls. She'll deal."

Emma crosses over to her closet and starts to thumb through dress options. She selects an azure-blue wrap dress and pairs it with a bright red sweater. That's Emma: seems sweet, but then she punches you in the face. I wish I had her confidence.

But confidence can also mean stupidity.

"You can't tell her." I find her eye in the mirror, make sure she sees how serious I am. "Lie and say you got deferred from Brown. She doesn't have to know. Yet. We'll figure something out."

"What, you'll lie about who got in? That's dumb. She'll find out eventually. Anyway, friends shouldn't lie to each other." She purses her lips, concentrating on tugging on a curl so it spirals gracefully down her shoulder. "Not directly, anyway. Lying by omission is one thing. . . ."

"That's what I mean. We just . . . don't tell her for now."

But Emma shakes her head. "No, it's better to rip the bandage off. I'll tell her at the party, so Avery can get drunk, put on her big-girl pants, deal, and move on. We can cry it out or some shit."

It amazes me that Emma thinks Avery is going to cry anything out with her. This can only lead to carnage. But the most horrible part of me is glad Emma is willing to come clean, so I don't have to. My number one goal at the party will be to confirm another Harvard acceptance to assuage Avery. My own version of lying by omission. The safe kind of lying.

I realize I've just done the same with Emma. She spilled her terrible secret, and I kept mine. Now to maintain the charade with Avery, for the rest of my life. . . .

Emma and I arrive perfectly fashionably late to the ED day party at Whitley Hall. It's 8:15 and music is throbbing through the double-paned windows. I know there will be a keg inside, plus a smorgasbord of liquor, even some wine for the classier among us. I am rarely classy. The administration, namely the faculty in residence and our RAs, look the other way on ED day, which is how the boys are able to hold such a barn burner on campus, on a Tuesday night no less.

On the outside, Whitley Hall is stately vintage 1850s, but inside it's renovated. Everything works like new, particularly the heating and plumbing, essential at a school with such entitled students. Whitley is the most popular upper-level dormitory for boys. It boasts suite-style living on the upper floors and a spacious lounge and chef's kitchen on the ground level, perfect for debauchery. We find a towering stack of pizza boxes on the generous kitchen island. I search through five boxes until I root out the pepperoni and help myself to two slices. Always start a party with a good cheese base.

Emma locates the drinks station immediately and pours us each a vodka cranberry. Coach will raise hell if she finds out I've broken the dry-season promise, but it's ED day. I will, at least, leave the party early to get to bed on time. The price of rowing is you become a de facto early riser. Conditioning starts at 6:00 a.m. sharp.

"Hey, aren't there usually five of you?" A boy wearing a sky-blue polo and self-satisfied smirk materializes in front of us. He grabs a red cup and depresses the keg handle.

"Screw you, Chase."

"Wow, Olivia, bad news today?" he clucks. "I was joking. If you want to find the rest of the Mean Girls, they're in the lounge."

"And where are you going next year?" Emma chimes in, perfectly on mission. I already forgot I need to ask Rebecca Ito about Harvard. I stare at my vodka cranberry accusingly.

Chase, who I expected to squirm, grins at us instead. "Don't worry, I'm not in your way. Was deferred at Duke, and now I can apply to Notre Dame, too. Not your kind of schools."

Emma shoots him a middle finger and he sidles off, ogling Sierra along the way. She shouts after him to "fuck off," then skips to my side and slips her arm under mine.

"Hey, teammate." Sierra's voice is now perfectly sweet. "Ready to make the rounds?"

"Already?" Emma groans. "I need to find Margot, then."

"Calm your tits, Em, I'm here." Margot swans in from the

lounge. She deposits her Solo cup on the drinks table and reaches for Malibu and Diet Coke for a refill. Margot is the kind of girl who wears thousand-dollar suede boots out in the snow, sniffs when they get ruined, and simply buys another pair. Luxury items are disposable to her, like tissues. Yet at a party? She goes full-on wasted sorority girl with a single drink. Already her cheeks are flushed a bright red.

"Let's go get this done quickly." Margot smooths a hand over her immaculate French braid, grabs her drink, and leads Emma away.

"That girl is on the hunt." Sierra moves in to refill her own drink. I notice her dutifully pour only Sprite. The back of my neck burns with shame. "Watch out, Milo. Speaking of, you ready for Rebecca?"

"I guess so."

Rebecca Ito has been a thorn in the Ivies' side for years. She was our fiercest competition for valedictorian and salutatorian until first semester junior year, when a bad breakup sent her reeling and she fucked up both her AP Chem final and AP US History paper. She's lucky Milo McNamara is a dick. He saved her from further suffering the Ivies' wrath. Avery was satisfied to see Rebecca's class rank fall several spots, and I had secured enough demerits for her sneaking out for hookups that it cost her a Model UN spot last year.

She's not our biggest fan.

"You should circle anyone else you think might have applied." I say, shooing Sierra off.

"You mean, like *you*?"

I shoot her a look. "Let's just get this done."

Sierra drops the attitude. She can only rib me for so long. "Yeah, fine. I'll talk to some people. After all, if you were able to go rogue and apply, other people probably were, too. I thought that new college counselor was a dumbass. Not from our world."

Our world. It warms my insides momentarily that Sierra includes me. Sometimes she's the only one who makes me feel like I belong.

"Let's go out there for thirty minutes, then forget about Avery's stupid assignment and have fun, yeah?" Sierra snaps me out of my musings.

"You leaving early?" Like I have to ask. Sierra is more dedicated to rowing than I am. Unlike me, she's recruitable. Yale sent her likely letter ages ago, and sure enough, today she got in. Though I had great promise when Claflin scouted me, I never got good enough for top colleges to recruit me. I'm just glad Claflin hasn't booted me for being such a disappointment. Despite being average, I love the water.

"Ten-thirty?" We agree on the time to leave and then make our way into the main throng of the party to find our quarries.

The kitchen abuts the lounge, which runs the length of eight towering windows and wraps around a grand staircase. The ceiling is vaulted and high, a real boon to a party packed with fifty seniors and an obnoxiously loud sound system. The staircase leads up to the second-floor landing, which affords a full view—and earful—of the lounge below.

They've dragged the study tables to the sides of the room and pushed all the overstuffed leather chairs and two couches into a cluster in the middle of the room. At the far end, a group is playing *Mario Kart* on a seventy-inch screen affixed to the wall. That's where I find Rebecca. And, much to my surprise, Margot. Even more shocking: Margot is kicking ass at Rainbow Road.

I join the crowd, hovering at the back of the couch, waiting for their turn to end. When it does, Margot swaps places with Nisha Khan so she can take her turn, then jumps into a lively conversation with Jason Wang. Avery confirmed he was rejected ED (Washington University in St. Louis), so Margot will be sussing out his RD plans. Rebecca taps in Diana Klein, and I take the opportunity to pounce.

"Hey, Rebecca. Good game."

She narrows her eyes at me. "What do you want, Olivia?"

I concede, offering a pathetic grimace. Behind me, Diana screams at Nisha, who just launched a shell at her. "Can we, um . . . ?" I direct her over to the windows, away from the Mario madness of the couch. But once we are reasonably ensconced in the corner, my mind goes blank. I don't know how to start.

Hey, how did ED go for you?

Did you get good news today?

Did you get into Harvard, or not?

Luckily, Rebecca does the job for me. "Avery sent you over here to ask me about Harvard, I'm guessing? You want to know if your sabotage paid off?"

"Uh—uh," I stammer, and Rebecca rolls her eyes and huffs.

"I could never prove it, but we all know you guys are rotten. Milo was a low blow. But please reassure your queen that I didn't even apply to Harvard. Changed my mind about attending school with her. I got into Stanford today."

"Oh! Congratulations." I mean it, because *Stanford* and also because she's legit smart and talented. Game respects game. But

44

Rebecca's news is a sharp pinprick to my balloon as well. I am back at square one. Rebecca catches my crestfallen expression.

"She didn't get in," she hisses through her teeth. "You're trying to find out who did. Oh, shit, that is hilarious." Rebecca straight-up giggles. "I don't know who else applied, sorry. What about you?"

"What?" My whole body washes cold.

"Where did you apply?"

It's a normal question. She doesn't know. I smile and practice my lies. "Penn. I saw speculation on the ApplyingToCollege subreddit that decisions will drop tomorrow."

Rebecca nods politely. "Well, good luck. Hope you didn't have to sleep with anyone to get there." She makes her exit on that zinger, a bridge too far. No, I never had to sleep with someone for the Ivies. We're not *that* bad. Although there *was* Ingrid . . . but I forget about her for now. Sophomore year was a million years ago.

Now alone, I lean against the window frame, surveying the room. Sierra has infiltrated the video-game clique, now talking animatedly with Diana. Across the room, I see Emma batting her eyelashes at Chris Hardin. The RD mission is in full swing. Margot now seems to be in deep conversation with Milo McNamara. Sierra was right. Guess she's got a thing for him. Avery is nowhere to be seen.

I check the Google Doc on my phone. The ED/RD list is getting filled out. For RD, Jason Wang is applying to Carnegie Mellon as his top choice. Eden Hannon to Tulane and Tufts. Seth Feldstein to Cornell and Georgia Tech. Autumn Hollander got into Emory. Avery's added a comment. **Following her ex-girlfriend to college? Pathetic.**

I input Rebecca's Stanford information and check the second sheet. The Harvard tab is empty. I don't even know who to talk to next, so instead I nurse my drink and watch the racing matches until a gurgling suck indicates I'm empty.

Back in the kitchen, I find Avery shoving Fritos into her mouth by the handful.

"Stress eating?" I ask, grabbing a refill. I'm generous with the vodka this time.

"Want to join me?"

She knows I do. This is what Avery and I have the most in common. Self-soothing through food. She has to be in a very bad place to carb load on junk food, though. Usually her version of stress eating is swapping out her light balsamic salad dressing for creamy ranch.

I tuck in with her, grabbing another slice of pizza for good measure. We nosh and sip for a good two minutes. I'm afraid if I speak first, I'll blurt something stupid. Instead, she does.

"Where are you applying RD?" she asks. I bristle.

"Penn decisions aren't out until tomorrow. I might get in."

"I know." I can hear the obvious doubt. *She* didn't get into Harvard, so why would *I* get into Penn, right? "But if you don't?"

"Northwestern. Boston University. Syracuse."

"No Ivies?"

"They'll have filled their spots with ED, don't you think?" It is the cattiest, bitchiest thing I can say, and I know it. I'm mad at her for the Penn dig. "And I'm focusing on a journalism school strategy. The best ones aren't the highest-ranked elites."

"Sure." What Avery really means: *That's what you tell yourself.*

"Rebecca Ito's going to Stanford." I change the subject. Kind of. Shit-talking others' college prospects feels comfortable.

"So she didn't take my spot. Good."

"I can't figure out who else would have applied," I say. Somehow I led myself right here, precisely to where I didn't want to be. "Maybe Sierra will have more luck." I nervously eye Emma across the room. I wish she'd drop the bomb already.

The music changes from a rap song to a country-pop crossover. Avery hops down from the barstool.

"I'm going to dance. You coming?"

"In a minute." I decide to enjoy the rest of my drink first. The sooner I switch to water, the better.

"Hey, Olivia." The familiar voice fills my stomach with butterflies. I turn inelegantly to find Ethan. He reaches past me to grab some chips. "Why are you by yourself?"

"No reason, why?"

"Hey, it wasn't an accusation. Though it is odd to see you without your friends."

I feel a pang of resentment. I am capable of operating alone. "What are you doing here?" I flip it back on him.

"I live here, remember? I'm always invited to parties as an anti-snitch measure." I raise an eyebrow. He shrugs. "Everyone assumes that because I'm Canadian I'm a Goody Two-shoes."

"Let me guess—you're hiding some deep, dark secret that'll shock us all? Some dastardly criminal enterprise?"

Ethan chuckles awkwardly. "I'm not that interesting," he says, humoring me.

"That's not true. Your dad's an ambassador, and your mom works for MSNBC. That's pretty cool."

"You writing my biography?" Ethan's eyes glint with amusement, but I feel my cheeks heat. Did I just blow my crush cover? I shrug it off, pouring myself another drink. Screw my two-drink limit. I'm fucking stressed. But I smile at Ethan, and we clink our drinks together in a cheers.

"I know a lot of things about a lot of people," I say, attempting a save. "We're journalists, remember?"

"Calm down, Ronan Farrow. I think we have to go to j-school before we're really journalists. The *Ledger* doesn't count."

"Is that what you're gonna study at Toronto?" I ask. "Do they have journalism schools in Canada?"

"Technically, you can major in anything and become a journalist. My mom studied economics. And I don't know what I want to do yet. I like classics, poli-sci, maybe even sociology."

My vision goes momentarily white. Maybe it's the long draw of vodka cran I just took, or maybe it's the cold, bitter fuel of my ambition, but for a second I hate Ethan. He doesn't even *care* about becoming a journalist. Why did he make me fight him for the editor position? For what? Avery had to bribe the outgoing editor, Stina Perez, to get her to vote in my favor, which in turn made *me* owe Avery. Sure, in the end it didn't matter, because Vasquez overwrote Stina to split the position, but *still.*

"Livvy, have you seen Emma?" Tyler appears from behind us, eyes heavy lidded and sweat on his brow. He smells like crisp night air and weed. It snaps me out of my rage haze.

"She's in the lounge," I reply, choosing not to comment on his using my nickname. It's too familiar for him. "Let's go find her." I suck down the rest of my drink, then heave myself up and off the barstool with a wave to Ethan.

That's when the screaming starts. Wild, high-pitched cries rise over the rest of the party sounds. Enough people stop talking for us to hear "YOU BITCH!" echo into the kitchen.

There's no mistaking that voice. It's Avery's.

CHAPTER FIVE

I beat Tyler to the scene by a few seconds, my bony-as-shit elbows finally coming in handy as I'm able to push through the semicircle of onlookers enjoying the fight. Avery's half-on-top of Emma, who is crouched over, trying to protect her head and face from Avery's freshly manicured, talon-like nails. Emma gets in a good jab to Aves's stomach, but Avery retaliates with a swift kick to the backs of Emma's knees.

Tyler falls in beside me, panting, eyes now alert. We give each other a short nod before rushing forward. He takes Avery, and I go for Emma.

Tyler wrests Avery away, lifting her by the torso up and off Emma, who falls forward into my waiting arms. Feistier than I gave her credit for, Emma twirls in my embrace, fists flying in the direction of Avery's flailing limbs, but they don't connect.

"Hey, stop it!" I shout in Emma's ear. "Both of you!"

Emma's gone limp now. I can hear her sobbing into my shoulder.

"Why can't she just be happy for me for once?" she wails.

"You stole my spot, you bitch!" Avery retorts. Tyler's barely holding on to her now, but I can see she's accepted defeat. The physical portion of the fight is done.

A few of the lookie-loos snigger, and then the whispers start. Avery turns, shooting daggers with her eyes. "Yeah, you fuckers, I didn't get into Harvard. You happy?"

"YES!" someone shouts from the back, setting off laughter and a few gasps.

For a second, I think Avery's going to launch herself into the crowd, root out the culprit, and flog them. Instead, she narrows in on Emma.

"How could you? You're supposed to be my friend. There are rules. One school per girl, so this very thing doesn't happen! You. Took. My. SPOT!"

"Avery, I didn't know, honestly." Emma grips my forearm so tightly that I fear it might break. "You're a triple legacy; I was so sure you would get in, especially with that SAT score!" Emma throws her a beseeching look. Avery scowls harder. "I wanted to see if I was good enough, and I wanted to maybe go together."

"I don't want to go anywhere with you!" Avery screeches. "I could kill you!"

I'm struck with a sickening déjà vu, an out-of-body sensation. It's like Avery's screaming at me. My secret turns acrid in the pit of my stomach.

Avery isn't done. Her voice drops lower, her murderous focus on Emma more intent. "Don't think I don't know how you did this, you little snake. Does Tyler know? Maybe I'll tell the whole school."

Emma retreats as Avery advances, forcing me to step back as well. I can feel Em shaking. From fear or rage, I can't tell.

"Hey, Aves, let's go outside for a minute. Get some air," Margot cuts in, touching tentative fingers to Avery's arm, then gripping more firmly when Avery doesn't haul off and hit her. "And maybe you should leave, Em."

Emma shoots Margot an *et tu Brute* look. Then something in her shifts. She hardens like steel.

"I don't have to go anywhere. I didn't do anything wrong. Just 'cause someone wasn't good enough to get in doesn't mean I have to feel bad."

Everything happens quickly. Avery grabs a Solo cup from a girl in the crowd, hurls it at Emma. Emma's reflexes are on point, but I'm a second too late. I take a full cup of booze to the face and torso.

"Shit!" I yell, partly because it's cold and partly because I'm pissed that my favorite dress is ruined. Sticky brown liquid stains my chest and drips down my body and onto the floor.

Avery doesn't even apologize. She giggles. Then she grabs Margot by the arm, and they make a hasty exit.

"Liv, I'm so sorry—"

I cut Emma off. "Just stop. I told you this would happen. Listen to me next time."

Her eyes go as dead as Avery's did a moment before. "Fuck you, Liv." And then she storms off, Tyler following after her, and I'm left alone in the middle of a goddamn crowd, the lights of their phones already eating up my humiliation. Screw this party. I push my way back into the kitchen and locate my coat and purse in the cupboard where Emma and I stashed them earlier. Stupid Emma. She's tossed a bomb into our friendship circle, and now mine will have to remain inside my chest, ticking away until it blows up and probably kills me.

"You okay, Olivia? Want me to walk you home?"

Of course it's Ethan. Of course he saw that. And now he's staring at my chest, which makes my entire body heat from head to toe. It's all far too embarrassing.

"No, I'm fine. Thanks for offering. See you tomorrow." I swipe the vodka bottle, now only a quarter full, and make a hasty exit through the back corridor before Ethan can protest. He doesn't follow me, and a swoop of disappointment stirs in the pit of my stomach. I fill it with another swig of booze.

The crisp coldness of pitch-black December nights is one of my favorite things in the universe. Claflin is two hours from any big city, which means brighter stars, darker nights. Immediately, I feel a degree calmer. The party is behind me, the din fading with every step. I tilt my head up as I walk the winding path around the back of Whitley, until I rejoin the main gravel thoroughfare that cuts through campus.

The path here is better lit, though the towering lights are positioned strategically and regulated by a timer so as not to disturb dorm residents' sleep. Every two hundred feet or so there's a pole with a blue box affixed to it—the campus blue phones. Pick up the receiver on any of them and you're connected directly to campus security or can dial out to the police in town. It's a relic of the pre–cell phone days, though who hasn't had their battery die on them, so I guess the blue phones are still good to have.

Their gentle glow is comforting. Every few feet, I step out into the next pool of blue light. I count my steps in the blackness between them—one, two, three, four. I reach the mid-thirties before I start over again. It calms me down. On the way, I text Sierra.

> Aves and Em had huge fight, and I ended up doused in someone's drink. Heading back early to shower & sleep. See you at practice, tho!

And I do precisely that. By the time I'm under my covers, I'm exhausted and also more than a little drunk. I should be ecstatic.

I got into Harvard. *Harvard.* But Emma and Avery's fight has shaken me. I feel nothing. I glance at my phone before drifting off; it's just shy of 11:00 p.m.

I wake to my bed shaking, swaying beneath me like a mattress riding a wave. *Earthquake?* My sleep-deprived brain panics. I take a second, two, to orient myself. Logic tells me, no, it's not an earthquake; my mind is playing tricks on me. This happens sometimes when I go to sleep drunk. Unpleasant middle-of-the-night wake-ups.

My heart thunders in my chest, so hard I can feel it in my fingertips. My eyes seem glued shut. I force an eye open, then the other. It's dark, but the shadows playing on the ceiling and wall are familiar. I'm in my room. I must have had a nightmare.

The wisps of the leftover dream don't leave quickly, though. I was somewhere cold and inky black. An amorphous place, but a strong feeling: someone was with me, and I was afraid. They were trying to kill me. A classic anxiety dream. At least it wasn't the one where a psycho chases me through a hedge maze.

But I'm fine now; I'm safe. I tell myself that. My brain knows it, but my heart thinks I'm a liar. Too spooked to go back to sleep, I fumble on the side table for my phone, depressing my thumb into the power button. I squint against the brightness to catch the time. It's a little past 2:00 a.m.

I roll over as my eyes adjust, more dynamic grays slowly edging into view, and that's when I finally notice: the bed across from me is empty. Emma's not here. Is the party still going on? No way, curfew is 11:30. Not that there aren't ways around that.

Now I throw back my duvet, allowing a flash of cold to wash

over me, wake me more fully as I swing both feet out over the edge of the bed and sit up. I scan the room. My heart leaps into my throat. The door is open, just a crack. I grasp the fluffy down cover tight to my chest, like it could protect me from an intruder. I look for hulking shadows crouched by the desks, hiding in the closet. Nothing. Everything is normal. No one is in here with me. I release a breath, and the tension rolls off my shoulders. But then why is the door open? I definitely closed it before I went to sleep, right? I try to remember pressing hard against the metal until I heard that satisfying click of the bolt.

Suddenly I'm parched and in desperate need of Advil. I go to the mini fridge to grab a bottle of water. The fridge light illuminates a slice down the middle of the room. It falls on Emma's desk chair. Her cherry-red sweater hangs over the back of it.

The sweater Emma was wearing at the party. Which means she came back to the room. I heave a sigh of relief. She's probably in the bathroom and didn't want to take her key. It's definitely late for her to be getting back, and she'll regret it in the morning, but that's her problem.

I gulp down the water like a dying man in the desert and then check my phone to see what I must have missed. Instagram first; I tap through Stories, looking at the time signatures to figure out if there's an after-party somewhere in Bay. But the last images from the party are hours old, and there are no after-party snaps. I open my text app and go into the Ivies' group text. Radio silence. Avery's clearly on strike, given everything that happened with Emma, and the rest of us are too cowardly to take a side.

Emma's not back yet. Weird. I cap the half-drunk bottle and place it on my bedside table. Slink toward the door, open it carefully, and poke my head into the hallway. Listen for running water

54

or the sloppy shuffle of my drunk roommate moving around. There's nothing but an eerie drip of a loose faucet.

A chill creeps up my spine. I rush back into the room, swipe my key card from atop my dresser, and pad down the hall to the communal bathroom.

"Emma?" I whisper, leaning through the doorway. Her name echoes. The faucet drips. No answer.

I go back to our room, shut the door behind me out of habit. Click. Locked and safe. I check my phone again, but there are no new notifications.

I think. Emma must be staying over with Tyler. Yes, that's it. She came back here to change and then snuck out, forgetting to close the door in her haste. Risky to hold an overnight—there's a reason the 5:00 a.m. hookup is popular—but maybe the administration would let it slip for ED day. I bet a lot of people are illegally staying over in their significant others' rooms tonight. Normally Emma texts me if she's staying over, but she was drunk and upset last night. Probably forgot. Right.

I move to Emma's closet and tap my phone's flashlight on. Her blue dress isn't there—I swing the light over to Emma's pop-up hamper—or there. She didn't change her clothes. Why come all the way back just to drop off a sweater?

Something is wrong. I feel it in my bones, like when you enter a room and know people were just talking about you. Or like a ghost walking over your grave. My mom always says that, though it doesn't really make sense. And yet . . . that feeling.

I sit on my bed and text her.

> Emma, are you okay?

55

I wait a minute, then two, sucking down water and coming more awake with every second.

I get up and cross to the window, cupping my hands against the cold glass and peering out. Our room faces the gravel path; half the security lights are out now. I squint to the left, searching the pool of light a hundred yards away for . . . I don't know what. I repeat the sequence to the right.

Then I'm pulling on wool socks and shoving my feet into my boots before I can change my mind. I don't bother to get dressed or even put on a bra. I zip up my heavy down coat, stuff my ID card and phone into my pockets, and slip out into the hall. I tip-toe past the dozen doors on the way to the elevator bank and stairs. Stairs will be quieter, and as I make my way down the three flights, I keep my hand on my phone, willing it to vibrate with an incoming text. It remains motionless in my palm.

The whole building is alarmed from midnight until 5:00 a.m. The front door, back exit, and all the windows. Except one. The story is that some intrepid soccer player and the Girls Who Code club founder took advantage of a snowstorm blackout four years ago to disconnect the system from the large bay window in the ground-floor study room. Now the study room window is the only way in or out of Bay Hall after hours without risk of detection by the administration, making it popular with troublemakers and romantic partners.

I reach the ground floor and find the study room door hanging slightly ajar. I slip inside, creeping past study carousels and spongy armchairs, and step to the window. Then I second-guess my entire plan. It's not even a plan. It's an impulse. I need to find Emma. Crouching down at the window, I look for evidence she's gone in and out this way. I feel the dingy carpet. It's damp from someone's feet; I can just make out a footprint in one spot, the mud from someone's tracks imprinted on the pile. Looks like a woman's boot, a much smaller foot than mine. Emma's.

Light glints off something shiny and small underneath the nearest armchair. I crawl over, pick it up between my forefinger and thumb. A diamond stud earring.

Don't you think they're a bit matronly? Avery had sniffed in disapproval.

Emma was unflappable. *Tyler says they're family heirlooms. I think it's sweet.*

Emma came through here for sure. I pocket the earring to return to her later. Once I find her.

I open the window carefully, quietly, and sit on the wide lip of the windowsill before slowly lowering myself closer to the ground. There's a five-foot drop, and I need to narrow the gap by a few feet to make the landing easier on my knees.

I suck in a breath as my arms stretch painfully at the shoulder sockets; it's now or never, but the ground still feels so far away. *Let go, you wuss,* I scold myself. And squeezing my eyes shut like the coward I am, I let go. Frigid air whips my hair back, and the second of free fall seems to stretch on forever. Then I feel the sting of impact in my knees. I stumble forward, barely avoiding a faceplant.

The study window spits me out on the back side of Bay Hall, a blind spot of external security cameras. I walk the dirt path around the building and reach the main path. The superfine gravel crunches under my feet. I'm about three yards from the honey glow of a streetlamp, half-shrouded in dingy gray, half-illuminated. I turn, surveying in all directions. Bay Hall looks out onto the lake, and if I go left, I will end up at the boathouse and the river. Going right will take me into the heart of campus, and toward Whitley.

Emma must be with Tyler. I go right.

Frigid wind blows in off the water and cuts me in two. In the distance an owl gives a low, long hoot. My feet crunch on the pathway, and for the second time that night, I count the steps between blue boxes, hating the way my heart is easing its way up my esophagus. This is how a slasher film starts.

A crack in the distance. I walk faster, scanning for the nearest blue phone. A hundred feet. I break into a jog.

And then I'm standing in front of Whitley. No light from any window. Everyone is asleep. I pull my phone from my pocket and bring up the home screen. Still no texts.

I crane my neck back, my eyes searching for Tyler's window. I think it's the first one from the right, on the third floor. Tyler has a single, and those are always on the ends. The lights are out.

I know there's a way to sneak into Whitley. Girls do it all the time. But I've never had a reason for a hookup during off-hours, so damned if I know how. I imagine myself creeping around the boys' dorm, finding my way to Tyler's door and, what? Knocking? Trying to explain why I've pulled him and my roommate out of a deep sleep—or, worse, *sex*—to assuage my stupid fears?

Suddenly I hear the unmistakable sound of wheels on gravel. Shit. Paul, the night security guard, must be doing his patrol. The scene comes into crisp focus. It's 2:30 in the morning, freezing, and I'm standing in the middle of campus—breaking curfew!— staring up at a slumbering building. Paul seems to like me well enough; we shoot the shit in the office sometimes. But no way he lets me go without a demerit.

I'm an idiot, jumping to conclusions, letting myself get

spooked by a stupid nightmare, an errant sweater, and a lost earring. Emma is probably asleep in Tyler's room right now. I turn around and head back toward Bay. First, I speed-walk; then I sprint. I just want to get back to bed.

Everything looks the same when I return to my room. A part of me hoped I'd find Emma here, tucked into bed, and we'd laugh in the morning about being two ships passing in the night, me sneaking out and her sneaking in. I definitely plan on giving her an earful.

I lie in bed, eyes dipping shut, trying to grasp at the feeling that sent me out into the frigid night. But it's gone now. And all I know is sleep.

CHAPTER SIX

The gentle wind-chime tone of my alarm sounds at 5:15. I swipe the snooze option twice before dragging my butt out of bed with a groan. I take my duvet with me, wearing it over my shoulders like a cape. It's freezing in here. The central heating is on a timer and won't start blasting for another hour. The delights of being a rower. Under my warm cover, I shrug out of my pajamas and into my sports bra, top, spandex pants, and formfitting jacket.

Rap, rap, rap, comes Sierra's knock at the door. We leave in ten minutes.

I throw the duvet back onto my bed, grab my toiletries basket, shove my ID into my jacket pocket, and hurry down the hall to the communal bathroom. Sierra grunts a hello mid-toothbrushing, and I claim the sink next to hers. We're no fuss for early-morning practice: brush teeth, smooth hair into a ponytail, and go. No need to bother with makeup that we'd sweat off. And we always shower afterward. You start the day twice when you have morning practice.

Sierra and I meet at the elevators, then take one down to the lobby. No need to sneak around now. We only talk once we're outside.

"So, uh, are we gonna talk about the shit that went down last

60

night?" Sierra asks almost as soon as our feet hit the pathway. In the heart of winter, we walk under cover of darkness; the sun won't begin to peek above the treetops for another two hours.

"Sorry about leaving you at the party like that." I shove my hands into the pockets of my coat and duck my face down into my scarf, even though it muffles my voice. "I couldn't find you. Where were you, by the way?"

"I got tired of watching a bunch of drunk idiots while I was stone-cold sober, so I took a walk." She waves me off. "Anyway, you know that's not what I mean. Emma *also* got into Harvard? Did you know?"

"Only for a bit before she told Avery," I say. "I told Emma not to say anything, but she insisted. She was so sure Avery would be happy for her."

Sierra groans. "That girl lives in her own universe, where she's the smartest and nicest person, *tee-hee,* and how could anyone ever think otherwise? Always pushing shit too far and then acting innocent when things blow up."

It's a surprising amount of vitriol. I guess Sierra and Emma have never been the closest, but still.

"Emma is . . ." I chew on my defense of my roommate. What can I say? Sierra's not entirely wrong. Emma does swan around like a princess and is pretty oblivious to how she affects others. Avery's guilty of it as well, and Sierra wouldn't speak a word against her. "Listen, clearly we both decided to see how far we could push it with ED applications. What's done is done."

"So you're going to tell Avery, then?" Sierra picks up the pace to a light jog, and I follow her lead. Coach expects us to jump right into conditioning, so the brisk trek to the boathouse *is* our warm-up.

"Absolutely not."

Sierra rolls her neck as she bobs. "You'll have trouble convincing her they only gave away one spot ED."

"I know." I mimic her actions. "Will you cover me?"

"Do I have a choice?" She stops suddenly then, squaring across from me and locking eyes. "This is pretty fucked up, Olivia. Last night, after you left . . . Avery was pissed. Like, unhinged angry."

"What happened?"

She squirms. "Nothing. I mean, she ranted a lot. She wants me to hack into Ms. Bankhead's files to see who else got her Harvard rec. She assumed Emma was Tipton's only outlier. I covered your ass. You're welcome."

"Are you going to do it? Hack the counselor files?"

Sierra purses her lips. "I don't know. I'm hoping Avery cools the fuck down over Christmas break so I don't have to."

We fall back into a run, the path curving around the lake until the Swiftensell Boathouse is in view.

I pray Sierra is right and Avery will feel her feelings and deal. It isn't worth destroying our friendship over something as stupid as college admissions. And yet our entire friendship has been based on college admissions, so . . .

"Come on, we're going to be late," Sierra says, lengthening her stride. But we're never late, because Sierra keeps us meticulously on schedule. There's no one on the path ahead of us, and as I suspected, when we get inside, it's clear we're the first ones here.

The Swiftensell Boathouse is not exactly a boathouse. More like a state-of-the-art training facility. It was built fifteen years ago, about fifty feet from where the original boathouse still stands. We use that one for extra storage now. Swiftensell is three stories high and multifunctional. On the ground floor is every piece of gym equipment imaginable, from weight machines to treadmills to custom indoor rowing tanks that sit alongside dozens of ergs.

Upstairs are sleek locker rooms equipped with rain showers and steam rooms, so you can sweat out the day's practice before heading down the hall to one of three conference rooms-cum-lounges. In season, we gather around large tables and Coach runs over practice and race footage on the one-hundred-inch 4K Ultra HD TV screen. I really should be a better athlete, given all the amenities.

Downstairs are the boats in a half dozen cavernous bays whose doors open onto docks right on the riverbank. From November to January, we do the majority of our training inside, away from the harsh hand of winter.

We drop our bags and coats in the girls' locker room one floor up. Sierra preps protein shakes for us so they're ready for later. We head back downstairs, Nora Patrick and Indigo Jackson offering groggy nods as they pass us on the stairs. Three more girls trudge through the doors when we hit the landing. The rest of the team should be here soon. There are fifteen of us on girls varsity, and boys varsity boasts a similar number. They'll arrive at 6:30 a.m., because why not let the boys get an extra half hour of shut-eye, right? It's fine by me—whoever gets the late shift is stuck on the shitty old equipment with broken monitors, loose chains, and wonky seats.

The rowing room is pitch-dark, so Sierra heads over to the control panel as I walk down the center aisle by instinct. My destination is the farthest erg on the right, which affords me a perfect view of the river through the floor-to-ceiling windows. When the sun starts its ascent, throwing dusky purples and sweet peach-pinks into the sky, I will have a front-row seat.

The lights come up as I'm halfway to my quarry. I skip ahead, unzipping my jacket as I go, then tossing it over the seat of my favorite erg, claiming it.

"Sierra, come on!" I turn and gesture to her to come grab the one next to mine. But Sierra is frozen at the door, staring at something in the middle distance. I follow her eyeline to the shallow pool to my left. Tangled between two oars is a person. Someone is facedown in the water, auburn hair floating around her like a halo.

"Hey, that's not funny." I move closer to the wannabe mermaid. This is someone's idea of a hilarious prank, putting on a bad Ariel wig and timing her submersion perfectly to our arrival. But as I move closer, she doesn't jump up, yell "Got you!" She's still.

"Liv—" Sierra's steps are halting and tentative. Fear is etched across her face. I get close enough to see, really see, the body. Because it has to be a body. It's not moving.

It. When do you cease to be a person and start to be a body?

Sierra rushes to *her* side, shaking a lifeless arm. With trepidation, I inch closer to take in the details. Red hair, blue dress, black leggings, and then . . . my eyes catch on her shoes. She's wearing boots, expensive boots. No one ruins genuine leather designer boots for a prank. Not these boots. The soles are red, because half the point is so you know they're Louboutins. I was with Emma when she bought them.

Emma. Emma has auburn hair. Emma was wearing a blue dress over black leggings, and those boots.

Emma is in the rowing tank.

Emma is a body.

Emma is dead.

A scream rips from my throat. And then I vomit onto the rowing-room floor.

CHAPTER SEVEN

Boots aren't enough to ID a body, not officially. So when the cops arrive, they turn Emma over and have Coach Gray make the positive identification. I volunteered to do it, but every adult snapped an emphatic *no* at me, and a ruddy-faced cop ushered me into the lobby to wait. Everyone else is being corralled upstairs so they can take our statements. They can't keep me from hovering outside the rowing studio, though. Emma was my friend, and we deserve to know what's going on.

Was.

Emma is in the past tense now, I guess.

I collapse hard on a wooden bench, my tailbone radiating pain up my spine. I check my phone. It's 7:15. Emma has been dead for an hour and fifteen minutes. No, longer. God, I want them to tell me something, anything. How long was she floating in that pool? When did she die?

My vision swims, the sour taste of stale vodka rising in my throat. I squint my eyes shut, plunging myself into pleasant nothingness. I break into a cold sweat. The anxious swirl in my stomach told me something was wrong yesterday. All of this, last night. Like I knew.

Why did I turn right, toward Whitley? What if I'd come to the boathouse instead? Could I have saved her? Or maybe I'd be another victim.

I pinch at my thighs, trying to bring myself back. My stomach remains knotted, my skin clammy and cold, but I can stop the horrible, negative tapes playing the what-ifs over and over. It's not productive to think that way. I narrow in on the practical instead. Like Emma's sweater, folded neatly over her chair. When did she come in? Why did she go back out? And why the boathouse? Emma didn't row.

The questions itch up my throat, make my tongue weigh heavy in my mouth. I need them out, spewed at the first detective who will listen to me. The answers will fill me up, sate the acid churn of hunger clawing at my stomach.

"Tell me it's not fucking true." Avery crashes through the lobby doors, eyes wild behind a chic pair of glasses. No time for contacts means she rushed to get here. She snaps a finger in front of my face. "Olivia!"

"You're not wearing makeup." My voice is dreamy as I marvel at a constellation of pimples on Avery's cheek. I've never seen her without her mask.

"I got a text. It said Emma is dead. What the hell, Liv? What the fuck is going on?"

I blink up at her. Swallow hard. Then I stand and pull her into a hug. "I'm so sorry." Like it's my fault, my job to apologize for the inconvenience.

Avery pushes me away. She's not a hugger, and I forgot. "What happened? Who found her? Did you see? Why didn't you text me?" She sneers the last question, like an accusation.

"Sorry I didn't think to pull out my phone while I was scream-ing over her dead body, Aves."

She inhales sharply. "You did see her. It's true."

"Yeah, it's true." I stare down at the floor. If I look at Aves, I'll start crying, though maybe that would be a good thing. I haven't cried yet. Upstairs, a dozen girls are sobbing; every so often their histrionics echo down the stairwell. Snatches of grief when some-one opens a door. And I'm down here, dry eyed. You can't cry if you don't feel anything.

Avery plunks down on the bench. "The last thing I said to her was that I hated her."

Actually, it was that you could kill her. I don't make the cor-rection. This is a rare sighting, a vulnerable Avery. Twice in twenty-four hours. I'll have to note this in my Mean Girl Field Journal.

December 16, 7:20 a.m.: Avery displayed feelings today. Re-markable.

I sit down as well, and we spend the next few moments in our own stunned silences. I catalog a dozen more questions to ask. Avery scrolls through her Instagram feed.

The door to the rowing room swings open, and both of us jump to our feet. A woman emerges, careful to shut the door be-hind her so we can't see the body.

Emma, I correct myself. So we can't see *Emma.* I won't let her be a body. She was a person only hours ago.

The woman looks at us, grim faced. Her frown accentuates a hawklike nose and severe chin, but her eyes—big and brown—and the aura of seriousness she carries remind me of my mom. I peg her for mid-thirties, and her messy ponytail and the way her makeup has separated around her nose and mouth tell me she was called here at the end of a long night shift. She looks tired.

"I'm Detective Cataldo," she says, offering a push of her chin in lieu of handshakes. "Which one of you is Olivia Winters?"

I raise my hand as though I'm still in class and this is nothing more than a teacher calling roll.

"I've known her since we were six." Avery sniffs, as if she needs to one-up me.

Detective Cataldo ignores her. "You discovered the body?"

I bob my head. "Me and Sierra Watson. She's upstairs." Last I saw her, she was curled into a ball on the locker room floor, alternately weeping and hyperventilating.

"We'll need to bring both of you down to the station for formal questioning—"

Headmistress Fitzgerald rushes through the rowing-room doors, as if she was eavesdropping on the other side. "Detective, I must insist any questioning take place on school grounds, with a Claflin representative present and our grief counselors on standby. We take the well-being of our students very seriously."

What Carmen Fitzgerald actually takes very seriously is the possibility that one of her students might say something that reflects poorly on Claflin or, god forbid, incriminates a staff member or a student with well-placed parents. I imagine phone calls have already been placed to lawyers and board members, who are no doubt on their way.

"I have an AP Calculus final today," I say. It's the first thing I think of, for some reason. Like nothing could be more important than a test. I feel stupid for having said it, but Headmistress Fitzgerald makes the point moot.

"Classes are canceled for the rest of the week. We'll reschedule everyone's exams, don't you worry."

Obviously classes are canceled. Someone died. Get it together, Winters.

The detective clears her throat. "Ms. Fitzgerald—"

"Headmistress Fitzgerald."

"Headmistress. You and I can discuss the particulars—"

The main boathouse doors burst open. "Where is she? Where's Emma! Oh god, where's Emma?"

It's Tyler. His eyes are rimmed red and frenzied. Fresh tears streak his cheeks. It strikes me that I don't know if I've ever seen a boy cry. Certainly not one like him—beautiful, rich, and confident. But now he's a wreck, because of course he is.

He makes a break for the rowing-room door and manages to grab the handle, but Detective Cataldo stops him.

"Excuse me; you can't go in there."

"But she's my girlfriend! They're saying she's dead! Is it true?"

I catch Avery, paragon of empathy that she is, rolling her eyes at him. My heart is breaking all over again. I am hollowed out. Tyler is shattered. Emma's poor parents. God, what will I tell them?

"You have to let me see her!" Tyler's knees give out, and he crumples to the floor. He ends up sobbing into Headmistress Fitzgerald's jacket collar as she drags him to his feet and over to the corner of the room.

Detective Cataldo clears her throat. "Miss Winters, one of my officers will need to speak with you as soon as possible. And Miss . . ."

"Montfort," Avery huffs, like it should be obvious.

"You'll need to leave. This is an active crime scene. Him, too."

The headmistress's mouth twitches. She has a good fifteen years on the detective and at least three class rungs.

All our eyes swivel to the rowing-room doors as they open again. A man walks backward through them, leading a gurney into the lobby. Emma looks so small on the metal slab, the outline of her body clear through the black body bag. There, she's become a body again. It's morbid, but my first thought is to wonder whether they salvaged the Louboutin boots or if she still has them on.

I'm going to hell.

Tyler begins his sobbing anew, and Avery gasps beside me. It's real to them now. They're getting the sanitized version of her death, a staid and respectful body bag being pushed past us, outside to the waiting ambulance. The image of Emma's lifeless body floating in a shallow pool will cling to me forever. But at least I get to live.

The questions scratch at my throat again.

I turn to Detective Cataldo. "Where should I talk to your officers?"

Fitzgerald frowns. "We will arrange for your people to interview all of the girls crew team, starting with Miss Winters and Miss Watson, at Austen Hall in one hour," Fitzgerald addresses Detective Cataldo. "That's the administration building. And you'll not speak to a single student a moment before that. There is breakfast at Austen, which you are welcome to avail yourself of."

Rightly cowed, Detective Cataldo dismisses herself with a solemn press of her lips and a nod. She goes back into the rowing center, presumably to dust for prints or whatever it is detectives do. Fitzgerald tells Tyler to pull himself together and return to his dorm. Avery gets a similar instruction. I get an assessing look.

"A grief counselor should be here by nine," she says. "Don't speak to any police officers without my express permission." Then she heads upstairs to corral the other girls.

Tyler, Avery, and I are left staring at the negative space where, moments ago, Emma's body rolled through. Tyler has stopped crying, but now he's clutching at his jacket above his heart, as if to rip it from his chest.

"Tyler, are you okay? Can I help?" I ask, though I stay firmly put, awkward as usual. Because I think it's what I'm supposed to say, rather than it being a natural instinct. I'm relieved when he shakes me off, ducking his head into his coat collar and heading for the exit.

"I just need some time."

Avery and I have a view out the glass double doors to the curve in the path where Emma's body is being loaded into the vehicle. Day is breaking, the sky throwing drowsy pinks, blues, and purples over the rooftops of the nearest school buildings. It's going to be a beautiful day. A joke made at our expense.

Tears prick at my eyes, finally. I am not a sociopathic monster. With friends like Avery, I worry sometimes.

Beside me, Avery stares ahead at the ambulance. The back doors are closed now. The paramedic hops into the passenger side. Funny that they sent an ambulance and not the medical examiner. We told them on the phone she was dead. Maybe it's standard protocol? Wishful thinking? Or maybe Claflin wouldn't let them send a mortuary vehicle past the school gates. What a bad look.

"Maybe Harvard will reconsider now." Avery's voice is soft. Wistful.

My stomach roils. She's thinking about her spot at Harvard? *Emma's* spot.

Poison slips past my lips, into my bloodstream. It thrums through me, spreading.

The ambulance drives away. Avery stands, brushes off some invisible dust from her pants, and leaves.

A thought, the tiniest supposition, pushes to the front of my brain.

What if Avery killed Emma?

CHAPTER EIGHT

If Dealing with Your Friend's Death were a class, I would have an A. Need to maintain that GPA, right? I've been smiling just enough but not too much every time someone asks me how I'm doing. I've got my platitudes down.

It's so awful, but I'm fine, thank you for asking.

I'm doing okay; taking it one step at a time, you know?

I haven't cried again, even on the phone to my mom, telling her what happened. *She* cried, though. I remained calm, a rock, and reassured her. I was fine. She didn't need to come get me. I'd be home in less than a week, anyway.

Really, I'm numb. Wednesday, the day we found her, was spent attending mandatory counseling sessions and going over the basics with a red-faced officer named Murphy. *How did you know the deceased? How did you find her?*

I tried asking my questions but got shut down. *We just need the facts, Miss Winters.*

I know there are stages of grief, but I can't peg which one I'm in. I'm not in denial. Emma is dead. It repeats in my head, again and again, all day. I see her, blank eyes staring at the ceiling after the police turned over her body. People die with their eyes open all the time; the ruddy-faced cop told me when I asked. I can feel the cold clamminess of her skin, which I touched, fruitlessly trying to find a pulse. It was macabre, but I drank it all in that morning, every detail of her death. It's all so surreal.

I'm not angry, I don't think. Tyler is. He's been screaming at people to do more. That if they'd done their jobs, Emma would be alive. Bargaining. What's the point? Nothing we say or do will bring her back. Depression. No. I feel fine.

But I haven't accepted it, either. I can't. Not with that lingering question: Did Avery kill her?

It's too awful to think your friend might be a killer. But it's also too awful to think your friend is dead. Someone did it. I was there when one cop said to another in a hushed tone that I could still hear, "No way it was accidental, even if she was drunk. Definitely homicide."

That was before they rushed me out of the room, like I was some delicate flower. But I'm not an idiot. Obviously, someone killed Emma. She didn't drown herself. Not the day she got into Harvard.

The day Avery got rejected from Harvard.

By late afternoon Wednesday, they announced the assembly. On Thursday morning all Claflin students were to report to the Colman auditorium for an update, an expression of grief, a makeshift memorial. They had to do something with us. Exams are postponed. Jordan Kingston, the other office work-study, texted me that parents have been calling nonstop. I'm dreading my next shift.

But I'm handling this death thing really well, remember, so I put on my best black dress, comb my hair into a ponytail, and meet the Ivies in the lobby of Bay so we can walk over together.

The remaining Ivies, I mean. We feel off-balance without Emma, even though four is a much neater number. There's no one to be in the middle of our formation (Avery was always in the point before). We're merely two pairs of friends walking in a line. I'm on the far left, Sierra thankfully between me and Avery. I think if I'm too close to her, I'll blurt out an accusation.

Yes, I am handling Emma's death very well.

You know it's a time for healing when the school lawyer opens the assembly with a ten-minute warning against posting anything defamatory to social media or speaking to the press. I check the time on my phone. It's a quarter past nine, so just over a day since I found her. I wonder how they told Emma's parents, how they're doing. It's funny, the thoughts that come and go, and when.

A tired Headmistress Fitzgerald follows the lawyer and introduces the Claflin board, sitting in the front row. I can feel Avery tense two seats over. Her mom is here. Fitzgerald reads stiffly from a prepared statement before handing it over to Detective Cataldo.

"Hello, everyone, my name is Maureen Cataldo, and I am the head investigator working the Russo case."

She chews on her vowels and skims the *R*s. Massachusetts born and raised, I would guess. Got here quickly yesterday, so local-ish. Maybe from down in Northampton, or Amherst. We don't get a lot of murders up here in the sleepy, leafy parts of the state, where they like to build schools like Claflin. It's idyllic. Murder-free.

"Unfortunately, this is a homicide investigation." Cataldo's words spark a cascade of whispers that ripple through the student body from front to back.

"We ask that anyone with information about Emma Russo's death come forward immediately. No information is insignificant, so please don't dismiss anything you might know."

She rattles off a tip line and an email address. I see a few students surreptitiously take notes on their phones. I wonder what any of them could possibly have to say, but then I feel the eyes. Glances stolen in our direction.

"It's important that we piece together Miss Russo's last day. Every detail counts. I'll be conducting additional interviews this afternoon. Thank you."

And then Detective Cataldo looks right at me. No, at us. *The Ivies.*

The seniors are invited to an exclusive reception after the assembly. A rehearsal room off the auditorium has been tastefully decorated, and caterers swim about the room, appetizers hoisted high on silver trays. There is a table laden with fancy cheeses and crudités in the corner. I want to say it's for the board's benefit, but I know the headmistress could have been murdered and Claflin would still pull out an impeccable spread on short notice.

It is a bizarro version of the ED day party. All the same people are here, except everyone is wearing black and no one is happy. It hasn't even been forty-eight hours.

We've commandeered a cluster of chairs arranged in a semicircle before a large bay window. Avery and Margot sit on the cushioned window seat, while Sierra, Tyler, and I slump in armchairs facing them. Tyler is an unexpected addition, but he keeps bursting into noisy tears, so we feel bad telling him to leave.

"I wish they'd let me speak. I had something prepared." Tyler pulls a small leather flask from his suit jacket pocket and takes a swig. "Maybe I'll plan a memorial service, a proper one, for next week. I miss her so much." He swallows hard and looks at the floor. Then he passes me the flask, even though I didn't ask for it. Why not?

Bourbon burns down my throat, nearly choking me, but I recover smoothly. Tell myself to enjoy the sour-sweet scorching a trail to my stomach. "Do you think they'll reschedule exams for after break?" I cough out. Today is Thursday. We were supposed to go home Saturday the nineteenth, after exams finished. But exams have been canceled, so we're stuck in "when can we leave campus?" limbo. And now there's a murder investigation, to boot. I think about my nonrefundable flight home to Maryland and how much it'll cost my mom to reschedule. I take another swig and then pass the flask to my left to Margot. Since she's facing out, she needs to be extra careful the adults don't see.

"They can't cancel everyone's exams indefinitely. Certainly not for us seniors. There are strict deadlines for first-semester grades at all our schools. No way we're being released Saturday." Avery puffs up her chest, sliding easily into know-it-all mode. I think I'm the only one who notices her deflate slightly at *our schools*. Avery doesn't have a school. I remember to look moderately upset. I pretended to get deferred at Penn yesterday.

Katherine Montfort appears like a witch, prim and perfect in a little black dress and a chic updo. "Don't worry, Avery darling, I've already spoken to the headmistress about your exams. It'll be uncustomary, but I'm told a special senior exam schedule will begin tomorrow and go through Monday."

My stomach clenches and I grab for my phone, ready to text my mom. She'll be pissed. Ms. Montfort goes on.

"Tragedy or no, it's critical you all get in those grades on time. Especially now." Her mouth freezes in an imitation of a smile, eyes flashing tightly at her daughter. *Especially now that Avery has failed to get into Harvard.*

"Thanks, Mom," Avery says. We all grumble our own thanks, even though we are anything but grateful that now we'll have to take our finals over the weekend. And again, so soon after our friend's murder. Have they forgotten about the murder?

"Tyler, dear, don't cry." Katherine lays a comforting hand on Tyler's shoulder. He sobs around a mouthful from his flask. His stepmother doesn't even comment on the alcohol.

"I'm sorry, Mom. This is all simply so much."

Avery's jaw clenches tight. I caught it, too. *Mom.* They've only been a family for, what? A year? I wonder if Tyler's doing it to piss off Avery. They always had an academic rivalry, then fought for Emma's time, and now they wrestle for Katherine's scant attentions.

"Now, Avery, I've called Megan back in, so you'll need to start on your essays right away. Don't forget to write about Hillary for the Wellesley 100."

I stifle a snort. Like Avery could forget to mention her family connections to the Clintons. And, god, Megan. She's Avery's twenty-grand-a-year private college admissions counselor. She told Avery shit I could have imparted gratis, like how writing about her trip to build a school in Haiti was a terrible essay topic. I nearly choked on a laugh when she pitched it to me. Poverty tourism, with a side of white savior narrative. Rich white people are the worst. Most of the students here have their own Megan. I use Reddit, which is free.

"Olivia," Ms. Montfort says, like a belated greeting, but it's really an admonishment. I didn't hide my giggle very well. "And Margot, Sierra. So lovely to see you, as always." And then she swans off to speak with a member of the board.

"God, give me strength," Avery says through gritted teeth.

Tyler shoots Avery a cutting look and pushes back his chair with undue aggression. His voice warbles as he says, "I need some air."

My stomach gurgles. "And I need food, apparently. Anyone want anything?" The girls give terse headshakes. I bob and weave through the crowd, passing Rebecca, whose not-quite-whisper to Autumn Hollander I catch:

"Thank god I applied to Stanford ED instead, or that ruthless bitch would have killed *me*."

Autumn barks a laugh. "Instead, they just fucked you over, literally."

Their laughter fades behind me as I find the snacks table, but the implication sticks to me like slime. Guess I'm not the only one who suspects Avery Montfort. But by "they," did Autumn mean the Ivies?

At the heaping cheese platter, I reach for a gooey block of Brie at the same time that the man next to me does. Our hands brush while going for the cheese knife, and I rush to apologize.

"I'm sorry I—" My head snaps up to his face. "Oh, hi, Mr. Tipton." The Claflin college counselor blinks back at me. I don't tell him he has crumbs in his beard, though really it's more of a scruff on his chin, like he can't quite manage a fuller growth.

"Hey, Olive, what's up?" His smile is just a bit wobbly, and he indicates I can go for the cheese. I smear a half-inch-thick slice onto a cracker, hand him the knife for his turn.

"Olivia," I correct him, taking a bite of my cracker.

"Right, of course. How are you holding up?" The Tipton I'm used to is confident, like a frat president on pledge night. He's that adult who tries a little too hard to be your friend. Now he's soft and awkward, and his juvenile act tugs at him like an ill-fitting suit.

I fall into my good-mourner script, well practiced by now. "It's hard, but I'll get through it. How are you?" The question tumbles out because that is what you do in situations like this. Mutual status checking. But Tipton appears shocked. Has no one asked him that question yet?

"I—" His eyes are cast downward, and he mumbles, "It's pretty hard. I've never known anyone who died."

"Yeah, me neither. Not really, I mean. One of my uncles died when I was young, but I wasn't, like, there or anything."

Tipton hums under his breath. "And you found her."

My throat goes tight, constricts around my words as the image pushes forward in my mind. The one I've had to force myself not to think about so many times in the past twenty-four hours. "She was so stiff. It was like a horror show."

He winces, takes a step back. Fuck, I did the wrong thing. No one actually means it when they ask. They don't want to hear the gruesome details. Hastily I paste on a smile to try to put him at ease. "I'll be okay. They don't think she suffered." That's bullshit, because no one has said it to me at all, and I am pretty sure she did. The visuals start rushing back.

No, stop. I wipe the thoughts from my mind. I refuse to spiral. If I spiral, I'll start sobbing.

Desperate to put an end to this conversation, I look over to the Ivies, hoping to catch Sierra's eye to rescue me, but am surprised to find a new face standing at the edge of their circle. Officer Murphy, the cop who took my statement yesterday, stands imposingly over the group.

"She was just a great person, ya know?"

"Huh?" I turn back to Tipton. I forgot he was there.

"Emma. She lit up a room." His sincerity almost hurts.

"Sure," I say, turning back to my friends.

But the chairs, the window seat, are empty. Have they ditched me?

Then Sierra appears and tugs gently on my elbow. "Come on. Emergency meeting."

CHAPTER NINE

"What the hell is going on?" But Avery snaps her fingers three times in quick succession, cutting me off, and Sierra and Margot hup to like the lackeys they are. Margot crouches in front of the first stall, looking for a pair of errant feet. Then, just for good measure, she bangs open the door in case someone's being sneaky.

"Surely that's not necessary—"

"Out!" Margot commands a girl in the stall, who cries, "What the fuck!" but finishes up quickly nonetheless, scuttling past us with her eyes averted.

"Wash your hands next time, you monster!" Avery shouts after her with a giggle.

I tug Sierra's sleeve. "Did something happen?"

Sierra yanks her wrist from my hold and shushes me. Her attention is glued to Avery, who hops up onto a sink, kicking her legs back and forth like a kid on a swing. The girls' bathroom isn't an ideal meeting place, but it does in a pinch. I try to hide my annoyance and lean back against one of the stalls, knowing there's no way one of those sinks would take my weight. Margot and Sierra stand on either side of me, creating a semicircle formation so Avery can preach to her disciples.

"We need to get our stories straight," Avery begins.

"Why?" I ask. The other three share a Look. No one answers my question.

"What time did you and Emma get to the party?" Margot asks, fingers poised over her phone's screen. Pretty sure she's started a Google Doc already.

"I think around eight-thirty?" Sierra supplies.

Margot notes the time. *I* note that they didn't ask me, despite the fact that I was the one who walked with Emma to the party. At 8:15. But they've already moved on.

"The fight was around nine-thirty; we should double-check people's Stories to be sure," Avery says. She says it so casually, like it wasn't a fist fight in which she threatened to kill the victim. I mean, Emma. "You left after that, right, Liv?"

"Uh, yeah," I say.

"We stayed at the party until around eleven," Sierra throws in. "I didn't see Emma at the party after the fight, personally."

"She went off with Tyler. I watched them," Margot says, adding it to the timeline.

"And we were in bed by eleven-thirty," Avery finishes. She points at Margot, who is swiping furiously at her phone, like we're done.

"She came back to Bay at some point." Three pairs of eyes whip around to me. I swallow hard. "Her sweater was in the room when I woke up. The red one she wore at the party. She must have come back and left again while I was asleep. It didn't look like she got into bed. Maybe there was an after-party?"

"If there were an after-party, we'd know about it," Avery snaps.

I do not point out that maybe Emma decided to spend the

rest of her evening with people who hadn't punched her in the face that night.

"Just don't go spinning theories with the cops," Avery continues. "We stick to the facts. Now, about the fight." She's looking right at me. "Let's not tell them exactly what I said."

"Wh-why?" I stammer. The looks I get back clearly indicate the other Ivies think I'm an idiot. Right, because murder threats might make Avery look bad. I shake out my shoulders, sit up straighter. "We have nothing to hide. None of us killed her, right?"

Avery and Sierra answer immediately:

"How could you even ask?"

"Of course not!"

And Margot starts to cry. I've seen her cry on cue many times, so I can't tell whether it's genuine. And I feel slimy as shit that my first thought is that she's faking it. But that's where I am with this shady bathroom meeting and what feels like my three "friends" ganging up on me. What are they playing at?

"We tell the truth," I say. "Because we have nothing to hide."

Avery flinches.

The lead weight of doubt settles in my stomach. The question *Did Avery kill Emma because of Harvard?* is feeling less and less ridiculous. Avery is hiding something. And Sierra and Margot may be in on it.

The door swings open.

Avery hops down from the sink, eyes flashing. "Get the hell out— Oh, Detective Cataldo. So lovely to see you." Her transformation from she-demon to sweet as pie is uncanny. Cataldo saunters in, drinking in the scene. Our formation makes clear this isn't merely four girls going about their normal business.

"Good morning, Miss Montfort." She nods to the rest of us. "Ladies." Her smooth control makes my defenses go up. I spy the other girls, who appear unrattled.

"How nice to find you all here. I guess it's true what they say, girls do go to the bathroom in pairs . . . or packs, in this case."

"We were just, uh—" But Cataldo doesn't let Margot finish what was sure to be an inadequate excuse.

"It's fortuitous, really. I wanted to be sure you didn't miss the announcement. I'll be conducting student interviews in a few moments, and you're up first." She crosses the room and turns on the faucet nearest Avery. I stifle a laugh as water splashes onto Avery's finely pressed dress, forcing her from her seat. Cataldo decidedly ignores Avery's squeals of indignation.

"You'll need our parents' and *lawyers'* permission to talk to us," Avery states coldly. I must have heard her use that line a hundred times to get out of trouble these past three years. I wait for Cataldo to fold like all the rest.

"Harker Pharmaceuticals, right? Interesting. Excuse me, dear." Cataldo reaches across the sink, forcing Sierra to take a step back as she grabs a paper towel. "Yes, I will need their permission, but luckily Ms. Fitzgerald is reaching out to the correct contacts now." She dries her hands carefully. She strikes me as the kind of woman who does most things in her life carefully. "And many parents have already responded. Including yours, Olivia."

"What?" I'm no actress like Margot. Panic flashes over my face in an instant.

"You are eighteen, so we don't need her permission. Regardless, your mother assured me that you would have no problem answering our questions."

"I—"

"As I understand it, you girls were Emma's closest friends," Cataldo continues.

"We were best friends." Avery is defiant.

"Then I know you'll help me find her killer," Cataldo answers smoothly.

Cataldo has us in the snare; now she only needs to snap the trap closed. I see the girls bristle. Beneath even Avery's bravado I catch a waver of fear.

But isn't Cataldo right? All I've wanted to do since I found Emma's body is to find her killer. So why does this feel like a trap?

"Yes, ma'am. Whatever you need," I say, like the good girl I used to be. Teacher's pet, great with adults, all that jazz. Deferring to authority. The only thing that's changed at Claflin is whose authority I mind.

"Wonderful." Cataldo tosses the paper towel into the bin. "We have a room in Austen already set up for"—the detective checks her watch—"ten minutes from now. So, if you ladies will excuse me, I'd like to use the restroom without an audience. Olivia, if you wait outside, we can walk over together. The rest of you, I'll see you soon. I'm very much looking forward to it."

And just like that, we've been dismissed. I try to remember a time when the Ivies were ever told off by an adult at Claflin. We're prep-school royalty. It doesn't happen.

Out in the hall Avery grabs my arm, pushing me into the center of a circle formed by her, Sierra, and Margot in front of a locker. Rebecca and Autumn's conversation echoes in my ears: *That ruthless bitch would have killed me.*

"Don't forget what we talked about," Avery says. "We stick to the timeline. We weren't anywhere near Emma when she died, so we've got nothing to worry about."

"Right," Sierra and Margot echo instantly. Good little soldiers falling in line again.

"Uh, right," I add meekly.

That ruthless bitch would have killed me. That ruthless bitch would have killed me. That ruthless bitch would have killed me.

"And, Olivia." Avery's grip tightens on my arm. "Text us right after and tell us everything she asks."

I blink assent. With a questioning look and a flip of her hair, Avery leaves with Sierra and Margot.

Shit. I replay the whole conversation again. The bossiness, the taking charge—that was just classic Avery taking the lead in a stressful moment. She's always been like that. This isn't abnormal behavior for her. I shake away the thought. I'm letting Rebecca get inside my head. I need to tamp down these suspicions stat, or Cataldo will see right through me. The Ivies are my *friends*. They're ambitious, but they're not psychopaths. I can't throw them under the bus until I know more.

Yes, that's what I'll do. Play it cool until I find out more. But coolness eludes me. My throat feels uncomfortably dry. I need water—or cheese. Cheese makes everything better. I turn on my heel, right into a pair of outstretched arms, the only things that stop me from smacking into a chest.

"Olivia!"

I let out an undignified yelp. "Ethan! What are you doing here?"

"I could ask you the same thing. I saw you coming out with the Ivies."

I grab him by the arm, drag him across the hall into a doorway.

I can't run the risk of Cataldo hearing from the bathroom. "What do you mean? And since when do you call us the Ivies?"

"Hey, hey." He raises his arms in surrender. "I overheard them talking to you. And, uh, everyone calls you guys the Ivies. I don't say it to your face out of respect."

That brings heat to my cheeks, that Ethan knows who I am. He reads me like a book, my panic, and takes my hands.

"Hey, are you okay?"

Sweet Ethan. Good Ethan. He's still grasping my hand in his; it's sweaty. Or I'm sweaty? Am I sweating all over Ethan? I pull my hand back, wipe it discreetly on my dress.

"I don't know. Margot, Sierra, Avery, they're being shady about the night Emma died. I left the party before them, so I assumed they all went home, but maybe not? Ethan, I think they're lying. I think . . . maybe they killed her."

"Oh. Shit. Wow." Ethan's brow furrows.

"Sorry, I shouldn't have said anything. You must think there's something wrong with me. It's probably nothing."

"There's nothing wrong with you. And you're not the first person who's been pointing fingers."

This is news to me. I step farther into the doorway, pretending at privacy. "What?"

Ethan turns sheepish. "It's wild speculation mostly, since she was *murdered*, and so it was obviously someone on campus. I've heard everything from it was Paul the security guy to one of the teachers to—" He cuts himself off.

"One of her friends," I supply. Ethan's expression confirms it.

"Avery is the top contender, given what happened with the fight," he says. "I know people turned over their videos to the cops. Not that they had to, since they were public."

Ethan is very on top of this situation. Makes me wonder. "Are you writing a piece on this?"

"What?" He hesitates. "No, of course not."

I arch a single brow. "It's what I would do, you know, if I weren't embroiled in it."

Ethan coughs. "All right, you got me. It did cross my mind."

"Aha!" I brandish my finger at him, delighted to be proven right. Ethan narrows his eyes at me. Maybe I'm a little too excited to discover he's as ruthlessly ambitious as I am. Canadian Ken isn't too nice for the likes of me.

Ethan doesn't press further. Instead, he touches my forearm, sending shivers up my spine. His expression turns tender. "Are you okay, though? You lost your friend, and suspecting your only other friends . . ." He trails off. Whether crack journalist or caring friend, Ethan gets right to the heart of it.

"I don't want to," I say. "But they're lying to me about something."

"Well, have you considered asking them? One-on-one, I mean. As a group you're all rather frightening, but I've always liked you when I get you on your own."

I can't tell whether this is Ethan's version of flirting or his straightforward, honest nature. But he's not wrong. Instead of stewing, I should simply ask. Not Avery. No fucking way. But I could talk to Sierra, perhaps even Margot, and just ask them about the timeline.

Shit, the timeline. Cataldo. I hear the bathroom door clang open, imagine Cataldo searching the halls for me.

"Thanks, Ethan. This helped. See you later?"

I don't wait for his response before ducking out of the doorway. I have an interrogation to get to.

* * *

Detective Cataldo has set up shop in a small conference room in Austen Hall, a far cry from the cramped office in which the ruddy-faced and balding officer interviewed me Wednesday morning. The vast conference table for ten is cluttered with Filofaxes and stray paperwork. Although it's only midday, Cataldo's eyeliner is smudged, and she has the watery eyes of a long day's work.

"Have a seat, Miss Winters."

There are nine other chairs around the conference table, so I have my pick. I sit directly across from her. It gives me a view through the windows, where the noonish sun is obscured by gray clouds that have begun to spit snow flurries. The dense woods that edge the campus are dusted white.

The distance is odd, the table too wide to match my fantasies of being questioned by a police detective. On TV the suspect is always in a small, dingy room with a two-way mirror and a narrow desk. This feels like a job interview.

"Olivia, hello," Cataldo begins, smiling. Or is her expression a grimace? Her eyes dart to the corner. Then she takes a deep breath, suddenly more at ease. I crane my head around to look. A briefcase sits next to a lone chair, empty. Empty because I declined the need for the Claflin lawyer. I'm eighteen, so he's optional, and I know enough to know that asking for the lawyer can make you look guilty. And this isn't *Law & Order*. It's not dangerous.

The detective leans back in her chair. Offers a genuine, sympathetic lip press this time. "I know this is difficult, but please walk me through that night."

"Again? I told the officer the other day. . . ."

"Humor me."

90

I sigh and launch into the timeline I rehearsed with the Ivies.

Mostly I do it with the hope of making the detective feel more comfortable so that we might establish a rapport. I've heard my uncle James tell enough stories about all the things suspects do that tip him off. The line between suspect and witness. I must be the latter. Cataldo seems to be lapping it up.

"And then I went to bed," I finish. "Sorry, my night ended early because of crew conditioning the next morning."

Cataldo *hmm*s under her breath while looking down at an iPad. "Yes, they all stayed a bit later, until eleven, and then went to bed as well. The last time anyone saw Emma was around that time."

This is it. My moment. Do I mention the sweater, the door, the earring, or no? Is it meaningful? Should I have told her about Avery threatening Emma? I backed off at the last minute, but—

"What was the fight about?"

"What?" I'm confused by Cataldo going backward. She accepted my explanation of simply "Emma and Avery got into a fight" with no problems.

"It's unusual for two friends to get into a physical fight like that. Must have been about something pretty serious."

This is a game of chicken. A test. Luckily, I've always excelled at tests. She must know what the fight was about. People took videos of it.

"Emma got into Harvard. Avery didn't. It was a whole thing. Hard to explain."

Detective Cataldo's shoulders tense, and her mouth turns down in a frown. I'm distracted by her lipstick. It's the wrong shade of red. Too orange for her undertone. "You think I don't know how elite college admissions work? How competitive it is?"

Does she? I don't say that, but Cataldo seems to know what I'm thinking.

"I didn't go to an Ivy League school, but I'm not stupid. I've heard how cutthroat things are now. Avery Montfort accused Emma Russo of stealing her spot."

She's bluffing. I know her like I know myself. She's lower middle class at best, and she's approaching forty. She has the look of a comfortably single career woman, no high school–aged kids. When she was in high school, competitive college admissions wasn't like it is now, especially not for the working class. This whole process is like a foreign language to my mom, who applied to only three schools, was accepted to two, and didn't have to worry about six-figure debt.

Cataldo doesn't really know. I indulge her.

"Each of the elite schools can admit only so many Claflin students—two, maybe three," I say. "The quota's true of any high school, though Claflin has a higher acceptance rate than most. So, yeah, Avery would have thought Emma took her spot. The school is supposed to stop that kind of thing from happening, but . . ."

"Stop it how?" Now she's interested. Her spine goes ramrod straight and she leans toward me. It would be effective at the police station, but the too-wide conference table renders her act ridiculous.

"The college counselor is supposed to only endorse specific students with their recommendation for each school. They can't stop anyone from applying, but they don't have to give their recommendation."

"But . . . ?"

"What?"

"You said *but* before. What happened with Emma and Avery?"

Shit. I walked right into this.

"There's a new college counselor this year. He didn't know the rules. He let Emma apply SCEA to Harvard when he shouldn't have."

"SCEA?" she repeats, pronouncing it "skee-uh," as I did.

"Single-choice early action," I explain. "It means you're declaring a preference to the school, the only school you are applying to early, but if you're accepted, it's not binding. You can apply to other schools regular decision."

"The new counselor—that's Mr. Tipton?"

I nod. She *hmm*s again.

"So Avery and Emma got into a physical altercation. You and Mr. St. Clair intervened."

I'm not used to hearing Tyler referred to that way. *Mister* feels much too gentlemanly to apply to him. I confirm after a beat, and Detective Cataldo goes on.

"Did Miss Montfort make any threats?"

I can't read Cataldo's expression. Am I giving her vital new information or confirming what she already knows? This game doesn't work if she catches me in a lie. Liars look Guilty. As. Fuck.

"She was pretty upset," I hedge. Then I consider: If I tell her what Avery said, maybe the detective will actually look into it. A betrayal could earn me peace of mind. The question of Avery's involvement has been niggling at me, carving out my insides like a subtle poison. Detective Cataldo could solve it for me. I take a deep breath.

"Listen, she said she'd kill her, but that's just something you say when you're really mad."

Cataldo hums again; the sound is low and musical. She knew already.

"Tell me more about Avery. Your friend-group dynamic. Between her and Emma especially."

I swallow hard, suddenly desperate for water. "What do you want to know? Avery's smart, beautiful, rich. Emma was, too. So are Sierra and Margot, actually. We sound like a cult."

"And you?"

"I'm decently smart and not heinously unattractive."

Cataldo doesn't laugh at any of my quips. A professional. "You're here on a scholarship," she says.

"Yes. I'm from Maryland. My mom's a teacher. Uncle's a cop." I watch for it, the slight rise of an eyebrow, and yes, she's impressed. *I am more like you than I am like them,* I'm telling her. I don't know why I need her to know that, but I do.

"Is it typical for Avery to fly into a rage?"

"No," I say, telling the truth. "Everything was riding on her getting into Harvard. She's a triple legacy, and her mom is . . . a lot. So not getting in set her off."

"What other sorts of things 'set her off'?"

Uh-oh. I gulp. "Uh, nothing in particular. We fight about totally normal stuff."

What I'm really thinking: when things don't go her way. That'll trigger an Avery flounce, pretty consistently. But it's a huff, a scathing look, some choice words, not a rage. The other night truly was an outlier. Wasn't it?

"And what about you, Olivia?"

"Sorry?"

"I'm wondering if it's typical for you to be out of your bed in the middle of the night, wandering around campus."

Shit.

"You appear on the security footage in front of Whitley Hall at approximately two-thirty a.m. on the night of the murder. The other cameras were out, the ones by your dorm, Bay. Very odd, considering."

My breath comes fast, my heart pounding. How can I explain without sounding senile? "Considering what?"

"According to the medical examiner, Emma died sometime between one-thirty and two-thirty a.m. We checked the security footage, and there you are. Just you, no one else. The timing is interesting."

Interesting. The word hangs, rattles around in my skull. She's confirmed all my worst fears. I could have saved Emma. I should have gone fucking left.

The truth tumbles out of me in a rush. "I had a nightmare. Woke up and saw Emma had never come home. But her sweater was there. Something told me to go outside and look for her. I thought maybe the party had gone late, and she was stuck outside. I got to Whitley and figured she must have stayed over with Tyler, so I went back." I wait. The detective's mouth hangs open, and her eyes search my face.

"What about Emma's sweater?" Cataldo recovers. "Why was that significant?"

"It was the one she had on at the party. So it meant she came back to the dorm and then left again. And the door was open."

"But you decided she must have stayed over with Mr. St. Clair?"

"I . . ." I take a deep breath. Why did I change my mind? "It was the middle of the night. I had a bad dream, and I wasn't thinking clearly. I was out alone in the freezing cold. I convinced myself it was the only logical explanation. That she was fine. I couldn't have known."

Right?

"How did you get out of the dorm? We checked the Bay Hall security footage, the internal feed. You don't come in or out the front door. Neither does Emma, if she did return to your room."

Double shit. If I tell Cataldo about the unmonitored window, I'll ruin it for everyone. But I need an explanation. And isn't Emma more important?

Cataldo is staring at me. Not like I'm guilty, but not like I'm innocent, either. She's merely acutely interested. I really want that water now. I swallow hard.

"Listen, I don't really care how you snuck out, Olivia. I don't work here. I'm not your keeper. I simply need to corroborate that it happened the way you say it did, when you say it did."

"There's a window. It doesn't have an alarm." This is bad. I was outside right after Emma died, and they have no proof I left my dorm when I said I did. That I was even coming from the dorm. Wait. "Are you asking because you think I did it? Do you think I came from the boathouse? Why would I walk from there to Whitley, then back to my dorm?"

"Hmm." Cataldo shifts in her seat, leans back into the recline of the chair. "It's why I asked you why you were out there. Looking for a logical explanation, that's all."

The wheels in my head are turning. My questions choke up my throat again. "Were the cameras out all the way to the boathouse? You think her killer cut them out?"

She ignores my questions. "So, you woke up from a nightmare, realized Emma wasn't there, snuck out a window, walked over to Whitley, then turned around and went back."

"Yes."

She *hmms* under her breath. Again. It's irritating enough that I know it's on purpose.

"I know it sounds odd," I say. "But I found footprints under the window, Emma's size, and one of her earrings. She went through that window. I wanted to find her."

"An earring?" Cataldo perks up. "You're sure it was Emma Russo's?"

"Definitely. Tyler gave them to her as a gift. Diamond studs. Too fussy for most girls here, so they stood out. It must have fallen out when she was coming in the window. You know how studs are. The backs pop off at the slightest provocation."

"I don't own any diamond studs." Cataldo cracks a smile. "I'm curious why this didn't come up in your first interview?"

"I put it in my pocket, forgot about it until now. Everything from that night is kind of a blur."

"Do you know if she was wearing that set on the night of her death?"

"I can't remember, but I assume so, since I found the earring under the window."

"Emma wasn't found wearing any earrings," Cataldo says. I watch her, watching me. Know her wheels are turning. Mine certainly are. Did Emma lose that earring another time coming through the window? But the dorms are cleaned every week. What are the odds it got missed?

"Oh" is the only thing I can say.

"Have you told me everything about that night? Every detail? No other earrings in your pockets?"

I don't like her tone. It walks the razor-thin line between mocking and accusatory.

"Yes," I grind out. "I've told you everything. And I want you to know I would never hurt Emma." It's true, it's all true, but the only thing I can think is: Would a killer say the same things? Has a killer said the same things already? Cataldo is looking at me, total poker face, and I can't tell what she's thinking. It's maddening.

I suck in a breath to stop myself from crying.

Then I think. The cameras were out from Bay to the boathouse. Anyone from Bay might have used that as cover. Anyone, like Avery.

"Do you think Avery could have done it?" I blurt out.

Cataldo raises an eyebrow. "Do you think she would have killed someone for taking her spot at Harvard?"

"I don't know."

Yes.

"You said there were two, three spots? So Emma's not the only one who got into Harvard. Someone else got in, too, and Avery didn't hurt them."

Yet. I need to get Cataldo off this line of questioning, which will lead her straight to me.

"How did Emma die?" It's been gnawing at me. I've tried to imagine what it was like for her up until the very last. Morbid.

Cataldo narrows her eyes at me. "We're not releasing that information at this time. You can understand."

Yes. They are withholding it to use against the killer. Top-secret information. But I have to assume that means she didn't drown.

"Olivia, have you seen the grief counselor yet?"

Not a question I was expecting. I stumble through an answer. "Uh, yeah, I had to, for like an hour yesterday. Why?"

Cataldo presses her lips together with concern. "Some curiosity about your friend is natural, but it's okay to give yourself space to be sad. To mourn."

She pushes back her chair and gets up, gesturing for the door. "Anyway, I wanted some clarification on why you were out so late that night, and now I have it. Thank you, Miss Winters. I may very well have some follow-up questions about your middle-of-the-night adventures. We'll be in touch."

She's polite as punch, but why do I have the feeling this isn't over?

I think I may be a suspect.

CHAPTER TEN

Sierra is waiting for me outside the conference room.

"You next?" But she shakes her head.

"No, my dad insisted on calling in our family lawyer, so they have to wait to speak to me. Avery and Margot are using that, too, to buy time."

Yeah, *that's* not suspicious.

"I wanted to check that you're okay. How did it go?"

"It was really straightforward," I begin slowly. Sierra's smile seems genuine, but I can't tell if it's purposefully disarming. I can't help sensing that Avery sent her to check up on me, make sure I did what they asked. "I walked her through the timeline, but I was honest that I went to bed early and didn't see Emma after that."

"She didn't ask about us?"

Bingo. Reconnaissance mission for sure.

"Nope." I'm nonchalant. Cool as a cucumber. Then I remember what Ethan said. That I should simply ask Sierra or Margot, one-on-one, what's up. Sierra isn't the only one who can play games.

But not here. I scan the halls, think of Cataldo listening on the other side of the door. "Hey, since exams are back on, you up for a last-minute AP Calc cram sesh?"

Sierra looks at her wrist. An empty gesture—there's no watch on it. "Uh, sure," she stammers. "I can tutor you for a few hours."

Tutor. Not study. I'm not *that* bad at calc . . . but I'll take it.

"Meet you in the Bay lounge in fifteen? I want to change out of . . . all this." I indicate my shoes, which are pinching, and my pantyhose, which I'd like to burn.

Sierra agrees, and I head to the dorm, where I slip into mercifully soft, stretchy jeans and my Doc Martens. Then I go to the lounge and spot her at a table. Apparently, no one else wants to study immediately following a murder assembly—go figure—so the lounge is otherwise blissfully empty. Sierra and I dive right into some problem sets, and just to prove a point, I complete the first one on my own and nail it. Once I learn a concept, I'm good. I just sometimes need extra help, *mon amie.*

I catch Sierra checking her phone every few minutes. She'll bolt soon if I don't act fast.

"Hey, I was wondering. . . . What's with you guys being so anal about the timeline? None of us saw Emma after the party, right?"

Sierra's hand stills, pencil poised precariously over her notepaper. "No. Why would you ask me that?"

"Uh, because the detective is asking, and we had an emergency meeting to go over the timeline."

"We just wanted to get on the same page. You're being paranoid, Liv."

Her words echo. Familiar. When I asked them why they went into Northampton when they knew I had homework. When I asked if they went to a room party without me. Late brunches and early dinners and movies in Avery's room.

You're being paranoid, Liv. We didn't purposefully exclude you.

I wasn't paranoid then, and I'm not now.

But I smile, laugh it off. I am good, agreeable Olivia. "Yeah, sorry, the detective just has me spooked. She's kind of scary."

"I'm glad my dad called in our lawyer, then. Speaking of, I gotta go. I have a prep call in twenty minutes. Catch you later?"

"Sure, dinner?"

Sierra hesitates, then closes her textbook with a snap. "I was gonna order pizza and cram some more in my room. Rain check?"

"Definitely." My teeth hurt as I force a pleasant tone. I let her go, pretend everything is A-OK, even though I know that when I head out to the dining hall for dinner and knock on Sierra's door, she won't be there. Avery's Audi will be missing from its usual spot. My friends are a war council, and I'm not invited.

The Ivies aren't the only ones skipping dinner at the dining hall. It's half-empty when I roll in at six, enabling me to grab some primo options without the line. I order a custom stir-fry and head into the table area like it's the first day of school all over again. Awkward with a tray and unsure where to sit.

Then I spot Seth Feldstein, also alone. Hot shame and the thrill of the hunt wash through me at the same time. I know Seth is the perfect person to talk to, but I've also been fastidiously avoiding him for, oh, the last two years. Too hard to look him in the face after what I did. But he's an easy mark, an ideal place to start if I'm going to piece together Emma's last movements. Because I'm going to find out why my friends are lying *and* try to save my own ass from being a suspect.

And I've gotten nowhere on my own so far. Before dinner I checked everywhere—Instagram, TikTok, even a Hail Mary on

Facebook—for posts from the party. Most people's photos are from early in the night, everyone's faces pristine and their eyes bright before a long night and alcohol ruined them. Very little from later in the night is public. I need access to people's phones, to their apps, so I can check their archives manually.

Enter Seth.

I throw my shoulders back and stride over. I can be confident, flirty. I know what Seth likes.

He's spooning Cap'n Crunch into his mouth, even though it's dinner, while staring down at his phone. His shirt is rumpled, like he found it crumpled in a ball at the bottom of his closet, which he probably did.

"Mind if I sit here?" I don't wait for his permission, though he grunts it while I'm midsquat. "Have you finished your paper for AP Brit Lit?" I ask. It's as good a conversation starter as any. Our papers are now due Saturday.

"Nope. I spent all yesterday writing supplements."

"Oh, for regular decision?" He side-eyes me, like why am I even here and what do I want? Touché. "I didn't get into Penn," I offer. "Well, I was deferred. I'm in the same boat. There goes my Christmas holiday, right?"

"You're really thinking about college applications after what happened?"

Ouch. I twirl lo mein noodles onto my fork. "I don't really have a choice. I have to apply somewhere. And Emma . . . I want to know what happened. I left the party early. You were there, right?"

"I live in Whitley, so yeah."

"Did you . . . see her? Late in the evening, I mean. I left at like ten. Did you see her fight with anyone?"

"Uh, other than Avery? You were there for that." Seth shifts uncomfortably. "Why are you asking me? Aren't the police looking into all of this?"

"Did they question you?"

He shakes his head. "Not me, but a few of my friends. They told them the same thing I'll tell you: Emma was drinking, like everyone else. She was with Tyler some of the night, with your friends other times. It's not like I kept tabs."

Seth's hackles are up. Shit. I backpedal and play innocent. "Sorry, I only thought maybe you saw her before she died, could tell me she had a good time at the party. I really miss her. I'm sorry to bother you." I move to get up, but Seth clears his throat and motions for me to stay.

"No, I'm sorry. I get you. It's sick what happened. *Here.* Claflin is supposed to be safe." He cradles a glass of soda between his hands. Takes a sip. "Look, Emma wasn't my favorite person in the world, considering, but I'm sorry she's dead."

Considering? Dammit, that means he knows. Though, of course he knows. He'd be a moron not to have figured it out. But my part in the ruse? I look at him through my lashes, subtle. No ire seems to be coming my way. In fact, the next thing he does is apologize.

"Sorry, I know they're your friends, but to be honest, I never got why."

"What does that mean?" It comes out a screech without my meaning it to.

"One of these things is not like the others," he singsongs like a Muppet.

I scowl and cross my arms over my chest. "Because I'm poor?"

Seth laughs. "I was going to say nice, but poor works, too."

"I'm not nice," I say. It comes out petulant. What a horrible thing to say to an ambitious woman. *Nice* gets left in the dust. *Nice* doesn't catfish Seth Feldstein for three months to help Emma land the captainship of the FIRST Robotics team. But I'm not going to tell him that. It's my dirty little secret, the worst thing I've done as an Ivy. Seth can just continue hating Emma for that. After all, she did put him on the List. Ingrid is on her.

"All right, fine, not a backstabbing bitch, then. Whatever the opposite of that is, that's you. I don't think you know half of what your friends have done. We all talk, you know, about what the Ivies get up to behind our backs. Your name doesn't come up very often. And if you're asking me what happened later that night at the party, that means your friends aren't telling you shit."

He has me. I am on the hook. I need to know more about what people have said about the Ivies. Did they figure out we were the ones who set off that Whitley alarm before finals last year? Do they know how we got into all the best classes? Does Seth know about the catfishing but have a spectacular poker face?

"You're right," I concede, hoping it will gain me the upper hand. "They're keeping something from me about that night. Which is why I want to piece together Emma's final hours myself. I was hoping I could look at your phone."

"That isn't what I was expecting. And it's a big ask. One's phone is sacred." He holds it to his chest, raises an expectant eyebrow.

"Dude, one of my friends is dead, and the other three are lying. Don't be a dick."

"Fine, fine." He unlocks his phone and hands it to me. I go right for Instagram, click onto his profile page, and tap to create a new set of highlights. Select from archive, slight scroll, and there they are. Seth's Stories from Wednesday night. I select all of them and save.

I tap into the new highlight group and watch. Most of the photos and videos are inane: selfies with dumb stickers affixed on top and neon scrawl drawn with too-thick fingers, so the words jumble together; Boomerangs of people zippering; video bursts of students shouting "Chug!" at willing victims. There are a few of the fight, video I refuse to watch for more than a few seconds. I catch Margot draped all over Milo in a drunken group shot, and Avery in the background of another, talking intently on the phone. I'm nearly at the end when I see a flash of red in the background. Emma's sweater. I press and hold with my index finger, stilling the image. Emma's on the stairs, going up. Pin-straight black hair folded into an immaculate French braid peeks out from behind her right shoulder. Margot.

I feel heat at my back. Seth hovers over my shoulder, and I jerk away, craving my own space. "What time did the party end, Seth?"

"About eleven-thirty, because of curfew. All the girls left, and after that what's the point?"

I tap back out to the highlight. The photo is near the end of the set. So maybe it was 11:15. Why was Margot going upstairs with Emma? I do some housekeeping, deleting the party highlight, and slide Seth's phone across the table. "Thanks."

"No problem. You know, if you want to find out more about your friends, talk to Rebecca Ito. She has a lot of opinions. And maybe she saw more of Emma at the party."

There's a glint in Seth's eye that I don't like, like he's a trickster god, delighted to lead me down the path of destruction.

"See you later, Seth." I gather what's left of my dinner onto my tray for busing and turn to leave.

"I bet."

I save a single roll before I dump the rest of the tray and then head for the exit. I'm in the middle of an unladylike bite when Rebecca Ito passes by, heading toward the salad bar. Speak of the devil.

"Webecca!" I chew quickly, clear my throat, try again. "Rebecca, hey."

She's just placing her tray on the metal track and reaching for a plate. "Hey."

"Can I ask you something?"

She flips a shiny black curtain of hair over her shoulder. "I don't know, can you?"

I ignore the dig. "It's about my friends. Avery, Sierra, Margot, Emma."

"I know who they are. The Ivies. What about them?"

"I overheard you at Emma's memorial. You think Avery killed her?"

"Shit, Olivia, that's pretty heavy for dinner." Rebecca sets the plate on her tray, which she slides off to the side of the station. She leans in, dropping her voice. "Do *you* think Avery killed Emma? It's a weird thing to ask me, otherwise."

It's like there's baking soda mixed with Coca-Cola in my stomach, threatening to erupt. But I push it down, play it cool.

"Seth said I should talk to you. About them. He said something about you guys keeping score."

Rebecca smirks. "Yeah, we're not stupid. Obviously. Or else why would you guys be sabotaging our exams and grades. Taking out the competition. I'd be impressed with the depths to which the Ivies are willing to descend if I didn't hate you all."

"So what? We gave a few kids the wrong notes, turned in a

107

plagiarist or three, and angled for the best leadership positions. It's nothing the rest of you wouldn't do. Haven't done."

"Oh, honey." But nothing in Rebecca's voice comes close to conveying sympathy. "Do you really think that's all it was? Do you really want to know about your friends? I'll tell you. But you might not like it." She looks far too pleased by the notion.

Whatever Rebecca has to share can't be unheard. Right now, all I have is a feeling that my friends are keeping something from me. If I let Rebecca spill, I'll know.

But let's be real, haven't I always known? All the after-parties I heard about the next morning. Shopping trips they "felt bad' inviting me to go on. Emma is *dead*. Nothing is more important than finding out who killed her.

I make a decision. "Tell me."

"Not here. Follow me. And throw that away." She points at the remains of the roll in my hand. I'm about to protest, but I swallow my words, along with the last quarter of my bread.

Rebecca taps her student ID to the sensor, and the doors to the allergy-free room slide open. We slip inside, and with the slow closing *whoosh* of the doors, we're hermetically sealed off, safe from both gluten and prying ears.

"You guys are subtle, I'll give you that," Rebecca starts, hopping up onto the bread counter. Hopefully her butt doesn't count as contamination. "Half convinced myself I was just really unlucky. But then I talked to Seth, Autumn, Diana, Jason. . . . Go figure— we're all in competition with you and your friends for class rank or have been up for very specific positions in your clubs and activities. Anyone who gets in your way ends up with very bad luck."

"What was your bad luck, then?" My voice is small because I know. I got her those demerits for sneaking out to hook up with

Milo. Maybe this is all a setup, a chance for her to dig her claws into me.

"Margot Kim slept with my boyfriend and convinced him to break up with me the morning of finals last year. She got me a shit-ton of demerits for sneaking out and fucked me over in Model UN. And then she didn't even have the decency to start dating Milo after we broke up. That was the tip-off."

"I'm sure that's not true," I say, because, well, I know the second part isn't. Yet I don't rush to tell her it was me.

"Ask Milo. He'll tell you. After he broke up with me by text, I got the whole thing out of him. I'd tanked half my exams and dropped four spots in the class ranking by that point."

"Margot likes Milo, though. It was probably a normal hookup, not sabotage." My voice sounds meek even to me.

"Perhaps." Rebecca shrugs, but her heart's not in it. "There's a pattern of sabotage, however. You should talk to Autumn about varsity rowing."

My stomach plummets. "Why?"

Rebecca offers a minx grin. "We always assumed it was you who did it, to get yourself the spot, but you seem so flummoxed by all of this, so maybe not. Talk to Autumn and Jason Wang. And Seth can tell you some choice facts about your dearly departed Emma. Now I'm hungry." She hops down and grabs a gluten-free muffin, then presses the button to release the doors and delivers her parting shot. "Oh, and re Avery: I don't know if she's a killer. But I do know she's gotten someone expelled. The word *blackmail's* also been thrown around. In relation to you, actually." She hums "Hail to the Chief" on her way out.

CHAPTER ELEVEN

I test the waters on the Ivies' group text, say my interview went fine, ask, "How about you guys?" No one responds. Not last night, and not this morning. Still, I start the day with purpose. I'm going to talk to Margot about that picture. She went off with Emma, and I want to know why. Luckily, I know precisely where she'll be at 10:00 a.m.

A ghost passes through me in the doorway of AP Gov. It's a coldness that snaps down my spine, a surreal sense like I shouldn't be here. We always sat in the back-left corner. Now Emma's desk is empty.

Margot's in her seat, though. My mind flashes to that perfect French braid, Emma's red sweater, them going up the stairs just hours before Emma died. Rebecca's accusation hangs heavy in my mind. My blood begins to boil.

Still, I head over and take my usual seat.

"Hey," I say, offering an encouraging smile. *Talk to me,* it says. *Tell me the truth.* Even though that's ridiculous, because Margot has never opened up to me about a single thing.

"Coach Gray's not coming. Our paper has been moved to January." Margot yawns, like it isn't bonkers that we get a month's extension because our teacher is so traumatized. I also imagine Katherine Montfort will see red when our grades are held up.

"Do we have to stay here, then?" I stare at the empty desk at the front of the room. Half the class didn't show up. "Wanna go grab a coffee? I'm flagging."

Margot never says no to Starbucks. There's a franchise branch in the Austen student center, because of course. And I have a strategy. We leave class and have our orders in hand within five minutes.

"It's my treat," I say before Margot can pull out her phone to pay. She has, naturally, ordered the most nauseatingly extra drink, which costs me almost five dollars, but it's worth it to put her at ease. Except it doesn't. Margot raises her perfectly sculpted eyebrows once we've settled into a quiet corner of the main lounge and fallen back into a set of puffy armchairs.

"You never treat," Margot says, her words more venom than voice. Suspicious.

"I know." High-pitched. I'm full of shit. But I forge on. "It actually makes me feel more centered, in a way, doing something nice for someone else. It's a good distraction."

Margot blows into the slotted opening in the lid. "So, what do you want to talk about?" She misses nothing.

I wish I knew how to approach Margot. But of all the Ivies, she and I have always been the least close. Margot doesn't get intense and anxious about things like I do, and sometimes I'm certain she thinks I'm an alien. I'm always watching myself with Margot, so today is nothing new.

"How are you coping with everything? You know, emotionally?" We'll approach this like pretend therapy. Friends share.

Margot shrugs a cashmere-covered shoulder. "It's up and

111

down each day. Weird things remind me of her, and I forget what happened."

It takes all my strength not to say that it's barely been forty-eight hours.

For a moment she's lost in her own thoughts, remembering something specific that draws a hint of a smile. Then it becomes a scowl. "It wasn't supposed to go this way. We were going to get into all our schools and graduate top of the class and go be fucking titans of industry. But not Emma anymore." Margot sniffs, though I don't see any tears. "Sorry, I didn't mean to unload on you like that. Avery doesn't want to talk about it. I've been feeling . . ." She shakes her head. "It's nothing."

"No, no it's fine. I need to talk about it, too. Detective Cataldo doesn't think I'm acting sad enough. She doesn't get that if I don't hold it all in, I'll burst." It doesn't matter that I'm wary of Margot. It feels good to get out my anxious feelings.

"You are acting kind of weird, Liv." Margot pointedly takes a swig of coffee. I remind myself who I'm talking to. Margot is a bear trap—she lures you in and then snaps at the perfect moment. I came here to get information.

"It's not weird. I want to know what happened after I left. I feel guilty. The last time I saw her, she was digging her nails into my arm after I'd pulled her off Avery. I should have checked to see if she was okay. Did none of you talk to her after the fight?" A leading question I know the answer to.

"Emma was fine." Margot snorts. "Last I saw her at the party, she was heading off for a hookup. A good lay to cure all ills. Think about it, Liv. Emma had everything she wanted, just the way she planned. I'm sure she died happy."

Holy shit.

"What about you?" I hit back. Kid gloves off now. "Did you get lucky with Milo? I saw the pictures, and you two looked comfy."

Margot tilts her head, assessing me. "Why would you ask that? Are you into him or something? Sorry, but you're not his type."

"What's his type?"

She offers me a look that simply says *not you*. Rebecca was right. Time to wrap this up.

"So, you're saying Emma left the party with Tyler? What time was that? You told the detective?"

An exasperated look passes over Margot's pristine features. Still, she indulges me after a long drag of her sugary drink. She finishes with a wet smack, already standing to leave. "I never said it was Tyler." She throws her bag over her shoulder. "And yes, I told the police. You should leave the detective work to them and stop snooping, Liv. Interrogating your friends is a bad look." With that, she makes for the exit.

Friends. What a rich word. I'm not sure I have any friends at all anymore.

I arrive at the journalism lab ten minutes late. We're on an exam day schedule, so newspaper is before lunch. Or so I thought. The classroom is empty. I stand in the doorway, blink heavily, in case this is one of those dreams where you show up for an exam to find an empty classroom and then, whoops, you're also naked. But I'm fully clothed, and I didn't fall asleep.

"Olivia, hey."

My gaze snaps to the back of the classroom, where Ethan is half-hidden behind his computer screen.

"Where is everyone?" I unzip my coat and start to unravel

my scarf, and as I draw nearer to him, I try to slow my ragged breaths.

"Everyone turned in their stuff, and all that's left is layout, so Vasquez let them go."

"Where is Vasquez?"

"Early lunch."

I slide into my chair and turn on my monitor.

"Listen, I did some work on it yesterday," Ethan says. "It's almost done, so we'll definitely be able to traffic it tomorrow."

I bristle. "Ethan, you know that the print layout is my job."

He ducks his head, plays with the dark curls at the nape of his neck. "I know, but with everything that happened, I didn't want you to worry about making a stupid deadline."

Shit, he's really thoughtful. "Sorry," I say. "I'm just a bit sensitive with the division of roles. They won't need me if you can do my job." I'm only half joking.

"Hey, you could do my job with your eyes closed, so the feeling is mutual."

Then Ethan sighs deeply and leans across me. My breath catches as his arm grazes mine, and warmth spreads through me. Ethan grabs ahold of my computer mouse and focuses intently on the monitor, so he doesn't catch the flush that has surely deepened in my cheeks.

Ethan clicks open InDesign. "I also didn't want you to see this, or at least have to deal with it for too long." He clicks over to a new inside spread. On the left is a giant image of Emma with her full name, her birthday, and Wednesday's date.

Always in our hearts is written in a saccharine cursive font. To the right of it is an obituary.

"It was Tyler's idea, and Ms. Vasquez ran with it," Ethan explains. "He sent it to me yesterday. She's already approved the layout, so you don't have to bother with it." Now Ethan is the one with spots of color on his cheeks.

"Thanks, Ethan. It looks great." The compliment is genuine, though it comes out hollow. For a minute I get lost between Emma's dimpled smile and Tyler's byline. I skim the first paragraph. It strikes the balance between florid and factual, overflowing with Tyler's apparent affection. Looks like he got his eulogy. I wonder if he knows it's for a girl who cheated on him. I force myself to look away. I don't want to cry in front of Ethan.

Ethan clears his throat. "Mr. Tipton sent me the current ED list. We can update it with any last-minute additions tomorrow, but I figure we'll lay it in now so it's ready. Congrats, by the way. I was surprised but also not surprised, you know."

"Sorry, what?"

"Harvard. I thought you were applying to Penn. I mean, I'm not shocked by the acceptance. You're brill—"

"Fuck! Please tell me that Tipton did not email that to you. Has anyone else seen it?"

"Whoa, whoa." He presses his palms against the air as if I'm a bull about to charge. "He sent it to the editor email account. Only I've seen it, as far as I know. What's the matter?"

Panic and grief overwhelm me, and I burst like a dam, fat, ugly tears spilling down my cheeks as my breath pushes past my lips in a staccato rhythm.

I've transformed from charging animal to porcelain doll before Ethan's eyes. It takes him a moment to shift gears, but once he does, he performs effortless emotional triage. A solid warmth engulfs me, a hug I never would have admitted I needed, but now that I have it, it's a miracle elixir. And Ethan's soothing voice tells me everything's going to be okay, and I believe him.

"But please don't ruin my sweater with your snot."

I choke on a laugh through the tears. And then a fresh wave of embarrassment crashes over me, and I break away.

"Thanks. I'm fine now." I wipe dribble from my nose on the back of my sweater sleeve. "I don't want you to think I'm weak because I cried in front of you."

"Crying doesn't make you weak." Ethan grabs ahold of my hand. The gesture is intimate and unexpected, more so than the hug, and it jolts electricity through me. "I don't think you're weak. Most days you're pretty intimidating, if I'm honest. So for you to cry . . . Tell me what's wrong."

Ethan's eyes swirl with emerald and amber, glint with care. And as long as—

"You weren't hooking up with Emma, were you?" I blurt. My stomach turns sick at the thought. Stupidly, I think of him as mine. But Emma hooked up with someone that night, and Ethan told me that he was investigating. Was it for more than just a news piece?

"What? No! Why would you think that?"

And I can breathe again. Then it all comes tumbling out: how I applied to Harvard when I shouldn't have, Emma's and my twin acceptances, but our very different decisions about telling the truth. Ethan's eyes go wider as I continue, into my post-dream middle-of-the-night walk, discovering Emma's body, my chat with Cataldo, the security cameras being out. That I'm a suspect.

"And, I don't know, Avery and Emma got in that huge fight,

and now she's dead. Who knows what she could do to me? And I'm sure everyone is lying to me!"

Ethan gestures for me to stop. "This is a lot. Let's put a pin in the 'your friend's murder' part for now. Let me get this straight: you and the Ivies have spent the last few years sabotaging your classmates, but it turns out that your friends did even worse things than you thought they did?"

"Yeah, I thought we were just tracking class ranks and working the system, but now they're lying about the night Emma died. I don't know who to trust."

Ethan reclines his ergonomic chair, steeples his fingers in front of his mouth. Thinking. Processing. And I realize what I've done. He knows the deep underbelly of who I am now. Backstabbing boarding-school bitch. What if he finds out what I did to him to try to get editor in chief? Though after Rebecca's hint, I'm not even entirely clear on what Avery did on my behalf. Bribery or blackmail? Who cares that it didn't even work in the end. If Ethan finds out I targeted him, he'll hate me.

Finally Ethan speaks. "I'd heard you and your friends did stuff. Rumor has it one of you pulled the fire alarm in Whitley last year before exams. . . . Other stuff, too. Honestly, Olivia, it's a relief to hear you didn't know about the half of it. I always wondered. Worried."

He ducks his head, avoiding my gaze. Butterflies work their way up my esophagus. He worried about me? Sure, his concern was whether I was a sociopathic asshole, but nonetheless. He cares.

"That's the problem," I say. "I have no clue what half I don't know. Rebecca was cryptic. Talk to Autumn, Jason Wang."

"Well, hang on." Ethan hops up, jogs over to the portable whiteboard we use for story assignments. He erases the fading detritus of the December issue. Across the top, he writes my four friends' names: Avery, Sierra, Margot, Emma. I hesitate at Emma's name. It seems *wrong* to investigate the misdeeds of the dead.

"Do you think something shady that Emma did got her killed?" I ask.

Ethan frowns. "I hope not. But we're not very good journalists if we don't ask the question. Did someone say something?"

"She may have been cheating on Tyler," I concede. "And if Avery, Sierra, and Margot were doing heavy shit behind my back, Emma might have been as well. I'm not sure what to think anymore. Put *cheating* with a question mark under her name."

Ethan does as I say, then starts to fill out a column of names on the left side of the board.

Rebecca Ito

Autumn Hollander

Jason Wang

Tyler St. Clair

Seth Feldstein

Seeing Seth's name makes me break into a cold sweat. If Ethan finds out about the catfishing . . .

"Add Milo McNamara and Diana Klein, too," I say to distract him. More names, more threads to follow that aren't Seth. "We targeted them. And Kaila Montgomery." I swallow heavy at that one. When Rebecca accused Avery of getting someone expelled,

I knew exactly who she meant. Except Kaila got herself expelled, didn't she?

Together, Ethan and I fill in the board with what nuggets Rebecca offered. Margot slept with Milo. Autumn thinks (thought?) I did something for my spot on varsity rowing. Avery got Kaila expelled.

I leave one thing off. The blackmail accusation. Ethan can never know.

"So we need to talk to all these people," Ethan says, scanning the list before taking his seat. "I feel like the Ivies stuff is more your business, and I can handle the murder investigation."

"Excuse me, *we*?" I chide. "When did this become a joint operation?" When did it become an operation at all?

Ethan grins. "I mean, I was already poking around. And if this is about the Ivies, things just got bigger. You want to get to the bottom of who your friends really are. I want the story. I need you, and you need me."

I need you. I float on an upswell of giddiness. Then my ambition slams me right back down.

"I want to share a byline. This could get national pickup, far beyond the *Ledger,* and I could use that edge for college."

Ethan tilts his head in confusion. "You already got into Harvard, though."

We are right back to where we started.

"You're right." My voice goes quiet. "I got into Harvard. But that's not the same as being able to afford Harvard. I'm applying to other schools regular decision. And if Avery really did kill Emma because she got in, then I could be next."

Ethan's expression finally turns to one of gentle chiding. "Olivia, you sound like a character in a bad slasher film. This isn't some Ivy League–motivated serial killer. We won't print it, and I'll keep your secret, but not because I think Avery Montfort will murder you."

"You don't think she did it, then?"

"I'm not saying that." Ethan jostles his leg. Thinking. "Obviously, someone on campus did it. And the security cameras thing? That's a bombshell. Premeditated if they shorted the cameras ahead of time." More leg jostling. Ethan bites his lower lip. "You're right that it had to be someone Emma knew. The cheating angle is compelling. I'm sure the police are looking at Tyler. They always look at the boyfriend."

"And me," I remind him. "I was out of bed with no alibi."

"I'm sure you weren't the only one," Ethan tries to reassure me. "Leave the party timeline and afterward to me. I know the guys who were there, and I'll ask without making it seem weird."

"She went off with Margot around eleven," I remind him. "After that, Margot says she went to hook up, possibly not with Tyler. And it's been bugging me that there was no after-party. There's always an after-party."

"We would know, since we're never invited to them!" Ethan jokes. A frisson of anger stirs in my belly.

"My friends invite me when they can. But I have to go to bed early because of rowing."

Ethan places a reassuring hand on my arm. "Sorry, I wasn't making fun of you or implying anything. You're right. There's always a room party somewhere. I'll find out who hosted."

I offer a small smile. "Also, Emma came back to the room at some point. Her sweater was there, and she left the door open. I think it was after midnight. Any earlier, she would have woken me up." Now I'm the one fidgeting. "I should check with Paul in security. The feed outside Whitley wasn't tampered with—Cataldo saw me—so Emma should be on camera leaving."

Ethan shakes his head. "Not if she went out the back and stuck to the woods side. You've never snuck in or out of Whitley?"

"I haven't had reason to," I mumble. Code for *I don't have a boyfriend.* I can't bear to meet Ethan's eyes.

His reply is nonchalant, not judgmental. "There's a maintenance door in the basement with a busted lock. Advantage of one of the older buildings. We don't have to climb in and out of windows."

I raise a brow. "You sneak out of the dorms at night?" Does Ethan have a secret girlfriend in Bay? Or worse, Kisner Hall? Is he one of those skeevy guys who likes freshmen and sophomores?

"Uh, no." He laughs. "But my roommate does. He's dating Nora Patrick." Ethan uses air quotes around the word *dating.*

"Okay, so what about Tyler and the cheating angle?" I steer us back on task. "We can't go around asking people, *Hey, were you hooking up with Emma?*"

"Like you asked me?"

"And see how well you took it. And I had to ask. You said they always look into the boyfriend. Same goes for secret boyfriends."

"Hookups aren't worth killing over."

"And college admissions are? See what you can find out. They'll tell a guy, brag about it, but if I ask . . ."

"Are you trying to shunt all the investigation work onto me?" Ethan teases. I like this, us being playful with each other. It's distracting me from being terrified.

"No." I grin at him. "I have the hardest job of all."

"And what's that?"

"Going to war with the Ivies."

CHAPTER TWELVE

Ethan and I transfer the whiteboard to a shared spreadsheet so we can keep track of who is doing what. It feels like the weirdest group project of my life. My short list includes talking to Autumn, Seth, and Jason Wang ASAP. I put an asterisk next to Kaila Montgomery. I don't know where to start with her. We haven't seen her in years.

The rest are easy enough. I shoot Autumn a text asking if she has a moment after exams today. I throw in an offer to buy her coffee to sweeten the deal, and push down the panic from burning through my incidentals budget with all this coffee bribery. I'm not super close to Jason, so I send a more formal email. I give him a cover story about interviewing him for a *Ledger* article. As for Seth, I can pretend I talked to him and then feed Ethan a version of the truth. Avery catfished him. Keep me out of it.

The text from Autumn comes a minute later.

Drop dead.

Okay, so not easy, then. I shoot back a response, but Autumn remains decidedly quiet. I send a text to Ethan instead.

> SOS. Whatever the Ivies did to Autumn is way worse than I expected. She won't return my texts.

I send a screenshot of her message for good measure. My phone buzzes a moment later.

Oof. Must mean your friends are pretty bad. But good news is it'll make a great story if we can get Autumn and the others to talk.

> Ha. That's a big IF. And I have an exam in 5. Autumn may be off campus before I even find her.

Leave it to me.

> What are you going to do?

I AM co-editor for a reason. I'm not just another pretty face, you know.

I smile in spite of myself. Oh, I know.

After my final exam for the day, I emerge from Colchester into the late-afternoon sun, which is already sinking over the horizon, even though it's barely three. Freshmen and sophomores push across the quad, dragging heavy suitcases behind them, the grinding of luggage wheels against the concrete a rough symphony to the contrast of my clicking heels as I cross over to Austen. Less time sensitive, their exams have been pushed to next semester, and it's clear anyone who can leave is fleeing murder campus at their earliest opportunity. Bay already feels half-empty. Juniors with generous teachers or paper exams are also gone. The police threw a fit. Cataldo wanted the campus on lockdown to conduct a "thorough investigation." But in the end, irate parents with deep pockets won out. Money always wins out.

"Hey, Cathy," I greet the administrative assistant. Her hair— short, spiky, and mostly silver—is tipped with magenta today. Cathy may be a grandmother, but she's a hip one. "I thought I'd drop by to see if you need me, since I missed my shift yesterday."

"Oh, sweetheart." Her cinnamon-brown eyes crinkle at the corners. She reaches for my arm and gives it a squeeze. "You've been through a trauma. Bless you for coming in today at all. But I could actually use your help. We've received a ton of take-home exams that need sorting. You know the drill."

Indeed I do, and this is a small hitch in my plan, which was to chat with Mr. Tipton. It's also more work than I anticipated having to do, but needs must.

"Is Mr. Tipton here?" I ask, carefully nonchalant.

Cathy indicates that he's in his office, and I head back. At first I'm sure she is mistaken. Nothing but shadows spill through the glass window of Tipton's office. Maybe he left for the day. But as I get closer, I see the dim glow from his computer screen. I peer inside. He's staring at his monitor, sitting so still that the motion detectors powered down the overhead lights. As soon as I knock on the doorframe and step inside, they flicker on.

"Hi, Mr. Tipton."

Tipton blinks against the brightness, head snapping up to look at me in the doorway. He forces a smile. "Olivia, good to see you. What brings you here?"

I cross the tight space between the door and the two chairs that face his desk, then pull out the nearer one and sit down. "I need to speak to you about early-decision acceptances."

"Congratulations on Harvard. It's quite the accomplishment."

My jaw clicks tightly as I swallow a curse. "That's just the thing, Mr. Tipton—"

"Call me Joe," he interrupts.

"Joe," I grind out. "I know you emailed the *Ledger* the list this morning, and I was wondering how you knew about my acceptance."

"My buddies at Harvard admissions shot over the whole list. Perks of being an alumnus. Plus, one of the guys in admissions used to be my roommate. Probably gave you an edge getting in, so you kind of owe me."

He all but waggles his eyebrows at the insinuation. Wow, I hate this guy. "Well, I need you not to share the information with anyone else. Please."

"Why? It's Harvard. That's prime bragging rights."

"Because I don't want anyone else to know," I say, tone falsely bright. Why is he making this hard?

"If this is out of some kind of deference to Emma, I think she would have wanted—"

"You don't know what she would have wanted." I cut him off. Tipton corrects his too-casual posture and puffs up his chest, but I continue before he can get defensive. "You didn't know her, um, Joe. And you're the one who got us into this mess. Did you even talk to Ms. Bankhead about her recommendations? The numbers got fucked, and Emma paid the price."

Tipton's cheeks have gone pink. "Language, Miss Winters." He plays adult for 2.5 milliseconds, then gets back on his bullshit.

"And why are you mad that I got you, and Emma, into Harvard? Ms. Bankhead isn't the be-all and end-all of Ivy League admissions so none of the other counselors should bother trying. I'm good at my job."

"But what if doing your job is what got Emma killed?"

"Excuse me?"

I stop myself before I can say any more, though I've already said too much. Tipton is looking at me as if I've sprouted a second head.

"Is that why you want to keep your own acceptance a secret? Olivia." He says my name like it's a terminal medical diagnosis. "If you know something, you need to tell—"

"It's my own private news, which I should get to share how and when I want. All I'm asking is that you not tell anyone else. *Please.*" I try to force confidence into my tone, but under Tipton's pitying stare, I'm thrown off-kilter. Maybe my entire theory about Avery and Harvard *is* bonkers. That's what Mr. Tipton's thinking right now. Does Ethan think that, too?

I need air.

"Have a good holiday," I say, breaking from my chair and high-tailing it back to the front office. I pick up the stack of exams and haul them over to a dusty side room so that I can hide in case Tipton comes through here. I open my phone to shoot Ethan a text, but he's already messaged.

Autumn is a GO.

I'm shocked, both that he is still helping and that he got Autumn to agree so fast.

Explain later. Be at dining hall @ 6.

Relief spreads through me like hot chocolate. The kind with whipped cream and sprinkles. I confirm, then consider my next steps. Tipton's doubt has shaken me, but even if my Harvard-and-Avery theory doesn't hold water, someone on campus killed Emma. Piecing together her final hours is the key. By the time the stack of exams dwindles to zero and I deliver them to each professor's mailbox, it's nearly five. Security guard Paul should be on shift now.

Paul is a security cliché. Washed out of the police academy, came home, and landed the night shift at Claflin. The daytime woman, Officer Pring, was an actual decorated cop with the Boston PD—hence the better title and time slot, and the unlikelihood of her spilling any relevant details to me. But Paul likes me. He'd say I flirt with him. I'd say girls are socialized to be friendly, and I am perfectly friendly. Anyway, he's not a bad guy. One of the few here at Claflin who gets me, where I come from.

I approach with a smile, knocking in a syncopated rhythm on the doorframe of the security office. "Hey, Paul. How's it going?"

Paul's sky-blue eyes are disconcertingly pretty but a little too close together. He's a high school heartthrob type with just enough twists to ground him in the ordinary. Paul is flirty but not creepy—very important for the nighttime security guard—and he laughs at my jokes.

"Hey, Olivia. It's . . ." He grimaces. I notice the three-day stubble and bags under his eyes. "Well, you know. With the murder. Can't help feeling like it's my fault, you know?"

Oh no. I've walked right into an emotional hotspot. I decide to steer clear of anything smacking of counsel. Fact-based, open-ended questions are the way to go.

"What happened?"

Paul takes a long drag of what I assume to be coffee and launches into it.

"I was on my regular curfew patrol when the cameras went out. At least, that had to be when it happened. Everything was working when I left. Got back around twelve-thirty a.m. and noticed the feed was down on several screens. Tried a hard reboot, but that didn't bring them back. I . . . I did a second patrol at two-thirty . . . I should have gone back out, I know, but."

"But it's Claflin," I supply. "Nothing ever happens here."

"Yeah." He heaves a sigh. "Yeah. Until now. On my watch." Suddenly those too-close, too-bright blue eyes narrow up at me. "I saw you on there. On the tapes, way past curfew."

It's a statement of fact. Not accusing. I nod.

"Detective Cataldo's on my ass about it," I say. "I was looking for Emma, but then I psyched myself out about it. Thought she was probably staying over with her boyfriend. I wish I'd come and gotten you. I was afraid of getting in trouble, but now . . ."

"Hey, you couldn't have known." Paul frowns. "I should have known."

He says it for himself, not for me. He stares at the floor; I stare at the wall. The moment passes.

"Earlier in the night, did you see her on the feed? Leaving the party, maybe?"

He shakes his head. "Went over everything with the cops." His Massachusetts accent is strong, so it comes out *cawps*. While

I'm sure I sound equally ridiculous with my Baltimore *o*'s, I'm still tickled by the stereotype. "I got plenty of you kids going to the ED day party, but she never came out. Not where the cameras got her."

"Did they figure out what was wrong with the cameras from Bay to the boathouse?"

Paul pushes off the floor with his feet, shuttling his chair over to the cascade of video screens. Spins around, checks that the images of our dorm, the lake path, the boathouse are now where they should be. It's all red brick contrasted against milky-white snow, gradually turning gray.

"The faulty ones were live again before daybreak. Before they found her," he says, his back to me. "The police think they were hacked. I don't know." Paul spins around again, eyes searching the screen, as if he could rewind the time, do things differently.

Hacked. It's exactly what I was searching for. The how. And hacking means computer skills, so either a skilled adult or a savvy student.

Sierra's face pops into my mind. She's the best coder I know, president of Girls Who Code, and talented enough to hack our class schedules. I add it to the list of *shit my friends might have done behind my back.*

I hear a ghostly "Hello?" from the main office. Paul shoos me off. We both have work to do. I return to the front and find that Cathy's gone. Check the clock on the wall, a relic. It's past five. Still, there's Tyler, hand poised over the silver bell on Cathy's desk, which only the most entitled students ever ring.

"Tyler, hey. Can I help you?" Technically I don't have to, since it's after hours, but it is the season of giving.

"I need a new ID," he says. "I lost mine."

"Sure. It'll take about ten minutes. The machine is slow as shit." It's a half fib. The machine *is* slow. But it'll take five, not ten. At the work-study desk, I jiggle the screen awake, input my password, and open the ID software, making small talk while I pull up Tyler's student profile.

"How were your exams?"

"Fine," Tyler drones. His eyes are on his phone screen. Talking to me isn't on the agenda.

As I navigate the screen, I'm not surprised that this is Tyler's third ID replacement in the last year. He's careless with his things. He just got a new ID in September.

I click Print New and glance up at Tyler. The printer is in a secure room in the back. I have the timing down to a science. "Listen . . ." I bite my lip. "I know it's uncouth, but I was hoping I could ask you something about that night? With Emma?"

That makes Tyler break eye contact with his phone. "What about?"

"After the fight, after the party ended, when's the last time you saw her? Did she come up to your room?"

Tyler's eyes narrow. "Yeah, she came up to my room around eleven-thirty. The party was basically over. But then she left around midnight. I told the detective all of this already."

So Margot was wrong. Emma had been going upstairs for a booty call with her boyfriend. A short one, though.

"Did she say where she was going?"

Tyler's eyes begin to glisten. He sniffs.

"I'm sorry to bring all this up for you," I rush to say.

"It's okay." He waves me off. "It's just bringing back memories. If I'd known it would be the last time we were together, I would have savored our time more. Stopped her leaving altogether. But she got a text after we, you know, and said she had to go."

"Who texted her? Who was she meeting with?"

"Calm down, Nancy Drew. Emma didn't share it with me, but I figured it was an Ivies after-party. Or a war conference, more like, after that fight. Look, I don't like to get involved in Avery's shit. That all is your business, not mine. Is my ID ready?"

"I'll go check," I say, swiping the key from my desk drawer and then heading back toward the maze of admin offices. My mind is reeling. Tyler hooked up with Emma and then he thinks her friends texted to meet up. My friends. The Ivies.

I shove the oversized key into the lock, shoulder the heavy door open, and flick on the light. Tyler's replacement ID is sitting in the output tray of the boxy printer. I grab it, then head back to the front office.

Another possibility crosses my mind, and I don't like it. What if Emma was going from her boyfriend's bed to someone else's? She could have let Tyler assume the text came from one of us. I'm no further ahead than I was before. All I know is Emma received a text around midnight, and Tyler seems oblivious.

He's also gone. "Tyler?" I call out to the empty lounge.

"Oh, hey, here!" He emerges, breathless, from behind me. "I got thirsty, had to hit up the water fountain by the bathroom. Thanks!" Tyler snatches the ID from my fingers. I walk him out, locking the administrative office door behind me. As I'm extracting my key, a harsh buzzing vibrates my purse.

"Sorry, have to take this." I wave Tyler bye and fish my phone from my pocket to check the caller ID. It's my mom. Oops, I haven't called her since Wednesday.

"Mom, hey. What's up?"

"Livvy, why haven't you called me?"

So we're jumping right into bad-daughter territory. Swell. I duck into an alcove off the lobby and lean against the wall.

"Sorry. Yesterday was a blur with an assembly, and my police interview, and studying for finals." And launching a murder investigation, I add in my head. "I meant to call."

"I'm worried about you, and you're barely responding to my texts."

I resist groaning, because the scolding I'd get for daring to be annoyed with my mother isn't worth it. Plus, she isn't wrong. But how do I explain to her that I'm dealing with more shit than I can handle? She's already concerned enough with me being so far away, and she's never understood the appeal of Claflin. She doesn't get the Ivy game like I do. I don't need her to add my friend's murder and my grief to her plate. And, god, if she knows I'm a suspect? She'll be on the first plane up here. That'll really fuck things up. I can't very well solve Emma's murder with my mom tagging along.

"Sorry, Mom," I finally say. "It's been hectic here. But I'll be home Monday, so . . ." My mom does not take the hint, that I'd really love to end our conversation, table all of this until I am home for Christmas.

"How are the girls? Avery, Margot, and Sierra? That Avery's not as tough as she wants people to believe, ya know. I worry about you all up there. And I cannot believe they're still making you take exams."

"It's because of college admissions, Mom. They have to. And we're all fine. I'm hanging out with Avery tonight," I make up on the spot.

"That's good, Liv. I sent flowers to the Russos. You'll find out when the funeral is, so we can attend? I'll have to find some way to afford the trip. We'll make it work." .

"Yes, of course, Mom." I'm on autopilot now, letting my mom hyperfocus and whip herself into her Mom frenzy. I just have to agree at intervals with whatever she is saying.

Finally, there's a moment of silence. It hangs, and I brace myself for a Mom bomb. "Olivia, I want you to give some serious thought to coming home permanently. Your friend has died, and you know I don't like how you get when you're up there. You got into Harvard. You're done. You can finish your senior year at Highland. High school is high school. It doesn't matter."

"Mom." It comes out like ice. "You know I can't do that. I only have one semester left. It's *fine.*"

"Okay." Such a simple word, but we can load it with such meaning. My mom is backing down for now, but the war is not over. We'll discuss this again over the holiday. "I'll see you in a few days. I love you."

"I love you, too."

As I'm saying it, my phone buzzes, tickling my ear. My mother's goodbye gets lost as I look down at my screen. I end the call and pull up the text that just came in. It's Ethan.

Ready for our dinner date?

My stomach gurgles a yes.

See you in five, I respond, trying not to think too hard about the fact that Ethan used the word *date.* A hostile three-person, cornered-in-a-murder-plot date, but still a date. My first date.

Progress.

I should head straight to the dining hall, but something locks me in place. There's a buzzing, like a bee is trapped in my brain. I lied to my mom. Not the first time, but maybe for the first time about something that mattered. I tap into my text messages and pull up my thread with Avery. Our last solo exchange was over a month ago. I swipe a new message.

> You working on RD apps tonight? Maybe we could work on them together?

There. A lie made true. Now I can eat with one weight off my shoulders. Though I suspect Autumn is going to lob another anvil on.

I find her at the dining hall entrance right on schedule, hands stuffed into the center pocket of her Claflin hoodie, brown eyes carefully neutral. We're teammates, but she's always been chilly. I'd always assumed it was WASPy snobbery, but the last twelve hours have cast everything I thought into question. Ethan stands beside her, already comfortably in conversation. No frost toward him, it would seem.

"Hey!" I say, with a grade too much cheer in my voice.

The ice in Autumn's stare could reverse global warming. "I'm not doing this for you," she remarks flatly while grabbing a tray.

"Why don't we make it quick, in that case. After you." Ethan motions Autumn toward the buffet line and follows after her, putting a buffer between us.

We make our way around the food stations and buffet lines to the half hexagon–shaped atrium. The floor-to-ceiling windows overlook the athletic fields. I eye the Ivies' usual table. It's empty right now, as if our fellow students know to give us a wide berth

134

even when we're not in the room. Well, technically, I am an Ivy. Fuck it.

"Over here," I say, leading Autumn and Ethan over to the table. We slide our trays in front of three seats facing the window. We get the view, but a bit of privacy as well.

"Rebecca brought me up to speed," Autumn opens. "She thinks we might be wrong about what you did to me. I'm not as convinced." I find myself on the receiving end of a begrudging look.

I chance a glance at Ethan. "Well, that's just it, isn't it? I don't know what I supposedly did to you." With a steadying breath, I say, "Tell me."

Autumn takes a bite of her lettuce-wrapped turkey burger. Then she cracks a smile before taking a long draw of water to clear her throat. "You know, for a while I genuinely thought I was being paranoid. It was too silly, bizarre that someone would Mean Girls me. Though, indeed, spiking my protein shakes is a lot savvier than Kälteen bars. The weight just crept on, and before I noticed, well, I'd failed my conditioning and you got the spot on varsity." Autumn shrugs, seemingly nonchalant, but a shit-eating grin creeps through. "Real poetic irony that you didn't even end up being good enough to be recruited. That's kept me warm at night."

"You think I sabotaged your shakes?"

"Hmmm," Autumn hums around another bite of burger. "I did. Though now, given your playing-dumb shtick, I'm assuming it was Sierra instead. Smart, really, having someone else do your dirty work so you have deniability. I can only imagine what you've done for your friends in kind."

I become very interested in cutting my chicken breast, making sure to avoid Ethan's eyes. That *is* the Ivies' strategy. Deniability. I once wrote a scathing editorial on Margot's behalf, saying her theater rival warbled like a dying cow and blasting Claflin drama for not employing race-blind casting for shows. That choosing the less talented Diana Klein instead of Margot for the ingenue lead was clearly unexamined bigotry. Margot is better than Diana, though. It wasn't lying, and the editors on the paper let it go to print. I remember the pride I felt when I showed the draft to Margot, thinking maybe it would endear me to her. No such luck. But thanks to me, she was cast as the lead in every production since then and is a lock for this year's Jimmy Awards. I never gave one thought to Diana. Guilt pools in my stomach.

"How would Sierra get access to your protein shakes? Maybe you just weren't good enough, and the weight gain was incidental." Okay, so maybe I'm not ready to give up denial just yet.

Autumn snorts. "Short memory you've got there, Olivia. Surely you remember that brief, shining time you and Sierra were breakfast buddies with me? We made our shakes together in the kitchen at the boathouse. I started arriving fifteen minutes later to avoid you. Still do. And the weight melted off as soon as I altered my schedule."

She's right. It was all the way back in sophomore year, so not at the front of my mind but not forgotten, either. Sierra said Autumn was just bitter about not making varsity. Screw her if she didn't want to be on the Shake Squad anymore.

"So that's it?" I say, spearing a piece of broccoli with my fork. "Sierra put some weight-gain powder in your shakes, and I get told to drop dead? It's underhanded but hardly earth-shattering."

I don't miss Ethan's flinch beside me.

Autumn looks ready to explode. "Is that it?! Your *friends* almost cost me a college scholarship. No school would look at me since I wasn't on varsity. I had to spend the whole summer training with a private coach to get back into competition shape. Do you have any idea how much money that cost my parents? How stressed I was about not making the team?"

"I—" But I have nothing to say, because I didn't know. And even though I wasn't the one who sabotaged Autumn's placement on the team, shouldn't I have noticed? They're *my* friends. And I'm the one who stole her spot.

There's no time to apologize, though. Autumn is already forging ahead.

"And if that's not enough for you, how about poisoning Jason before the ACT? Not to speak ill of the dead, but that's what your friend Emma did. She slipped him laxatives. Last year, February sitting, he loses it right after Emma buys him a coffee. Confirmed."

"That's . . . insane," I settle on, hardly adequate for the mental images Autumn's story conjures up. I don't realize I'm shaking until Ethan's hand covers mine under the table. A moment and my heart begins to slow. I think. "But why would Emma mess with Jason's ACT score? He applied to WashU, not an Ivy." There's no point in even pretending that my friends and I weren't aggressively protecting our Ivy status. Clubs and class ranking transcended all school choices, but there was no reason to sabotage a test score unless someone was a direct competitor. We're not *villains.*

Autumn snorts. "Yeah, he switched to WashU because he knew if you guys thought he was still gunning for Princeton, there'd be a target on his back. After the laxatives, none of us wanted to even think of what you might do."

It takes my hand going cold for me to notice that Ethan's removed his. It's as if all the oxygen has been sucked from the room. Then Ethan hops up, wiggles his empty glass, and says, "I'm empty. Anyone else need a refill?"

Autumn and I wave him off, and my lungs slowly fill back up with air. I realize this is an ideal opportunity—the only one, really—to ask her my burning question.

"What about Avery? Rebecca mentioned blackmail."

Her triumphant smirk falls into a scowl.

"God, that bitch." Autumn's nostrils flare as she releases a huff. "Look, I'll tell you only because Stina's long gone, but if I hear shit about it, I will hunt you down and I will kill you."

As soon as the threat is out of her mouth, Autumn's eyes go wide and she smacks a hand over her lips as if to take it back. "Shit, you know I don't mean that. Given everything that's happened, with Emma. But . . ." She groans. "Just don't tell anyone, okay?"

I give her my word, now desperate to get this information any which way I can.

"Avery . . . hooked up with Stina. Led her on. And then Avery said that unless Stina endorsed you for editor in chief, she would tell Stina's very Christian, very conservative parents that she was queer. It's cliché as shit, and trust me, Stina is living her truth at Emory, but still. Her parents haven't caught up with the times, and they one hundred percent would have withdrawn tuition support and probably kicked her out, too. Serious shit. Avery is garbage."

"Shit." It slips out as I lean back in my chair. I suck down an Arnold Palmer, my mind a jumble. Avery gay-baited someone to get me the editor job? And then I didn't even get it! Well, not exactly. I preferred the version where she told me it had been brib- ery. Avery has money in spades. But integrity? You only get so much. Avery's is shot.

"How do you know all this?" I ask in a whisper. I look to the drinks station to track Ethan's position, but I don't see him.

"I caught them together. And then you got her endorsement, which I thought was weird, given she didn't even like you that much. Oh, no offense. I confronted her and she told me."

"I had no idea. I'm sorry."

"Oh, good, you're making up!" Ethan appears with a full glass of orange soda and a wide grin. Thank god he only caught my apology and not the reason for it.

Autumn snorts, finishing her turkey burger, then her water. "Making up, sure." She softens the slightest bit. "But thank you for apologizing. I'm still not exactly a fan of yours, Olivia, but it's good to know you were kind of in the dark about all of this. One less totally heinous bitch at this school. The Ivies, though. It was a matter of time before one of them ended up dead." With that, Autumn picks up her tray, leaving Ethan and me still sitting be- hind her.

Humiliation burns my cheeks. Even without the Avery bomb- shell, Ethan's heard enough.

"We were all ambitious," I say, as though that justifies any- thing. "I never thought they'd take it that far."

I'm all too aware of Ethan's warm presence beside me. I'm shocked he hasn't run away.

"Thank you for your help with Autumn. How'd you get her to change her mind?" I ask.

He shifts closer. I get a whiff of his piney aftershave. "Dough- nuts and free Drake tickets," he deadpans.

"Ha, ha," I retort. "Even you're not *that* Canadian." I know he's dodging the question. I wait for him to continue. After a time, he does.

"After Sierra did, um, what she did—though I swear to you I did not know the reason Autumn didn't make varsity—anyhow, I built her a recruiting website for crew. Posted some video clips, a few articles I'd written about her for the *Ledger,* and her stats. She said it helped her get college coaches' attention."

I'm quiet for a long time. "I'm not proud of it, you know?"

Ethan rests his head on my shoulder. "We've all done things we're not proud of."

My phone buzzes, breaking us apart instantly. It's a text from Avery.

> Yes!!! My room, 8. Bring snacks. I've got the booze.

Ethan leans over to take a look. "Guess you've got a date with a snake."

CHAPTER THIRTEEN

I am buzzed on a 2008 vintage pinot noir from Avery's secret stash of wine, which includes bottles that cost more than every item of clothing on my body combined. Avery tops off my cup, though it isn't even half-empty, and we clink the hard plastic together like fine ladies. Or tipsy sorority sisters.

Avery is leaning against a wall of pillows on her bed, laptop on her lap, and I'm sitting perpendicular to her near the end. Her calves are propped on top of mine, and they provide a perfect shelf for my own laptop.

My contribution to the evening's proceedings is a jumbo bag of cheese puffs from the school market. Avery hogs the bag, crunching on pieces in steady succession, sucking neon-orange cheese dust from her fingers reverently.

She doesn't look like a killer. Or a saboteur supreme.

We're on hour two of writing essays . . . or attempting to write essays. The wine helps until it doesn't; we keep taking detours, Avery sharing a piece of gossip on someone, me worrying about paying for college. And thrumming in the back of my mind are today's revelations about Avery and my so-called friends. I know

I should just ask her about what Autumn said, but I'm not even sure where to start.

Hey, Aves, did you hook up with Stina, then blackmail her?

Why have you and our other friends been performing truly heinous acts of sabotage behind my back?

That's what's really bothering me. Carving me up from the inside out. That they don't trust me.

The sting of exclusion leaves behind a gentle, familiar ache. Then I question myself: Why would I want to be included in such vile acts? Is fitting in that important to me?

Maybe, the tiniest voice inside me whispers.

My mom's voice rattles around my head, too: *I don't like how you get when you're up there.*

Me neither. But this is all I have. Claflin and the Ivies. I have to know who my friends really are. Maybe if I start Avery off with some small talk, I can work up to the big stuff.

"Are you looking forward to the holiday?"

Avery snorts. "Not really. Megan sent me a deadline schedule for my essays. It's pretty brutal."

The one nice thing I can say about Avery's essay coach is that she refuses to do any of the writing for her or Tyler. She sets deadlines, and Avery has to meet them, like homework. Avery is a talented writer, but I know Tyler has struggled. Though even the best of us struggle. For the aspiring journalist in the group, I sure am sucking at my supplements tonight. Everything's coming out stilted and trite.

"How's it going for you?"

"Writing is hard." I faux sob. "I wish I didn't have to do these stupid applications."

"You and me both."

"Shit. Sorry. That was insensitive," I say, expecting Avery to snap back, but her response is kind.

"No, don't worry about it at all. We're both nursing ED rejections. Or deferral in your case. Whatever. Solidarity."

I burn with shame. Avery is not the only bald-faced liar in the room.

"Are you still, uh, trying to talk to Harvard?" I prod at Avery's motive. She takes a swig of wine.

Avery makes an affirmative noise into her cup. It buzzes, like a bee is caught inside. "My mom is petitioning the admissions department to move my app to regular decision now that, uh, Emma can no longer attend. Switch my status to deferred instead of rejected, basically."

"Wow, that is cold." And what would Katherine Montfort do if she knew about my admission status? God, what if she finds out from her contacts?

"She finds my backup schools unacceptable. My whole life, it's been Harvard, and nothing but Harvard." Avery bites her lip. "No matter what I do, she'll be disappointed."

My stomach churns with uncertainty. Avery is a teenage girl. My friend, really, for all her faults. I'm second-guessing my little murder investigation, no matter how attractive Avery's motive seems. Though, does it hold water anymore if she's recovered so smoothly from her Harvard rejection? Wouldn't she be all for her mother's petition if she killed our friend to pave her way back into Harvard's good graces? I'm not sure anymore.

I'm drifting further and further away from my theory. I want to text Ethan, have him add it to our interview notes. I snort a laugh. Like we're detectives.

"What's so funny?" Avery raises a brow.

"Nothing," I chirp, even though I know she's not stupid and won't be satisfied with my answer. I grasp for something to say, something that will appease her. "I was just thinking about something Ethan said." My cheeks heat, the sliver of truth both an offering and too much to bear. "Don't call him Canadian Ken," I let out in a rush.

"That was Emma, not me." Avery's tone is clipped. Then she softens. "It's obvious you really like him. I don't care who you date."

I snort into my wine.

"Hey, it's true. As long as it's not Tyler."

I jostle her calves with mine. "Do you have, like, a thing for him?" I've always found her sensitivity about any of us dating Tyler odd. Like, *Cruel Intentions* odd. Once Emma started going out with him, Avery nudged at regular intervals about when it might end. *You can't take high school boyfriends to college,* she'd say.

Now she recoils as if I've slapped her. "Oh my god, Olivia, that is gross. No. Tyler is . . . ew, no."

"Okay, okay." I throw up my hands in surrender.

"Seriously, though, Liv, if Tyler starts flirting with you, ignore him. Go for Ethan. You two are perfect."

I know Avery claims she's fine with my crush, that "Canadian Ken" was Emma's thing, but I don't trust her. A week ago I would have been the subject of ridicule for liking someone so boring. Now Avery is practically playing matchmaker. And then there's the Tyler thing.

I decide to try something. A police tactic.

"Do you think he could have done it?" I ask.

"Who, Tyler?" Avery's mouth goes tight.

"They always suspect the boyfriend. They have to be looking at him."

It's a risk, showing my hand, letting Avery know how curious I am about Emma's murder. I want to see how she responds. If there's even a chance that she's guilty. Or if she knew about Emma's cheating. I'm fishing.

"They're looking at all of us," Avery says. "My mother warned me about that on day one. That we'd all be suspects." Her eyes go flinty as she levels her gaze on me. "But Tyler's been cleared. Mom gave me the happy news this afternoon."

"Oh, wow, that's great news." I sound droll, but I mean it. If the police have ruled Tyler out as a suspect, that's huge. They must have an alibi for him.

Avery hums underneath her breath. She takes a long swig of wine, then changes the subject. "Hey, can I run my Harvard essay by you? My mom said I should write a new one. Something reflective, for the appeal."

She says it so casually, I have to take a moment to orient myself. Ensure I've not traveled back in time two months to when we were working on ED apps. Avery's mom has been able to jump right into action, trying to get the Harvard admissions board to reverse its decision. How terribly convenient, with Emma's dying and all.

I think about Katherine Montfort's demanding to speak to the headmistress, railing against an unfair system. The picture from Seth's Stories, Avery on the phone at the party. Who would she have been talking to? All her friends were there except for me, and we didn't talk that night.

Is it completely outside the realm of possibility that Avery killed Emma at her mom's instruction?

"Hey, Liv, hello?" Avery snaps her fingers in my face. I'm forced to play ditzy, put on a smile.

"Sorry. Yeah, send it to me. Your essay. And can you read my Northwestern supplement?"

We exchange Google Drive links, and I try to dive into proofreader mode. It's hard to concentrate on Avery's new essay, about the challenges of a blended family, when all I can think about is a mother-daughter murder pact. This is the stuff of a true crime podcast. The darkest, most awful part of me wonders if it would be too late to start one for my college apps.

My phone buzzes with a text. It's from Ethan.

> You free? Can you come over? Whitley lounge in twenty? We should talk.

I check the time—10:45 p.m.—so cutting it fine on curfew. What could he need to talk to me about that we can't discuss tomorrow?

I find Avery leaning forward at an awkward angle, trying to spy my screen. "What's that?" I'm grateful Ethan didn't text anything of substance.

"Oh, Ethan has a question about something. For the *Ledger*. He wants me to come over to Whitley, but I really don't want to get dressed." We're rocking pajamas and fuzzy socks. My makeup, at least, is still on.

"You should go! I'm hitting a wall anyway on these things. I want to let them sit overnight before I send any of them to Megan."

I envision myself going back to my room, getting dressed, bearing the cold to trek over to Whitley. I don't want to do any of it, except for the warmth at the end of the tunnel—Ethan. And I'm terribly curious what the urgency is.

"Fine." I extricate myself from the sprawl of Avery's limbs and pack up my laptop. I sway on my feet, remembering that, oh yeah, I've drunk half a bottle of wine. My blood zings with possibility, lips tingling from the phantom sensation of would-be kisses. What if Ethan has romantic intentions for such a late-night summons?

I rush back to my room, put on dark-wash jeans and one of my newest and most flattering tops, just in case—purple and teal, with a plunging neckline. Then a frisson of terror streaks through me, and I add a black button-up cardigan as a modesty shield. My winter gear goes on top, and I'm out the door in ten minutes.

I tap into Whitley, making my way to the lounge. It's comparatively staid, now that the party layout has been replaced with a school-sanctioned study area. I find Ethan pacing in front of the television, his eyes scanning the floor, mouth moving as if he's reciting something to himself. I call his name and his head snaps up, smile so electric it sends a pleasant ripple of shivers through me. But then his gaze turns serious, and he beckons me closer.

"Hey, it was easier to meet here, but let's go up to my room."

My heart stutters in panic. He's already leading me toward the stairs.

"This is very ominous, Ethan. Are you going to tell me what's going on?"

"In a minute. Don't worry."

We turn left at the landing, and he leads me four doors down. His room sparks some serious déjà vu. The furniture echoes the pieces in my own double back at Bay: sand-colored wooden desk, bed frame, dresser set arranged from left to right, but Whitley has been standing for over a hundred years, so all the other room features are rustic and charming. A lush, deep cherry wood hugs frames of both door and windows, and there's a patch of exposed brick on the outward-facing wall.

I peg Ethan's side immediately, the right one, where a Toronto Maple Leafs flag makes it painfully obvious. To fill otherwise blank wall space, there's also an abstract art print and a movie poster. Some old Scorsese film about gangsters. His roommate's side is cluttered with posters of shiny cars, big-busted women, a different Scorsese film about gangsters, and a giant bulletin/dry-erase board crowded with class assignments and schedules. There's no roommate to be seen. I gesture at that side of the room.

"He's studying for AP Bio. He won't be back until late. We need the privacy."

"Ethan, what the hell is going on?"

He leads me over to the bed, giving a sweeping gesture for me to sit. I do, and he pulls out his desk chair, arranging it catty-corner to where I am. He leans close, even though we are alone.

"Sorry for the cloak-and-dagger. Also, you look really nice. That top is aces."

Ethan ducks his head to hide the flush in his cheeks, without success. Meanwhile, I go warm and bubbly all over.

"Anyway, after dinner I talked to a few people and got some more intel on the Ivies for you. Specifically, I got Seth to spill."

Acid pushes up my throat as Ethan throws me a solemn look. Then he turns to his laptop and pulls up our tracking document. Next to Seth's name and under Margot, Avery, and Emma's columns he writes **Catfished.**

Relief floods through me as I release a breath. He's pinned it on the other girls. He doesn't know it was me. Now it's time to play dumb.

"Catfished?"

"Seth *thought* he'd met a girl named Ingrid from Wheatford Prep on a subreddit. They DMed, emailed, texted for months, including some pretty intense sexting." Ethan grimaces. "He showed me and everything. So, Ingrid insists on meeting for the first time in person to . . . you know, and it has to be the Saturday of some huge FIRST Robotics competition. Seth chooses love over academics and then gets stood up, and Emma ends up team captain. Once Ingrid stopped returning any of his messages, Seth pieced together that she'd had an uncanny habit of keeping him busy during FIRST building sessions . . . so that's why he hates you guys. I get it, though. If someone did that to me . . ."

It's surreal to hear my own sabotage told to me like a story. Only I know that Ethan and Seth are missing a few pieces. Yeah, Emma put Seth on the board, but Avery and I created Ingrid together. We're the writers in the group. Ingrid was like my own personal smutty RPG. I burn red hot to think Ethan read some of my sexts.

"You look like you're going to be sick."

"I probably shouldn't admit this, but I've been drinking. I think it's catching up with me." Wine will excuse my flush, surely.

"Wish you'd brought some over. After plumbing the depths of humanity today, I could use it."

"Ha, no way I could sneak off with any of Avery's private store. She takes her French reserves very seriously."

"Speaking of, how did it go? Find anything out from Avery?"

"Not much, honestly. It felt normal. Maybe *too* normal? I can't tell anymore, though, looking at that." I gesture at the Ivies' ledger. It's beginning to fill up. "Maybe I never could."

Ethan points to a single word hovering under Avery's name at the bottom of the sheet. "Who did she get expelled? I know it wasn't Emma, but that's a damn good motive for murder."

I squirm under Ethan's too-earnest gaze. This one has been

bugging me. "It's Kaila Montgomery," I say. "She got expelled sophomore year, but it had nothing to do with Avery. Kaila called in a fake bomb threat to get out of exams."

Ethan arches his eyebrows. "That sounds oddly similar to the Ivies' tactics."

"Well, I know that *now*," I mumble. "It just seems extreme, is all. The only thing I could come up with that Avery benefited from with Kaila's leaving was that she had been the runner-up in the student body elections. So, technically, it's how Avery became junior class president."

"That's it, then!" Ethan lights up.

"Getting someone expelled for a club position is a bit much, even for Avery," I say. "Besides, Kaila went off the deep end. I saw it. She was ranting, paranoid, and she punched Emma in the face. . . ." I trail off. Ethan's giving me a look. Though I have trouble connecting cheese puff–dusted, wine-drunk Avery with something so diabolical . . . he's right. "Fine, put Kaila on that list."

"Under Avery *and* Emma," Ethan says, typing out **fake bomb threat** under both. "You don't get a fist to the face unless you did something. Could Kaila have come back to campus to get revenge?"

"She couldn't have hurt Emma." I shake my head. "They sent her to a wilderness reform program. It's where rich kids with expulsions go while their parents work to get them into a different boarding school." Despite my denials, I try to remember whether Kaila was local. Would she have a reason to be back in Massachusetts this close to the holidays? Could she have gotten onto campus last Wednesday?

"So, you're seeing what I'm seeing?" Ethan's eyes rake over the list. "Motives. I know you're set on Avery, but the Harvard thing is weak, I think. A few of these, though, are serious reasons to kill someone."

"But Emma only did a few of these."

"The overwhelming pattern from talking to people is that they don't like any of you. And no one is completely certain who did what." Ethan goes quiet for a moment. Then he says to his hands, "I'm glad you didn't know about any of this, though."

I don't deserve the zip of happiness his words inspire. "So, this is our new list of suspects? With Seth, Jason, and Kaila as our top three?"

"From this list? I'd really just look at Kaila. Jason had a bad test day, and Seth's pride is hurt, but those are nothing next to getting someone expelled."

"Men with hurt pride murder women all the time," I mutter darkly.

"Seth as a killer, though? I mean, on that subject, we can't rule out Tyler or the secret boyfriend."

I can't believe I forgot to tell him. "Tyler came into the office, so I talked to him a bit. Emma was with him after the party for a hookup, but she left around midnight. She got a text from someone and said she had to go. Tyler thinks it was one of her friends, maybe about an after-party."

"So, they *are* lying?"

"If Tyler's right about who texted Emma, yeah."

Ethan senses my hesitation. "You think it was the other guy?"

"The hookup Margot mentioned may have been Tyler, but her dropping hints that Emma was cheating . . . Margot is a Fort Knox of secrets. If she let it slip, it's probably based in truth. But after talking to Tyler, I don't think he has a clue. So the jealous boyfriend doesn't fit. The police seem to agree. Avery said they cleared him today."

"Really?" Ethan pulls a face. "That sucks. Jealousy's a great motive."

"So is revenge." I wave my hand at our growing list. "I'll try to get in touch with Kaila. Start there."

"And I'll keep digging into the timeline, since now we know Emma left to go somewhere at midnight. We just have to figure out where she would have gone between then and her death."

"It's a big blank," I say. "I talked to Paul, the security guy. He says the key cameras were hacked. Down for a few hours, the critical hours. There's zero footage of her leaving Whitley. Nowhere to go." Frustration builds, exploding like someone combined soda and Pop Rocks and shook. "This is hopeless!" I shove Ethan's laptop at him and jump off the bed, starting to pace.

"We're not cops," I continue. "We're barely journalists, either. A ton of people have motives, but we can't prove anyone was or wasn't anywhere at the time of the murder. We're stuck."

"On the bright side, that means the cops can't prove anything about you, either."

"Except that I was definitely out of bed at the crucial time. It's circumstantial, but it could be enough. We're back at square one."

"Let's sleep on it. Ask around." Ethan's voice is gentle. Reassuring. I stop pacing and sit back down. Ethan continues. "We still have the Margot lead to follow, whomever Emma was hooking up with. You'll reach out to Kaila. We're okay."

Ethan's the king of pep talks, but I still can't help feeling like we're spinning our wheels. However, I keep the rest of my anxiety spiral to myself, nodding when Ethan suggests we meet for breakfast.

A sharp triple rap on Ethan's door nearly makes me jump a foot in the air. "Lights-out in fifteen!" calls a voice I vaguely recognize. Ethan must catch my expression. "Mr. Tipton is the faculty in residence here." He looks to the door. "My roommate will be back any minute. You'll have to be careful sneaking out."

I don't waste any time, slipping out into the hallway when Tipton's back is turned. My legs manage long, quick strides to the main landing, but instead of descending the staircase in view of all, I steal along the perpendicular hallway that tees out from the middle of the building, all the way to the back stairwell. I take it down two levels into the basement to find the busted maintenance door Ethan mentioned, so I can slip out unseen.

The lights in the basement level are motion activated, and they tick on as soon as my feet hit the landing. The soft whir of a dryer to my left indicates the laundry room. I move in the opposite direction, assuming maintenance will be at the front of the basement level. I try the last door to the right, which opens out into a muck room of sorts. There are all kinds of physical plant bric-a-brac, from industrial cleaning supplies to rusting cans of paint, and an ancient lawn mower I am pretty sure is older than I am.

Metal shelves tower in the center of the room. After slipping down the middle of the corridor they form, I find the back door. I reach for the handle, praying this is the right one, when it swings wide open and Tyler barrels right into me.

"Olivia, shit!" There's a warbling sound as the ream of paper he's carrying cascades to the floor. I bend over to help him pick up the sheets and can't help but look at them.

"You're hosting a candlelight vigil for Emma?"

"A memorial," he corrects me. "It's too cold to plant a tree, and not enough time to order a plaque, but I wanted to do something before the holidays. Emma's parents are coming. I have to get the word out ASAP so people know to stay through Sunday night. I don't want everyone leaving early." He sniffles. "I was putting these up around campus and lost track of time."

I notice he doesn't question why I'm here, sneaking out as he's sneaking in. It's probably a common occurrence here. Tyler sniffles again, lingers, like he wants to talk. I'm a bottle-it-all-up-inside kind of person, but Tyler clearly isn't.

"That's really good of you," I say, grasping at grief small talk. "You must miss her so much."

Tyler seizes on my sympathy like a parched man being offered a drink. "I'm still in shock. I just can't believe she's gone, you know? And everyone's already moving on! Exams back on, and 'What are you doing on your winter vacation?' I want everyone to come to the memorial, to remember what we've lost. Emma was everything."

"I'll be there," I say, because I'm not sure what else to say. His devastation seems genuine, no hint at all that Emma wasn't his perfect, devoted girlfriend. There's no way he knew about the cheating. But he doesn't ask me how I'm doing or feeling, I note. He's myopically focused on his own grief. "Do you want me to put some of these up in Bay?" I hold up the posters.

"That would be amazing, thank you. I asked Avery to help, but she said the whole memorial idea was too weird. Anyway, I have to sneak up before lights-out. Night, Liv."

"Night, Tyler."

It's black beyond the door. I squint up to the clouded glass of the security light, bulb clearly burned out. After a minute to let my eyes adjust, I make my way across the greenish-brown grass, careful to step where yesterday's snowfall has been eaten away by the day's sunlight. Finally I reach the dirt path that snakes behind Whitley, around the Colman Performing Arts building, and over to Bay. Along the way, I look for cameras and find none. Security is truly an illusion on campus. Anyone could, and likely does, easily sneak around, the woods to one side and the back sides of the buildings to the other. I'm kicking myself for not going this way the other night. I could have avoided the entire fiasco with the cops grabbing me on camera.

And so could have anyone else that night. Including the killer.

A shiver runs through me, and I hurry toward the nearest blue phone. I count my steps between them, like I did the night Emma died. Then my butt vibrates, and I fish my phone from my jeans pocket. New email. I tap in and read the first line of the message. Stop in my tracks.

My whole body goes cold and taut, like antifreeze is trickling down my spine, pooling in my shoes like lead weights. I read the email again. It's six words, but they rattle around my skull like bullets.

> **From:** Meddling, Quit <backoffclaflin@gmail.com>
> **To:** Winters, Olivia <owinters@claflin.edu>
>
> **Subject:** Some friendly advice
>
> Stop digging or you'll regret it.

CHAPTER FOURTEEN

I peel myself out of bed too early, to meet Ethan for breakfast. On instinct, I check my email on my phone first thing, and there it is, taunting me: the warning from last night. I hoped I'd imagined it. I tap into it again, try to decipher any clues to who sent it. It's from backoffclaflin@gmail.com. And with the fake name Quit Meddling, they're really laying it on thick.

But I have no intention of stopping. Everyone around me is lying, and I have to know why. *Emma* was lying. I need to know if it got her killed.

While waiting for my foundation to oxidize and set, I utilize my best Google-fu to track down Kaila. I remember that her mom was a dean at Smith, and it doesn't take long to confirm that she still works there. A few more minutes and I have their address. I poke around Instagram, Twitter, and Snapchat, looking for signs of life. Kaila's social media is pretty dead. She hasn't tweeted in eighteen months, and her last Instagram pic is of a dandelion sprouting above a grassy patch with the caption *Plant me and I will grow.* It's from a year ago. We used to be Snapchat friends, but now her account is gone. I send her an Instagram DM, just in case.

Hey, don't know if you're back in town, but would love to talk.

Vague but truthful. It'll do.

I find Ethan in the dining hall, nursing a mug of black coffee. I help myself to a healthy serving of bacon and my own cup and join him. As I stir two packets of sugar into my coffee, I consider telling Ethan about Quit Meddling's email but ultimately decide against it. He might encourage me to stop what I'm doing, and I can't have that. But my discovery about the path behind Whitley is safe. Ethan groans through a sip, the liquid gurgling like he's a fish.

"So anyone could have snuck around, regardless of cameras."

I nod, nosh on a salty slice. "We're truly at square one. I did DM Kaila, though."

"And?"

I check my phone. "No reply yet. But her parents live in Northampton, so it's entirely possible she was around last week. We'll see."

"How was Tyler when you ran into him? Do we still think he didn't know?"

Ethan doesn't watch his volume, and I pop my head up like a meerkat, scanning the immediate area to ensure that no one heard and is watching. Then I lower my voice for my reply. "I can't tell. He's planning a candlelight vigil—I mean memorial—for tomorrow."

"I saw." Ethan's jaw flexes. "We need to figure out who Emma was cheating with, then confront him and see how he reacts. From what you told me, it seems like Margot knows who it is."

"I can't ask Margot. She made it clear yesterday she had nothing more to say."

He seems to think on that. I gnaw a piece of bacon. I watch the green pops in his hazel eyes dance.

"If you had a secret boyfriend, how would you contact him?" he asks.

"You're assuming I know how to contact an actual boyfriend." It's out before I can stop it. I talk faster. "Idon'tknowthough. Probably text or social media?" Good cover.

"Right, her phone." Ethan either didn't notice my first answer or is too nice to say anything. "If you have a secret hookup, you text them. Or message them. There has to be a trail."

"The cops took her phone. Laptop, too. They still have them." I hate to see Ethan's spirit dull. I take a swig of coffee, letting the acid slice through my guilt.

"Are you sure she didn't have another phone? A burner?"

"She wasn't a spy, Ethan. It's not a movie."

My response is automatic, Ethan's suggestion too easy to dismiss out of hand. But then I remember: Emma upgraded her iPhone last fall. She asked me if I wanted her old one, since otherwise it would sit in a drawer. Uncomfortable with being a charity case, I declined. My mother had bought my refurbished smartphone for a bargain price, so proud when I unwrapped my Christmas present and squealed with delight to finally have a touchscreen phone that wasn't an embarrassing pay-as-you-go. The Ivies noticed that kind of thing, off-brand discount-retailer phone, outside of contract.

And I noticed how all of them always had the latest fancy phone model the day it came out. I close my eyes, think about all the times I saw Emma on her phone in the past few months. Her old case and her new were nearly identical. The new one was pink. The old one was lavender.

I picture Emma texting furiously during dinner. On a lavender phone. It feels familiar, fresh—was it last week? The week before? Or am I forcing the mental image, fusing much older memories with newer ones?

"You look like you're thinking about something," Ethan says.

"I—" My throat catches as I conjure up a picture of our room. Where would Emma have stashed that old phone? Underwear drawer, maybe? "Emma might have had another phone," I concede. Ethan preens. "It's worth checking. But if it was in our room, the cops might have it, too."

"Or they might not."

He's right, it's something.

"I'll search my room between exams, and maybe we'll get lucky."

"Which ones do you have today?"

"Only AP German and Brit Lit, which is a paper."

"Lucky." Ethan rips into his toast and speaks midbite. "I'm dreading AP Bio and Art History."

"Art History?" I rib him. "So hard critiquing all those pretty ballerina paintings, huh?"

"Hey, it's all a bitch to memorize. Birth dates, death dates, moving-to-Paris dates, painting dates."

"That's a lot of dates."

"And yet somehow I'm still single." Ethan's eyes sparkle, and my breath nearly leaves my body. Hastily I finish my bacon, give myself time to craft the perfect retort—something magical, flirty, the perfect invitation.

My phone buzzes on the table, and I see the camera icon on the notification bar. Thwarted by Instagram. Ethan's looking away now, spearing a piece of melon. Spell's broken. With a sigh,

I swipe and tap, and my heart rate spikes so hard I feel my ribs ache.

Kaila replied.

Is this about Emma?

Shit. What do I say? Before I can type out a reply, another message appears.

I was sorry to hear what happened. I'm in Boston today, but I'll
be around tomorrow. Can you come down to Northampton?

I message back a hasty yes, asking her what time. Tomorrow is Sunday, with the final senior exams on hold until Monday morning, so the hardest part for me will be finding a ride to the train station.

"I'm meeting Kaila tomorrow," I tell Ethan.

"Do you need me to go with you? As backup?"

It's the first time it's occurred to me that I might need it. "She's not violent." I hope.

"Isn't the whole point of meeting with her to figure out whether that is the case?"

Kaila is, indeed, a wild card, and that's the very problem. Safety in numbers is smart, but who knows what Kaila will reveal about the Ivies, what grudges she holds. She wasn't one of us, but she was close. Used to date Tyler, in fact, so we all ended up at the same parties and lunch tables.

But I really could use the backup. "I'll let you know what time she agrees on."

"I've been thinking." Ethan leans forward. "About the security cameras. If the system was hacked, we should talk to Sierra." He pauses. "Though it's also possible she's the one who did it."

I'm quick to defend my friend. "No way. She wouldn't." Instinct pushes the words out of my mouth, but they come out hollow. The thought has crossed my mind.

He shrugs. "Maybe it had nothing to do with the murder. All a coincidence. But really anyone taking CS classes is a suspect."

"That's a lot of students."

"It is, but Sierra is president of Girls Who Code, the obvious expert we should talk to first. Even if she didn't do it, she's our best bet at knowing how someone could. I understand if you don't want to do it, given everything going on. I can talk to her."

"No!" I bring a hand down on top of his, stopping him from picking up his phone.

"I was only going to check the time."

I don't move my hand. His skin is soft. Finally I pull it back. "I'll figure out how to get to Sierra."

Ethan nods. "Okay then."

I complete my AP German exam in forty minutes flat—it's multiple choice, which is a gift. As I walk out the door, I can hardly believe that the most important thing to me less than a week ago was nudging my GPA high enough to go up a spot in class rank. Like it'll matter in ten years. Now all I can think about is finding Sierra. I walk through the plan as I head to my work-study shift. I'm so distracted that I miss the warm body blocking my path.

"What the—"

"Miss Winters!" Detective Cataldo hastily stows her phone in a navy crossbody purse and flashes a tight smile. "You finished early."

"Uh, yes, hi."

"I need to ask you a few questions."

"So you waited outside my class?" I can't help the accusation in my tone. My hackles are up.

Cataldo shifts uncomfortably. "Let me walk you to— Where are you going?"

"I have my work-study job."

"Austen Hall, then." She grimaces. Clearly not her favorite place. Wonder why.

I drag my feet, following her to the stairs, down them, and out into the chilly mid-December air. We shrink in our coats, each burrowing into the warmth. A few students mill about. A boy crosses the quad hauling a large beige suitcase behind him. Guess he's not sticking around long enough for Tyler's candlelight memorial. I wonder if the detective will be there.

Austen Hall is a short walk across the main quad, and Cataldo seems determined to drag out our tête-à-tête. She walks slow and talks fast.

"Did Emma ever share her passwords with you?"

"No. Why?"

Cataldo's breath puffs white in the frigid air. "We got into Emma's phone easily, but her laptop is another story. Her parents don't know it. I was hoping that since you were roommates . . ."

"In my experience, friends don't usually share their computer passwords with each other," I say.

"Okay, what about Tyler, then?"

"What about him?" Did she notice the high pitch of my voice?

"What was their relationship like? How often did they spend time together? Did they hang in your room, his? Were they sexually active? If so, how often?"

"Whoa." I stop short halfway across the quad. Round on the detective. "Are you really asking me about my friend's sex life?"

"It's standard procedure, Miss Winters. If there was a disruption in the regular rhythms of their relationship recently, I need to know. Sex is a powerful motive."

I answer perfunctorily and try not to squirm. "Emma was spending the night at Tyler's on a regular basis. No major change. I didn't pry into the more scintillating aspects of their relationship. It wasn't my business."

It wasn't, but that wasn't really why. Emma was having sex, I wasn't, and it was awkward. Emma went to Margot or Sierra about sex stuff. She stopped sharing, and I stopped asking. It was fine. But I don't like what Cataldo is implying.

"If you're trying to slut-shame Emma . . ."

"I'm not." Cataldo is quick to defend herself. "I want to get a clear picture. So, what about the nonsexual aspects of their relationship? Was he a good boyfriend? Did Emma ever complain to you? I've asked your other friends the same questions, but I want to hear it from your perspective."

I can only imagine what Avery had to say about Tyler and Emma. Cataldo's brown eyes are wide, oddly warm for a hard-boiled detective. Really, she's kind of soft, but I wonder if that's an act she's putting on to set me at ease. I hedge.

"They were great. Kind of obnoxious about PDA, but it was a perfectly normal relationship. Two hot, smart, warm-blooded teens who liked each other."

Cataldo's eyes narrow at my glibness, but she doesn't call me on it. "They liked each other? Weren't they in love?"

I fuss with my backpack strap, cursing myself for being too honest. Cataldo can tell she's got something from me. I huff air through my nose, savoring the warmth it blows onto the lower part of my face. "Emma thought undying teenage love was Shakespeare bullshit," I say. "It wasn't her thing."

"Not a fan of *Romeo and Juliet,* then?"

I shake my head. "They were fine. Just . . . most people don't take their high school relationships past high school. They weren't forever or anything."

Cataldo *hmms* under her breath. "You clearly don't attend anything like my high school. Plenty of people took those relationships to forever. Or at least their first divorce." She laughs to herself.

We start walking again.

"I thought Tyler had been cleared," I say, testing the detective.

Cataldo's eyebrows lift. "Who told you that?"

"Katherine Montfort told Avery."

Annoyance flits over the detective's features. "Then, yes, you heard accurately."

"So why ask me about them?" She squirms, and it occurs to me: police tactics. *Sex is a powerful motive,* she said. Does she think *I* was into Tyler? I nearly laugh at the thought. But any amusement fails to spark, dying against the steely truth: I'm still a suspect.

Cataldo's next statement does nothing to disabuse me of the notion.

"I read some of your text exchanges. You and your friends."

She lets it hang. I don't respond.

"You don't seem to fit in with them," she says. "Girls like us . . . it's not real. They let you hang around when it's convenient to them, but you'll always be outside looking in."

"They're my friends." I grit my teeth so hard I fear I'll chip an incisor. "I'm not like you." If I say it often enough, forcefully enough, maybe it will be true.

And she fucking *hmm*s again.

"Well, if I were you, I'd watch my back. I'm assuming you didn't tell them about your Harvard admission?"

The Georgian red brick of Austen looms above us. I stop short and drop my voice low. "How do you know about that?"

"I'm a detective, Miss Winters. Give me some credit."

"It's not a big deal."

"Weren't you telling me you suspect your friend Avery killed Emma because of her Harvard admission?"

When she says it like that, it sounds moronic. And paranoid.

"And did you use the same loophole your friend did? Your rule-breaking college counselor?"

I sigh. "I wish I'd never done it. It was stupid."

Cataldo tilts her head. "You regret getting into Harvard? Why? Because you got something your friend wanted? You think you owe her?"

I squirm under her gaze. Have to remind myself she is a police detective, not my friend. She doesn't know me. She suspects me.

When it becomes clear I don't plan on responding, she moves on. "What about Mr. Tipton? He's kind of cute, huh?"

"Isn't he a bit young for you?" I quip.

"How old do you think I am?"

I shrug. This is dangerous territory. "Older than he is, for sure."

"Is he too old for you?"

"Ew. Yes. I'm not an idiot. Twentysomething dudes who hit on teenagers are gross."

"Right answer." She nods approvingly.

I very strongly wish to end this conversation, so I turn and make my way up the brick stairs and into Austen. The detective follows me into the lobby and hands me her card.

"Call me if you think of anything. Or text. I'm hip like that."

I barely suppress a groan. She's kind of embarrassing. I shove the card into my coat pocket with my gloves.

"Detective Cataldo, what a pleasure." Headmistress Fitzgerald's tone indicates otherwise. But she's appeared for a reason. Fitzgerald casts an appraising eye on me, and I take my cue to scoot back. I linger just out of Fitzgerald's eyeline, pretend to check something very important on my phone.

"We're going to need you to return Emma Russo's cell phone and laptop to our office within the next twenty-four hours."

"Excuse me? Those items are logged into evidence, and my team—"

"Your team is a two-bit country outfit, which I hear hasn't been able to crack a simple laptop password. The board has called in a favor with the FBI. The Russos are in agreement. We need the devices back so the FBI can take over."

"*Ms.* Fitzgerald," Cataldo begins, "it is my pleasure to educate you on FBI jurisdiction and how the agency works with local law enforcement. *With* being the optimal word. I am happy to collaborate *with* the FBI as needed, and please communicate my thanks to the board for their thoughtfulness. But this is still my investigation, and I will not surrender important evidence."

"Certainly." Fitzgerald offers a strained, false smile. "You misunderstand me. Claflin has access to the best IT professionals in the state. We're simply offering to help. Plus, the Russos want their daughter's phone back, seeing as you've already accessed that and had ample opportunity to make a copy of the contents. They'll be here for the candlelight memorial tomorrow evening and have requested to pick up the items."

"There's a candlelight memorial?"

"Mr. St. Clair planned it, with my full support. Sunday was the only evening to do it, what with the new end of the term Monday midday."

"Interesting. And yes, I'm well aware of all your students and faculty jetting out of here in the next forty-eight hours. And I will consider relinquishing the evidence. Since it's a request and not a legal demand."

"Right."

I think I have just witnessed an epic battle. I'm not sure who won.

Fitzgerald retreats to her office, leaving Cataldo and me to awkward silence. She clears her throat, makes eye contact with me; I take a step toward the main office, eager to escape. Cathy saves me, appearing at the admin office door and calling over to me.

"Olivia, dear, is that you! We have a lost student ID, and I need you to make a new one."

"I have to go," I say, already moving away. "I'm the only one who knows how to work the ID software, so . . . bye."

I share an awkward departing wave with the police detective, who is trying to either manipulate me or mother me. I don't know which one is more concerning.

CHAPTER FIFTEEN

Now, where would I hide a phone? I'm standing in the middle of my room after work, surveying the landscape. I turn, spinning in a sloppy circle, rounding on Emma's dresser. I'm sure the cops searched, too, but I look anyway. Rifling through each of the drawers in succession turns up nothing. If this were a spy movie, there would be a secret compartment at the back of one of the drawers, but I know it's all dormitory standard issue.

Next I try her desk, which surely is the second place the cops also looked. The drawers are full of papers, Sharpies, thumbtacks, a stapler, neon Post-its, and an old box of Wheat Thins.

Under the mattress, under the bed, at the back of her closet—I try all those places and find nothing. I search the pockets of her coats, pull down her suitcase and check every zip pouch. I move strategically and tidy up after myself with care. It can't look like I've tossed the place. Talk about making me look guilty.

I discover Emma's Kindle in a basket by her bed, a device the police didn't take, and for one triumphant moment I think I've cracked it—maybe she exchanged secret messages on this!—but no luck. I'm about to try to unscrew the heating vents because that's always where people hide covert devices in movies, when a hunch prickles behind my rib cage. If I had a secret phone, I'd want it within easy retrieval distance. Somewhere convenient to me but unlikely for anyone else to discover.

An urgency ticks at me. The detective said it. Forty-eight hours until the semester is over and everyone leaves. Half the student body is already gone. A whole pool of suspects who will scatter across the country, possibly even the world, in a few days' time.

If Emma had a secret boyfriend, and his information is on a secret phone, I'm running out of time to find it.

I go back to Emma's desk and search from top to bottom again. My eyes catch on the box of Wheat Thins in her bottom drawer. A thing the cops likely wouldn't look at twice. The box is heavy, and something inside thumps against the cardboard as I lift it. I unfold the flaps and reach my hand into the plastic bag. Bingo. I pull out Emma's lavender-cased iPhone. Something cold grazes my knuckles as I pull the phone out, so I go back in to retrieve what turns out to be a key. I slip it into my pocket to deal with later. All my attention is on her phone.

A press to the power button does nothing. It needs a charge. Shit.

The normal spot where she charged her phone is empty, so I assume the police took her charger with them when they grabbed Emma's laptop. I'm an Android girl; none of my cords will work. And so I embark on another top-to-bottom search of the room, going through all of Emma's things once more. Naturally, I find a backup charger in the last place I look—the basket next to her bed. I plug in the phone, and a black-and-white battery icon appears on the screen, but I know it will be some time until it turns on. It's going to be a wait.

My bed is calling my name, so I lie down, close my eyes for just a moment.

When I startle awake, the room is all shadow. My mouth is gummy with sleep, my limbs heavy and achy. Not the kind of nap that refreshes you. I feel like death.

My phone tells me I've lost four hours. That explains the gray cloak that has fallen over the room.

There's a pounding on the door. That must be what woke me. I cross the room, wiping dried drool from around my mouth, sure I look a picture. When I open the door, Sierra eyes me up and down.

"You look tired."

"I was napping. Though I think once you pass the two-hour mark, it's just sleeping."

"You hungry? I came to see if you want to hit up the dining hall for dinner."

"Uh, yeah." I realize now that I skipped lunch, and I am starving. Is it worth the awkwardness with Sierra to eat? Absolutely. "One sec." I grab my bag, quickly unhook Emma's phone from the charger, and drop it into my purse so Sierra doesn't see. I want to power it up so badly. But instead I go with Sierra, making small talk about Christmas break.

"I texted Aves and Margot, and they'll meet us there," Sierra says as we cross the quad.

"Great." It's not great, and I hope Sierra missed the shade of panic in my voice as I said it. I sneak my phone out of my bag, figuring it's safe to check that one, though my fingers whisper over the textured case of the one I really want to look at. I have a few text messages. Ethan checking in on how my exam went and reporting that he survived his. And one from Kaila. She wants to meet tomorrow at 10:00 a.m.

"Why are you texting with Kaila Montgomery?"

I catch Sierra reading over my shoulder, too nosy for her own good.

"I was curious how she was doing, so I reached out," I try, casual as can be.

"Olivia, you are a terrible liar. What's going on?"

Sierra grabs hold of my arm, rounding us to a stop outside Austen. Two boys graze past us, opening the door and sending a heavenly blast of warm air our way. Sierra stands firm, making it clear we will freeze until I spill.

I debate how much to tell her. But then I think about Emma's secret phone in my purse. How much do I have left to uncover?

But this is *Sierra*. If I can't trust her, I am truly alone.

"I'm looking into people Emma screwed over. I've . . . heard some things from people since she died. Things I had no idea about. Like how Kaila might not have gotten herself expelled. I thought it was worth looking into."

"That is really fucking stupid. You're not a cop. And look." Sierra shuffles in place, nudges a toe into a graying patch of snow. "Things with Kaila got super dramatic, and yeah, we kept you out of it. Emma wasn't perfect, but Kaila's dangerous. You should stay away from her."

"So you admit it? You did shit behind my back? This is the angle the cops don't know about. All the crap we pulled, the stuff you guys did behind my back. I can talk to Kaila while she's got her guard down, find out if she was near campus last week."

Sierra considers me, a range of emotions passing over her face. Consternation morphs to pity.

"Liv, what are you doing? Why do you care so much about this?"

Her question knocks me back a foot. "Our friend *died*," I remind her.

"I know that," she snaps. "I was the one who found her, remember? We're all . . . broken from this." She blows out all the air in her chest in one long, slow exhale. "I'll never get her face out of my mind. I can't help but feel responsible. . . ."

"I know." I touch a tentative hand to her arm. "If we'd stayed at the party, not left her, maybe it would be different." For me, it's a genuine sentiment. For her, a condemnation, that the Ivies are lying about the timeline.

Sierra flinches. I drop my hand.

"Liv, all the things we did, whether you knew about them or not, are in the past. We did it. Admissions are all but over. Let it be. And if something Emma did got her killed, the cops will figure it out. There's no need to bring the Ivies' shit into it. And what if Kaila did do it? You're just going to meet with her alone?"

"I won't be alone. Ethan is going with me."

"Ethan Kendall? What have you told him?"

Everything. "Nothing," I say. "He knows Cataldo has me on the security footage outside Whitley. He offered to help. Overeager student journalist and all that."

"Wait, why were you outside Whitley? And why wouldn't you take the back way?"

That gets a raised eyebrow from me. "You know about the back exit?"

"Everyone does." She shrugs. "Everyone who needs to sneak in and out of Whitley, at least. That was dumb getting caught on tape, though."

"I wasn't doing anything wrong, so why would it matter?"

She takes a step back from me. "Are you a suspect?"

"No. At least, I don't think so. Not anymore. Cataldo keeps asking me questions about Emma's love life."

Suddenly Sierra is intently interested in the ground.

"Did Margot tell you? Or, worse, did you know?" I ask her.

"I . . . suspected."

"I lived with her and I didn't notice!"

"Well, you're not exactly the most observant when it comes to these things, Liv. No offense."

Sierra does mean offense, so for once I decide not to grin and bear it. I show her how observant I can be.

"The cameras were hacked, Sierra. You were always saying it would be easy to do if the school was stupid enough to connect the cameras to the internet. Any idea who might have done it?"

"Paul probably messed something up, hit the wrong button."

I shake my head. "The cops specifically said *hacked*. Someone turned them off for a few hours."

Sierra and I lock into a stare-down. I know she did it. She will not concede.

Finally Sierra heaves a sigh, breaks eye contact. "I mean, yeah, it wouldn't be hard. Olivia, why are you harping on this? I'm sure whoever did it was sneaking around, hooking up or something. Not killing Emma. You have to let this go. Come on." She powers up the stairs to Austen, not waiting to see if I follow. She reaches the top landing before she notices I'm not beside her.

"Aren't you coming?"

"Sounds like the Ivies prefer to meet without me, anyway." I turn on my heel, for once leaving her in *my* wake.

* * *

Embarrassment turns to rage as I tromp across campus back to Bay. How dare Sierra treat me like that. For what? Trying to solve the murder of our friend? So what if the Ivies don't like the reckoning that's coming for everything we've done over the last two and a half years? If it was something we did that led to this, we deserve to know.

Or if it was Emma's hookup, we need to know that, too.

Finally I get back to my room, and I wrest the phone that's been tempting me out of my bag. I check that the door is locked, even though I know it is, and curl up in the farthest corner of my bed, pulling my down comforter around me like a shield. I power on the phone.

And then the lock screen asks me for a passcode.

I curse under my breath, start cycling through potential codes.

Emma's birthday, both American and European style, doesn't work. I try as many other notable birthdays as I can recall—Tyler's and both her parents'. (I have to creep on Emma's Facebook to get those.) I'm running out of tries. The phone will lock me out after ten.

My eyes search Emma's side of the room, looking for clues. Nothing obvious with numbers jumps out at me. There's a large print of the Eiffel Tower at night, the *Marie Antoinette* movie poster, one of Degas's dancers. Emma had a thing for Paris—all things French, really. I zero in on the movie poster, for some reason. Emma wasn't merely a cream puff; she was fiercely smart and thoughtful about things, genuinely interested in history. She read not one but two biographies of the cake-loving queen (though, as she reminded me more than once, Marie never actually said that, not that way, referring to the famously misattributed quote).

It's silly, stupid really, but I find myself Googling "Marie Antoinette," pulling her essential details. And I take a chance, tap in the passcode.

1-7-9-3. Year of death.

It works.

I whoop in triumph as the home screen comes up. An angry red 11 shouts out from the messages app. I tap in. Three threads are clearly spam, advertising something or other in Spanish, and there are a few older ones labeled with names like Ashley and Brian, but there's only one that's an active conversation. There's no real name, unless her paramour's name is Beau. But I reckon it's a continuation on the French theme.

I take in a succession of gray speech bubbles filling up the left side of the screen. I read them from the bottom up, tracing panic backward.

Emma, wtf, where are you? Answer me, please. I'm worried.

Emma, are you OK?

I need you, babe. Don't keep me waiting!

Are you coming? (insert racy pun here)

I'm here, aching for you.

I gag, even though they're hardly sexts. *Aching for you?* No thank you. I scroll up through the chat history until I get to Emma's last message to Beau.

> I've had the worst fucking night.
> Need you. Usual place. 2 a.m.

I check Beau's final panicked text. It's from 2:30 a.m.

Back, back, back, I find evidence of at least three months' worth of flirty texts and references to clandestine meetings. There are some legitimate sexts, as well as more-intimate selfies of Emma and even a freaking dick pic that I did not need to see, ever, and will struggle to banish from my memory. Isn't this what Snapchat is for?!

I am able to deduce one thing from the dick pic: Beau is likely white. I never thought analyzing dick pics would be a life skill I'd develop.

Otherwise, his texts to Emma don't offer many clues. He always uses complete sentences and proper grammar, though his emoji game is also perfectly on point. He's generic, like every try-hard guy who pulls out cheesy, romantic bullshit from TV and movies because it's what he thinks girls like. Tyler calls Emma "babe," too.

All I know is that Beau lives on campus—there are no instructions about sneaking past main security. It doesn't mean much, since hundreds of students go here.

What I don't get is why Emma needed a whole other phone to text this guy. Who would be so bad that Emma would need to keep their texts attached to a completely different account?

I pull up Google on my laptop and type in the number. Most of the results are advertisements—*pay us for more information on this number!*—and painfully obvious things, like *Boston number information!* Like I don't already know it's a Massachusetts area code.

Then I pull up my phone, scrolling through my contacts to see if I have the same number in my phone. I'm not exactly a social butterfly, especially not with boys at school, but it's worth a try. Predictably, it yields nothing.

I throw the phone hard against my pillow. How did I miss this? Emma was my friend. We *lived* together. I had no clue any of this was going on. Is it like Sierra insinuated, that these things go straight past me?

Or, more likely, did Emma go out of her way to hide this? If so, why?

A low rattle makes me jump. Is Beau texting right now? I look at Emma's phone but realize it's mine instead.

Meddling, Quit has sent a new email. The message is once again short and sweet.

> You're stubborn. So was Emma, and look what
> happened to her. For your own sake, stop.

I need to find Beau. *Now.* Before Emma's killer finds me.

CHAPTER SIXTEEN

I text Ethan to come over ASAP, then pick up Emma's phone again. That last message Beau sent, at 2:30 a.m.—what if it was a plant? Sent to make him look worried about her. An alibi text. I check the one before that. There's a twenty-minute gap.

I zoom all the way to the top of the chain and read every message again, trying to discern any identifying details. I'm halfway through when my phone buzzes from my side table. Ethan is here.

> I'm downstairs. I don't actually know where your room is.

I let him know where to find me. I hate the way Quit Meddling's email clings to the top of my in-box. I get a jolt every time I see it. I swipe the email to archive it, put it in the back of my mind. I'm definitely not telling Ethan, not about this new message or the previous one. Tracking down Beau is far more important. So some dick is telling me to stop digging. It's not like they've overtly threatened me or anything.

There's a knock. I crack my door open, check that it's Ethan and he's alone, and then grab him by the arm and secrete him inside, even though it's not yet 8:00 p.m. and he's totally allowed to be here. But this feels so explosive, so wrong.

"Whoa, what's going on?"

"I cracked the code for Emma's phone. The one she used to text Beau." Before Ethan can ask, I clarify. "That's the code name she used for him. *Elle avait un penchant pour les choses françaises.*" Taking in Ethan's confused look, I translate. "She had a thing for French stuff."

"Can I see?"

We sit on my bed, side by side. I hand him the phone, but not before I scroll all the way back up to the top. "You can help me go through these, comb for clues to who he is. I'm lost." Ethan's eyes widen. Then he bows his head and starts to read. I scoot in closer so I can read, too. Excitement skitters up my spine, making the hairs at the back of my neck stand on end. He smells good, like lemongrass and clean skin. The thought makes me feel like a serial killer, and I hope he doesn't turn his head to look at me, because I am sure my entire face has gone pink. Also, that would put his lips in alarmingly close proximity to mine. And now I'm *certain* my face is raspberry red.

"Ah!" Ethan cries out, and my eyes whip down to the screen.

"Shoot, I meant to warn you about the dick pic!" Ethan turns his head toward me now, our lips hovering oh-too-close, but the look of numb horror on his face is anything but romantic. I suppress a giggle, pulling back a blessed extra few inches. "Sorry. I would have deleted it, because no one deserves non-con nudity, but it's evidence."

"I get it, but I'm also scarred for life," he says, his tone playful.

"So, there's one thing." He scrolls up to a text, shows me. "He must live in Whitley. She mentions she can sneak in to see him, that Tyler showed her how."

"Wow, mentioning her boyfriend to her . . . other boyfriend. Awkward."

Ethan laughs. "But helpful. This rules out most lower levelers, narrows it down to, say, sixty-five people?"

"Oh, great, only sixty-five," I drawl.

"I know, I know. But . . ." Then he rockets off the bed, cutting across the room in three long strides. He stops in front of Emma's whiteboard, which is affixed to the back of her closet door. He erases the "affirmation for the day," a cheesy thing Emma used to do religiously but gave up on at some point. A tiny space inside me aches as another vestige of Emma disappears forever. Even if it was a quote from *Mean Girls*.

Ethan begins to write out names, and I spot the pattern.

"Guys on the FIRST Robotics team, okay. You're missing Rajesh."

"Beau is white, remember?"

Oh, how I'd like to forget.

"She did tech for drama, too. Hold on." I pull up the school website and navigate to student organizations. Ethan adds the names of any junior or senior boys from the latest production photo. I backtrack to the FIRST team page in case we missed anyone. Ethan catches me frowning at the image.

"Something wrong?"

"Professor Butler," I say. "Do you think . . ."

"He doesn't live on campus, so no." Now Ethan frowns. "But Professor Griffin is one of the faculty in residence at Whitley. Drama sponsor."

Ethan adds him to the list.

We crawl through each of Emma's activities on campus, all her classes. We end up with twenty-two people, because Claflin is lousy with white dudes.

"Now we go through the list, narrow it down to who she would have realistically hooked up with, compare it to the texts. Maybe we'll spark on something," Ethan suggests.

Am I even the best judge of who Emma would be into? I'm basing it on the Emma I thought I knew. The roommate and friend who always had to be the center of attention (at least when Avery wasn't around), but you didn't fault her for it. Because she was fun, freewheeling, clever. Emma entertained, was never a stick-in-the-mud about things. Everyone liked her, I thought. Can I trust my own gut?

I read Beau's messages carefully. Then I see an exchange that makes my blood run cold.

Babe, what's the code again?

3724.

Then, after a ten-minute gap:

Now what?

Seriously? Boys' locker room, through the steam room. 1902.

"Ethan!" I call him over from the whiteboard, where he's crossed off a few names on his own. The less socially adept candidates. Emma had high standards. "Look at this. Three-seven-two-four. That's the code to the boathouse. That had to be their spot." I scroll up, double-checking. "Yes, this is when they started to hook up regularly."

Ethan peers over my shoulder. "What's in the boys' locker room, through the steam room?"

I leap into action, already halfway into my coat. "We're going to find out."

"Now?"

I plop down into my desk chair and slip on my boots. "Yep. Get your coat." The knit of his brows says, *Olivia, I think you have lost your mind,* but Ethan hops to it.

"Won't it look weird, us going to the boathouse at this time of night, after what happened?" Ethan asks once we're outside. I charge ahead of him, my longer legs and determination giving me a lead.

"It's still ages before curfew. And if anyone asks, I'll say I left something in my locker that I need to take home with me. With training canceled, I haven't had a chance to go back since—" I catch myself before I say it. Everything comes back to Emma. "It's fine."

I've walked this path a million times; my feet carry me by instinct. I'm so used to practice, my arms already ache in anticipation. I roll my shoulders, missing the burn. It hasn't even been a week. I glance up at a security camera. Presumably it's on this time. Is Paul watching me right now? Could Paul have been hooking up with Emma? Maybe his whole *Oh no, we were hacked!* shtick is a front. He turned off the cameras so there'd be no evidence of him sneaking out to the boathouse to meet with her. I share the theory with Ethan.

Instead of telling me I'm paranoid and I suspect everyone, he agrees. "It's compelling."

Wild theories don't seem so wild anymore.

We reach the boathouse, and I input the key code. The front doors click open, and we make our way into the lobby. There's still police tape over the rowing-room doors. A tug at my navel, like an invisible string, has me veering left. I touch the doors. Finger the yellow plastic tape. It's warped, like it's been stretched by someone ducking under it. I don't know what I want from it, from this place. To walk back through that morning, retrace every step? Find something I missed?

"Olivia?" Ethan's voice breaks me from my trance. He's poised on the bottom of the stairs, ready to ascend.

"Right. It's upstairs on the left." I follow him up, and then we cut through the locker room. The steam room also features a hot tub, and Ethan's eyes nearly bug out of his head.

"Does the girls' locker room have one of these as well?"

"Yep."

"I should have rowed crew."

I look him up and down. "You're tall enough."

Ethan breaks into a dopey grin. "You checking me out?"

"Merely an observation." I duck my head to hide a smile. "It has to be there." I point to the only other door, tucked away in the shadows beyond the hot tub. We approach, but with the lights off it's difficult to see the keypad. Plus, I've forgotten the code. Emma's phone solves both problems, the flashlight blindingly bright as I refer back to the second code and key it in.

Ethan and I tumble into a lounge. The lights flick on automatically, on a motion detector. They're low mood lights, but bright enough to illuminate the space. It's swank—leather couches and armchairs, wet bar, big-screen TV with gaming system attached.

"Those assholes," I mutter.

"What?"

"They knew about this place—or at least Emma did—and didn't tell me. This is a hangout spot."

"And probably a nap spot!" Ethan flops down onto one of the leather couches. He sighs into the supple black material, closes his eyes.

"You sure you want to lie on that?" I wrinkle my nose.

"Why?"

And Sierra says that *I'm* clueless. "This is a hookup spot." I raise my eyebrows knowingly.

It takes a second, but awareness washes over Ethan all at once and he nearly falls trying to get off the couch. I walk the perimeter of the room. "I bet Tyler told Emma about this place," I reason. He's captain of the guys' crew team. "And then she brought Beau here. Classy."

"Or Beau was on the team, too?" Ethan suggests, starting to walk the perimeter of the room. It's wall-to-wall shelves stuffed full with books, the kind with cracked spines and gold-embossed titles that clearly aren't meant to be read. "What are you looking for?"

"I don't know. Clues? We have to figure out who he is." I hold up Emma's phone for emphasis. Ethan crosses to the bar, starts to rummage through the supplies. I hear bottles clinking and join him. He's poured an amber liquid into a glass tumbler. "Are you drinking?"

"You think I'm going to turn down the chance to steal expensive whiskey from the rich douches at this school?"

"Good point. Make it two."

"Really?" But Ethan doesn't wait for confirmation before pouring one for me, too.

"I've put up with a lot of bourgeoisie bullshit over the years," I say as I accept the glass. "Fifth-wheeling luxury shopping trips and pretending to be fascinated by tales of spring break trips and summer vacations in Saint Moritz, Montenegro, Tokyo, Seoul, Paris, the Hamptons. No one gives two shits about how summer vacay went down in Lanham."

Ethan's gaze is keen. "You've been nursing that bitterness awhile, huh?"

"You don't know the half of it." I raise my glass to his, and we clink them together. A toast to the best and brightest of Claflin Academy. The progeny of the one percent.

"I never did think you fit in with them. You didn't make sense." Ethan narrows his eyes, thoughtful. Then he drinks.

His commentary slices through me, a dull knife opening old wounds. I hold my glass too tight, crystal etching grinding against my fingers. It's meant as a compliment, but that doesn't erase how desperately I wish I belonged. And with all the Ivies have kept from me, it's glaringly clear that I don't. I never will.

I toss back the whiskey in one go. A mistake.

I double over, hacking wet, heavy coughs between gulps for breath. The liquid burns and stings like a wildfire spreading from inside out.

"Whoa, Olivia!" Ethan slaps his hand on my upper back, trying to help, but all he does is disrupt my rhythm. I cough harder and reach for a nearby waste bin in case my dinner decides to come up with the whiskey.

"Hey," I rasp, sucking in my first proper, deep breath in what

185

feels like centuries. "Someone burned something in here." Tentatively, I reach my hand inside, feeling the partially scorched remains of black fabric. Finally good to stand, I set the container on the bar and use both hands to carefully pull out the charred remains of a sweatshirt.

The stitched lettering across the bust has been well ravaged, but some threads remain. I recognize the color immediately. It's not even necessary to figure out the letters.

"It's Avery's," I say. "Her Harvard hoodie."

"You're sure?"

"If it were Yale, the stitching would be white. Princeton is orange. Harvard is crimson. That shade of crimson."

"The depth and specificity of your knowledge is very weird." Ethan fingers the raised embroidery of what I think is an *H*. "Okay, so this is a Harvard hoodie. Couldn't it be Emma's? We know she was here."

I shake my head. "No, Emma does have a Harvard hoodie, but it is maroon with white lettering. And it's in her closet right now. I checked the pockets earlier today for the phone. Avery's hoodie is black."

"So that means she was here."

"The night Emma died." I search the room for something to carry the sweatshirt in. I'm not leaving it here.

"How do you figure?"

"The wastebasket hasn't been emptied. The whole building has been shut down since it happened, so it had to have been left here the night of— Aha." I find a plastic grocery bag under the coffee table. "Otherwise the cleaning staff is in here Mondays, Wednesdays, and Fridays. Emma died Wednesday morning."

I burn under Ethan's assessing gaze as he watches me place the hoodie into the bag.

"Are we turning that over to the police?"

"I wasn't planning on it."

"And the phone?"

Unease crawls up my spine. "Why are you giving me the third degree?"

"Emma had . . . a lot of secrets." He squirms under my gaze. "I think this is getting a bit intense. That phone is evidence of a crime that may have led to a murder. We're in a secret room that places your friends at the scene of the crime. I feel like we're in over our heads and we should hand this stuff over to Cataldo."

Logically, I know he's right. Normal, everyday people logic. But we're embroiled in a freaking murder. Someone we know, someone *I* know, killed my friend. "I can't hand over half-baked evidence, not when it will make me look even more suspicious for doing all this digging instead of giving Cataldo information. No, we have to keep looking, take these clues to their natural conclusion and *then* hand stuff over."

"I want to state for the record that I object," he offers with a wink.

"Duly noted," I return with a salute, going warm and fuzzy with relief. "Come on, let's go. This place gives me the creeps." In point of fact, it gives me a hollow feeling that gnaws at my insides. My friends hung out here and never told me. Another lie by exclusion.

We slip back out into the shadows of the steam room, the plastic bag crackling against my thigh as we move. I haul open the tempered-glass door to the locker room, and that's when we hear them. Voices, echoing up the stairs.

I react on instinct, grabbing Ethan by the arm.

"What—"

"Shhh!" My destination is the shower room. It's the closest place to hide. Ethan catches on quickly enough, pulling me toward the nearest stall, but my strength bests his. I tug him to the left, to the third stall in. Another tempered-glass door—preferred boathouse aesthetic—creaks on its hinges as we scurry inside.

"Why—"

I cut him off again, this time with an explanation. "They could see us through the door. This stall is out of the direct line of sight. Now hush." I strain to listen, a hair shy of pressing my ear to the door. I can't, for fear it will swing out, make noise.

"Hold up! Your legs are longer than mine!"

"It's not my fault you're slow."

My body goes stiff with recognition. Margot and Avery.

"Why are we even here? It doesn't matter, does it?"

And that's Sierra. Avery responds to her. "It matters to me! We can't let the cops find it."

They move through the locker room, bickering, and then their voices muffle as they reach the steam room. I turn to Ethan, planning on telling him we should sneak closer, see what else we can hear, and suddenly we're touching—full-on bodies touching. Shower stalls are meant for one person, not two. I wonder what it would be like if I were a dainty girl, how much less space I would take up, but right now I love every inch of myself. My breath hitches as Ethan's hand grazes my hip, not intentionally, I'm sure. The stall is so small. That's why I rock forward on the balls of my feet, grabbing hold of his arm to steady myself. The world narrows to the warm pressure of Ethan's hand where our thighs touch, to the inch of space that I'd need to close in order to press our lips together.

Then the damn bag crinkles, the dry crackle earsplittingly loud. Shit. I have to hope the Ivies have keyed into the secret room already, that they didn't hear the sound. We have to go. The spell is broken, anyway. I tip my head to the door, signaling Ethan.

I push the stall door open slowly. The hinge exhales like a drunk toad. We make a break for it; I clutch the bag to my chest so it won't swing and rustle. Every sound is a gamble.

We steal back through the lockers, into the upstairs foyer, and down the stairs. It's a mad dash; I fly out the front door, barely waiting long enough to ensure that Ethan is still behind me. Once outside, I break into a run. I half convince myself this is like any other conditioning exercise; I savor the burn in my lungs, the throb in my disused calves. Coach would be ashamed of how quickly I slow to a stop. I tell myself it's to check on Ethan. He's gasping for breath, doubled over a few feet behind me, hands clutching his knees and thighs.

"What . . . ," he pants, "just . . . happened?"

I stare down at the boathouse, imagine my so-called friends rooting around that secret room for the charred sweatshirt I now clutch to my chest. "Avery put herself back at the top of the suspect list, that's what."

CHAPTER SEVENTEEN

The next morning, Ethan and I take a Lyft to the train station and the 9:10 a.m. commuter line to Northampton. It's a nauseatingly cute college town with New England flair. It's a short walk from the station to the wide expanse of Main Street, where the vintage buildings have had a modern facelift by way of hip shop signs.

Kaila is supposed to meet us at Starbucks. We're early, so Ethan holds down a prize corner table next to an outlet while I grab us drinks. I can see all the aspiring writers giving him the evil eye when Ethan fails to produce a laptop. They can suck it up. The table will provide the closest approximation to privacy we can get in this place.

"Oliver?" the barista calls, somehow butchering my painfully common name. I'm unique enough at a small school like Claflin, but I was one of no fewer than three Olivias in my class at my old school. "Caramel macchiato with whip and a soy latte?"

I fetch our drinks and slide into the seat next to Ethan, which will force Kaila to sit across from us, interrogation-style.

"I'm impressed you haven't made fun of my drink." Ethan takes a sip of a caramel concoction.

"I'm not an asshole," I say with a shrug. "And I think gendered expectations for beverage consumption is stupid."

"Remind me again why you're an Ivy?"

"They adopted me. Everyone needs friends."

"But with friends like these, who needs enemies?" a new voice chimes in, raspy and wry. Kaila. My chin whips up, and I feel my eyes go cartoon wide. "Different, right?" She does a showy spin.

To an outsider's eye, nothing about Kaila would seem out of the ordinary. She's a tidy five-foot-six in slouchy jeans and a green cable-knit sweater. Her deep brown hair is shorn in a pixie cut. She must fit right in at Smith, visiting her mom. This Kaila is earthy with a boho-chic flair.

But the Kaila I knew prized nothing more than her luxuriously wavy hair, which she grew, grew, grew until it nearly reached her butt. Proto-Kaila dressed like an Instagram influencer, with the account to match. She wore makeup.

Bare-faced Kaila plops down across from us, now-unruly eyebrows raised at Ethan. "You brought your boyfriend?"

Ethan and I answer in unison.

"He's not—"

"I'm not—"

"Then he's your heavy? In case I flip out?" Kaila barks a laugh. "Don't worry. The whole point of reform school is that I am reformed. No more punching people in the face. Even if they deserve it." Challenge dances in her brown eyes. Then she melts into a shrug of contrition. "I was sorry to hear Emma died, though."

"Thanks." I offer a thin smile. "Did you read about it in the *Globe*?"

"Nah, it hit the East Coast boarding gossip circuit by Thursday afternoon. I go to Wheatford now." Kaila answers my next question before I can ask. "Haven Ridge was only for a year. I transferred last semester."

"What's Haven Ridge?" Ethan jumps in.

"I spent nine months hiking twelve miles a day and living in the woods, basically. Group therapy three times a day, too."

"Wait, what about classes? APs? Taking the SATs?" I am appalled at the thought of falling so far behind.

"That's not the point of a therapeutic wilderness program. Think of it as a gap year. I'm a junior now, so I'll graduate a year behind you guys. It's no big."

"You seem so . . . Zen."

"That would be my no longer hating myself and my friends. You should try it." Kaila smirks, then seems to catch herself. "Sorry, old snarky habits die hard. You know, at my new school, everyone thinks I'm super nice."

"I always thought you were nice," I say, bending the truth a bit.

Kaila laughs. "You were afraid of your own shadow, and definitely of mine. It's okay. I know what I was like. But Haven Ridge changed my life. I loved it."

"You loved reform school?" Ethan remains riveted.

"I had to deal with my shit. Spent a lot of time alone and in my thoughts. It was good for me. So, I guess I can thank Emma for that."

I almost forgot why we're here. Time to dive in. "You don't blame her for what happened?"

Kaila takes a measured sip of coffee. "What exactly is it that you think happened? And why are you asking me? You think I killed her?" She rolls her eyes, not exactly the reaction I was expecting. "I was at Wheatford, fully alibied, thanks. And I don't give a shit about what Emma did anymore, though yes, I do blame her. She took me down. Ruthless, she was."

"You know it was Avery, right?" I have to correct her. "I mean, you were expelled and she got your ASB spot."

"It's cute that you think that. What happened to me went way beyond the student council. Emma wanted me out, and she took me out."

"Took you out?" I snort. "Why would she do that?"

"I was her roommate, I'm not an idiot, and, well, I was dating Tyler."

Now I'm rolling my eyes. "You think she got you expelled for Tyler? That catty-girl bullshit wasn't Emma's style."

Kaila narrows her eyes. "Why did you text me?"

The question catches me off guard. I stumble into my answer. "I heard from someone. A rumor. They said that Avery got you expelled. I wanted to know the truth from you. . . ."

"Well, now you know I didn't kill Emma, so are you good?" Despite the finality of the statement, she doesn't move to leave. Kaila's eyes twinkle with something. Like she wants me to ask her more questions, but they have to be the right ones.

"How did she do it?"

"I've thought about that a lot." Kaila tears off a cube of zucchini bread and tosses it into her mouth. "She must have jacked my SIM card and cloned it, and then she used a duplicate phone to call in the bomb threat the morning of exams."

"That sounds like something from a spy movie. Emma wasn't a computer genius."

"No, but Sierra is. Emma was my roommate, so she had easy access to swipe my stuff. I Googled it. It's not that hard to do."

Kaila's mention of the roommate connection sends a chill of

unease through me. "So, what, they traced the call back to you, and that was it? Why didn't you defend yourself?"

"Surely your family brought in a fancy lawyer or something to appeal?" Ethan chimes in. "I cannot tell you the number of times I've heard guys say they have a family lawyer on retainer to come down to the school for even the most minor infraction."

"I wasn't exactly myself," Kaila says. She fusses with the short hair at her temple, urging it to lie flat against her forehead. "I could never prove it, but . . ." Her brown eyes lock on mine. "Did Emma ever make you drinks? In that pitcher she keeps in the minifridge?"

"Sometimes," I say, trepidation behind the response. Unsure of her point. "Arnold—"

"Palmers," she cuts me off, finishing my thought. "Well, I hope she didn't lace yours with Adderall. I'm pretty sure that's what happened to me. I drank those things like a fish leading up to exams. By the time I was framed for the bomb threat, I felt like I was vibrating out of my skin. Not myself. Admin thought I was crazy. *Unstable.* That's the word they used with my parents."

"That's a pretty massive accusation." Ethan leans forward; I see his journalistic instincts roar to life. An urge to fact-check. But this isn't a story to me. It's my friend. I lay a hand on his forearm, urging him to back off.

"And Emma didn't take Adderall," I say.

Kaila smirks. "Avery Montfort's family runs one of the biggest pharmaceutical companies in the world, and you're questioning where Emma could have gotten some spare drugs?"

Heat creeps up the back of my neck. "It's just so extreme."

Kaila quirks her brows and tilts her head, as if agreeing. "I was pretty shocked to find myself on the receiving end. I thought they were my friends. What surprises me is that you didn't know about any of this."

"Well, it turns out the Ivies did a lot of things I didn't know about," I mutter into my soy latte.

"I wondered if they ever warmed up to you after I left. Guess not." Kaila's eyes are shrewd but kind. "What other things have you found out about?"

"Why do you want to know?" Ethan squares his shoulders, cracks his knuckles.

"See, he's your heavy," Kaila teases, then shrugs. "I'm just curious. They must be bad enough that you reached out to me. I want to know what my former friends have been up to."

The set of Ethan's jaw tells me he disagrees, but he doesn't actively stop me from pulling up our list on my phone and handing it over to Kaila.

Slowly but surely, Kaila's brow disappears into her bangs. "I see drink sabotage is a theme. Though it's weird that Emma was taking the ACT in February last year."

"Shit!" Ethan exclaims, trying to save his coffee cup but failing. Caramel macchiato slides across the table, and Kaila has to skid her chair back to avoid a lap full of coffee. I grab for the few napkins on the table and throw them on top, but it's not enough.

"I'll get more." Ethan rushes to the sidebar and grabs a thick handful of napkins. As he returns and mops up the mess, Kaila hands back my phone. It's dry, thankfully.

"Well, I feel better knowing I'm not the only victim of Emma's vengeance. How are you feeling?"

Pre– versus post–Haven Ridge Kaila jumps out at me again.

I think I've made more eye contact with her in this ten-minute conversation than I did in an entire year at Claflin. Her concern seems genuine.

"I'm okay," I say, finding it difficult to articulate my swirl of emotions, especially to a near stranger. "I'm not even sure what to say to them, knowing all this now."

"Watch your ass. That's my best advice. Keep your head down, graduate, and never look back. I wish I'd stayed out of their way."

"Avery?" the barista calls out, and I nearly jump out of my skin. Scanning the room frantically, I look for her familiar blond head moving toward the pickup bar. But it's a short brunette who grabs the proffered drink. False alarm. It strikes me how annoyed Avery would be to have a name twin out in the wild. She prides herself on being singular.

"Ethan, would you mind getting me a scone for the road?" I ask. "I'll text you a screenshot of my Starbucks card." If Ethan thinks it's strange I'm using him as my lackey, he doesn't say anything. Dutifully he joins the end of the line, which is ten people deep, so it'll take him a bit. By design.

Kaila leans in, a knowing smile plucking at her lips. "Something you want to ask me privately?"

"Are you really saying that the reason Emma did all that to you is because she wanted Tyler for herself? It wasn't about getting Avery that ASB spot?"

"I think the ASB spot was likely cover. Gravy. It wasn't about Tyler per se. . . ." Kaila sips her coffee, I think as an excuse to go no further.

"Why can't you tell me?"

Kaila's expression turns grim. "You don't want to get any more involved in it than you already are, trust me. Emma was a complicated girl. She had secrets. Don't let her take you down with her. I'm glad I escaped with little more than an expulsion no one will care about in ten years."

"Emma's dead. What can she do?"

"You're thinking too small. You're caught in a web and don't even know it." Kaila finishes her zucchini bread and crumples the waxy paper bag into a ball. Then she downs the rest of her coffee, finishing with a wet smack. "Back off, Olivia. That's my advice. But if you don't want to . . . I've given you everything you need." And with a pitying look and a small salute, she bids me farewell.

The words *back off* echo in my ear. Quit Meddling's first email came before I ever contacted Kaila, so she can't be the secret emailer. There's no way. But she's saying the exact same thing.

Stop digging.

"Did she leave?" Ethan looms over the table, a bag with my scone in hand.

"Yeah, let's go." I push back to leave, and immediately a hipster dude with a laptop appears to take the table. Vultures.

Ethan and I walk back to the train station in uneasy silence. I suspect he knows I sent him on an errand to give me time alone with Kaila. He doesn't pry into what we discussed, but his jaw keeps flexing, gloved fingers ticking against his thighs. He wants to ask. My wheels are turning. Emma had secrets upon secrets, but they're like wisps of smoke dancing away from my fingers as I try to grab hold.

We wait on an empty platform for the 11:15 train back, frigid wind cutting through the station and through our coats. There's a shelter down the platform, but neither Ethan nor I make a break for it. I think we both need to feel the burn of the cold.

"What do you think?" Ethan asks finally. All that silence, and he opens with such a widely fielded question.

"I think if Kaila got the worst that Emma did and she didn't want to kill her, then the revenge motive is thin. Unless Jason Wang was willing to kill over some abdominal distress." I stare at a point across the platform, eyes trained on a tattered two-sheet ad for a concert that took place three months ago.

"My guess, it's all about Beau," Ethan says.

I unconsciously thumb Emma's phone in my bag. "The candlelight memorial tonight—you're going?"

"We have to, lest we look like heartless assholes."

"Right, which means Beau will be there, even if he killed her," I reason. "I have the phone, so I have his number. So we set a trap at the memorial. I'll text him, and you scan the crowd to see who is on their phone."

"Why would he answer a text if he knows she's dead? He'll know it's a trap."

I begin to pace, an improvement on leaning forward every twenty seconds to check if the train is coming. "We don't need him to text back. Just look at his phone. React. It'll give him the fright of his life, even if logically he knows she's gone. We'll get him."

A two-toned wail signals the approaching train, cutting off any protest Ethan might make. We move to the end of the platform, ready to board. "Meet me there. It'll work," I say, trying hard to convince myself.

CHAPTER EIGHTEEN

I'm crossing the quad with Ethan when Cataldo calls my name. We stop, Ethan asking with an apologetic look to leave me to it. I let him go with a wave and paste on a smile as I turn to find the detective jogging toward me. A laptop bag is slung over her shoulder and looks to be bumping painfully against her hip.

"Hey, how are you?"

"Uh, fine."

"Are you going to Austen again? Can I walk you?"

I eye Austen, then the laptop bag. Emma's laptop bag. I wasn't heading to the admin building, but I nod. If there's anywhere I can find out the depths of Emma's secrets, it's in her personal files. This might be my only chance with her laptop.

"Isn't that breaking the chain of custody?" I indicate the bag.

"So you *were* listening?"

"Couldn't help it."

"Yes, but no. Claflin's lawyer was happy to explain it to me this morning. I am merely dropping off the laptop into Claflin's custody until tomorrow, when an FBI tech, who is assisting with the investigation—not taking over!—will help us crack the password."

I try my luck. "I can take it in for you if you want."

"I have to deliver it myself to a secure location."

"Of course."

"I'm glad I ran into you. I'm piecing together the timeline for the night Emma died, and I have some questions."

I let her go on.

"What was Emma wearing at the party?"

"Blue dress, red sweater, black leggings, her black boots, and a navy-blue peacoat."

Cataldo stops. We're outside Austen again. Déjà vu. "So that's why you felt she had returned to your dorm room, correct? Because of the sweater."

"It was on her desk chair when I woke up. And the door was open, remember."

"Can you think of why she'd return to your room only to drop off her sweater and not otherwise change her clothes? That's odd. What time would that have been? That she came back? If she did?"

"I don't know. I was asleep. Could have been anytime after eleven-thirty but before two-fifteen."

"The missing time between the party and her death." Cataldo releases a long breath, which blows like smoke between us. "So the sweater indicates that she did go home after the party. What I'm stuck on is what made her leave the dorm, if she did go back to your room. There were no texts on her phone from anyone arranging a meeting."

I think about Emma's secret phone and the texts from Beau.

"Are you sure you didn't wake up while Emma was there?" the detective continues.

I scoff. "And what? Make plans to go to the boathouse with

her?" It shoots out of my mouth before I can think. Sarcastic to a fault.

Cataldo raises her eyebrows. "I was thinking more along the lines of your waking up momentarily but not remembering, seeing her get ready to go, maybe her telling you who she was meeting."

"That didn't happen," I mumble. And I know who Emma was meeting. Beau. After the Ivies. A full social calendar. I'm not ready to hand over my Beau lead, but my friends . . .

I chew on the thought for a moment, and then I decide. "Did you find out about the secret room in the boathouse? Emma used to party there. Maybe that's where she went."

I'm going to burn my friends. Maybe they deserve it.

Cataldo's eyebrows disappear under the rim of her winter hat. "Excuse me?"

"I only found out yesterday. Guess I wasn't cool enough to be invited. But that's probably why the security feed was out. They were sneaking out there to party that night."

I give her a single puzzle piece, watch her eyes go wide with surprise. I don't know if this is smart or colossally stupid.

"Where is this secret room? What do you mean, you only found out yesterday?"

"It's behind the boys' steam room. You need a code to get in. It's one-nine-zero-two. I found a text exchange I wasn't supposed to know about and realized my friends hung out there without me." Half-true. I'll tell her about Beau later, once I've figured out who he is.

"And who is *they*, exactly?"

This is my last chance to turn back. To be a good friend.

But good friend to who? My friends who ditched me on the regular to party in the boathouse? Who committed acts of sabotage that turn my stomach?

"The Ivies," I say with one big exhale of breath. "Avery, Sierra, Margot, Emma."

"And you. You're an Ivy, aren't you?"

It seems like a trick question.

"Technically." It's an offering. Giving Cataldo an inch on our conversation the other day. "But I wasn't invited to the boathouse. Like I told you, I only found out yesterday. Tyler said the Ivies texted Emma after they hooked up."

Cataldo does a double take at that. "I interviewed all three of them, and no one said anything about an after-party in the boathouse."

I narrow my eyes at her. "You think they'd tell you the truth after someone got murdered?"

"You suspect your friends?"

"I didn't say that. But . . ." What *am* I trying to say? "I know they were at the boathouse that night, and I know Emma went to meet them. Or maybe she was there meeting someone else, and they saw something. I don't know."

How did it work? Emma partied with the other Ivies and then texted Beau to meet her there? When would she have had time to come back to the room? But she did. Sweater, door, boot print, earring. Cataldo said Emma wasn't wearing an earring when they found her, but when else would it have ended up on the study room floor?

The timeline doesn't make sense. At least, the timeline I'm *assuming* doesn't make sense. I don't actually know when the Ivies were in that room. When Avery burned her hoodie in effigy. And Tyler said there was a text, but Cataldo doesn't know about it. It had to have been deleted. Was it them?

I'll have to ask them.

But first I need to hack Emma's laptop. "Shall we go in?" Cataldo follows me into Austen. I don't work on Sundays, but I hope Cathy won't say anything and blow my cover.

I escort the detective into the admin office, where, thankfully, I find the front desk vacant.

"Shit." Cataldo drums impatient fingers on the desk, peers around for someone.

"Who do you need?"

"Someone named Cathy is supposed to secure this for me. They said there was a place for it."

God bless Cathy and her smoke breaks I am not supposed to know about or disclose to Fitzgerald. Everyone has secrets at Claflin, even the staff.

"I know where they mean. We have a secure tech closet. I have a key." I fish said key out of my bag. I smile at Cataldo, dangling it between my fingers for her to see. "I'll show you."

I suck in a breath and hold it as I go to lead her back; if she follows, then she trusts me. Perhaps I am not a suspect after all. But if she doesn't . . .

But no, she does. I can breathe again. We make our way to a small room off the main hallway, tucked between the faculty lounge and the security room. It's long and rectangular, really an oversized closet, lined on three sides with floor-to-ceiling shelves that house state-of-the-art projectors, MacBook Pros, LED televisions, and the like. Really, it's a tech graveyard, but I hope

Cataldo doesn't notice. It is true that we keep the room secure, though. The ID-making machine sits on a cart against the back wall.

I find a spot on one of the shelves near the doors, move a small box of wireless mice so Cataldo can slide the laptop case into the space.

"Her phone is in there as well. The FBI wants, the FBI gets."

I give a watery smile to her tepid joke and usher her out. I lock the door and hurry back out front. I need to get Cataldo out before Cathy returns, so I can slip into the tech room unseen.

"I'll see you tonight at the memorial?" I ask. I want her there for when I nail Beau.

The detective gives a belabored sigh, lingers at the doors. "Yeah, I'll be there."

A shrill ring sounds. "I have to get that." I smile brightly and wave. "Bye!" I answer the phone, quickly placing the caller on hold, and then watch Cataldo until she disappears down the hallway. Whoever called will have to try again later. I spring into action, go back to the tech room, but I hesitate at the door. Am I really doing this? Definitely breaking the law. Also maybe betraying my friend. If my theory about her laptop password holds, I'll have access to Emma's private files, everything.

Something niggles at the back of my brain. I have my key in my right hand. It's a clunky thing, big square handle.

Like the key I found in Emma's desk. But there's no way . . .

I dig into the pocket of my jeans, for once thankful I own only two pairs, and the key I slipped in there the other day meets my fingers, cool to the touch despite my body heat. Hold it up against my own key. Identical.

Motherfucker.

I slide Emma's duplicate into the secure tech room door and feel the heavy door give. Any guilt I felt about hacking Emma's personal files dissolves. I want to know why the hell she copied my key. I slip inside and close the door behind me.

First, I fish out Emma's phone from the laptop bag's front zip pocket. Cataldo said the police cracked Emma's phone password easily, so all I have to do is try her birthday—European style, because she was sophisticated—and her home screen appears. I find the Ivies group text and wince reading back our messages. All caps intensity, carefully chosen emojis, vicious words about peers, each other, exchanged in an endless thread that scrolls back and back and back. Did the cops read every single one of these?

Reading through it, I see the signs I missed. Where I chimed in on something or brought up a new topic, and everyone else just . . . ghosted the convo until one of them, almost always Avery or Emma, changed the subject. So many times, it's like I was texting into the ether.

I swallow bile and switch to Emma's thread with Tyler. It's lots of nauseatingly cute back-and-forth, also some choice emojis— lots of eggplants and peaches, vom—but nothing suspicious. No accusations Emma was cheating on him. Tyler seems like a perfectly good boyfriend.

What I don't find is a text chain from the Ivies, the group text they must have had, minus me. I'm sure it exists. They texted her that night.

I put the phone back where I found it and finally slide her sleek MacBook Pro from the case. I scoot with my back against the door and settle the laptop on my thighs. I open it up, flex my fingers until my knuckles crack. It's stupidly simple, typing the same passcode from Emma's secret iPhone into the prompt box.

But it works. There are only so many passcodes a person can remember. The cops had no way of guessing this one without knowing her. Or, at least, the surface of her.

The missing text chain is bugging me. I have to know if I'm right.

I've watched my friends fiddle with their iPhones and Macs over the years, so I know exactly what to do: check Emma's iCloud backup. If I'm unlucky, everything was perfectly synced, and if a group text existed but was deleted, it would have been deleted everywhere. But if I'm lucky, Emma may have turned off iCloud backup on her Mac, preserving any messages sent on this device. Or there will be a backup I can restore.

I have to try. And then I'll dive into her Google Drive. All of Emma's secrets are at my fingertips now.

Power, warm and electric, fills my body, wars with the sticky goo of self-loathing that pricks underneath my skin. I'm losing sight of myself, of the me I pretend I am most of the time—my best self—while the other Olivia settles in. The version of me who is not simply an Ivy but a damn good one. This is where I excel. At suspicion and hypothesis and investigation. Connecting dots and forming a picture and enacting my vengeance. I don't like liars. I don't like false friends.

It takes a while. Several false starts and stops. I'm not Mac-native. But then there it is. I restore the last backup and find a text thread that wasn't on Emma's phone. It's months old, not up to date, the messages exchanged in the lead-up to Emma's death lost forever. But it's proof: Emma, Avery, Margot, and Sierra had a separate group text. It's titled *Rich Bitches*.

With friends like these, indeed.

Emma's Google Drive is easier to navigate. I find a spreadsheet labeled Move for Good. I have no clue what that is, but it's at the top of the page when I sort by last modified, so it must be important.

First, I skim the column headers: donor name, pledge amount, date to pledge, pledge request, location. Then the names and donations. It's a who's who of Claflin Academy. Several jump out: Raj Jain, Chase Masters, Eden Hannon, Chris Hardin, Margot Kim, Avery Montfort. Avery's name is highlighted yellow; I don't know what that means. In total there are twenty names and donations in amounts that make my eyes water. Not one donation comes in under 10K. The highest one is 18K. I know Claflin kids are rich, but no way these students are making those sorts of donations for . . . what? A charity I know Emma wasn't involved in?

The strangest data point is the "pledge request" column. I run my finger over the numbers. 1360. 1420. 1570. 1550. 31. 34. The hairs on the back of my neck stand on end. My eyes rake over the date-to-pledge values. I know some of these dates. Too well. October 5. November 2. The dates I took the SAT to try to raise my score. February 8. The only spring testing date that wasn't canceled because of COVID-19—the ACT when Jason Wang got poisoned.

SAT and ACT dates and scores. A laundry list of Claflin seniors. And a fuck-ton of money.

Emma was running a goddamn SAT scam.

CHAPTER NINETEEN

Sound rushes in my ears as I push Emma's laptop away from me like it's poison. Breathe in, breathe out. I try to steady my racing thoughts.

I think back to all those times Emma kept me company at work. I'd leave her out in the bullpen while I made copies, stuffed faculty mailboxes, brewed coffee. Clues slam into me: Emma had a duplicate of my key. Chris Hardin said he needed to thank Emma for something on ED day. Tyler needed a new ID when he'd just had a replacement made in September. In time for the October test date, perhaps? Though, no—I pull Emma's Mac-Book back into my lap and check—he's not on the list. But I bet if I look up every one of the students on this list, I'll find they had duplicate IDs printed shortly before their test date.

All you need to take the SAT or ACT is a valid school ID. And I handed Emma the keys to the castle.

Is this why Emma became my friend? Why she suggested we move in together? To keep an eye on me, her mark?

And she took the test for Avery and Margot. They both knew. Laughed at me behind my back, I'm sure. Rich bitches, indeed.

I scan the list three times just to be sure my eyes aren't playing tricks on me. But no. Sierra's not there. Thank god. I need one of my friends not to be a total garbage human. But Avery and Margot. And Emma, of course. I fucking hate them. The whole time I was struggling, Emma was handing our fellow Ivies scores in the mid-1500s. For the sweet price, friend discount, of 10K and 15K, respectively.

I can't believe my friends sank so low.

I piece together how she must have done it. There are Claflin-specific SAT and ACT days on campus. So she couldn't possibly take the test for someone else at school, not with faculty as proctors. Thus, all the national test dates. I scan the location column, town names from all over Massachusetts jumping out at me. She must have driven to places where she wouldn't be recognized.

But that only explains the girls on the list. Since there are boys, too, Emma didn't pull this scam off alone. She had to have a male test-taker. I check the spreadsheet again for any indication of a co-conspirator. What if *he* killed her? With the amount of money the scheme raked in, it would be a good motive. Off Emma, keep all the proceeds. I tally the money column. Over two hundred THOUSAND dollars. What. The. Fuck.

I might kill someone over that. . . .

I screenshot the spreadsheet and text the image to Ethan.

> I found what Emma was hiding. SAT scam. I have a new theory.

The Instagram logo winks up at me. I tap in, navigate to my DMs and to the thread with Kaila. She dropped every hint, I realize. That it was odd that Emma had been at the February ACT exam to poison Jason Wang. And she was dating Tyler, she'd said. I type a message.

> Emma was running an SAT scam and Tyler was her male test-taker, right? I found her secret spreadsheet, and she had a copy of my key for the room with the ID maker at the office in Austen. Is that why she became friends with me?

I have to stop myself before I word-vomit more of my thoughts and feelings into the thread. A door slams shut. Shit. Someone's out there. Hastily I hop up, flip the light switch to stop light from spilling through the crack under the door. With nothing but the screen's illumination to guide me, I download a copy of the spreadsheet and email it to myself, making sure to delete the sent email from the cloud, just in case.

I think about Cataldo finding Emma's tracker. The FBI. Should I delete it, protect Emma's memory and the college admissions chances of everyone involved? Does Emma even deserve it? Do any of the cheaters on her list?

My finger hovers over the delete command. I *do* have a copy of the spreadsheet now. . . .

Deleting evidence echoes in my mind. I can't. If I'm lucky, the FBI will miss it. Assume Emma was really into charity.

My phone vibrates, and I nearly jump out of my skin. Ethan's texted back: Are you sure? Meet me in the atrium ASAP.

I slam the laptop shut and shove everything back onto the shelf. Peek my head around the corner and see that Cathy is blessedly not back yet. I make a break for the main door and walk on autopilot. I text Ethan.

I don't notice the hush that has fallen in the atrium. I look up to find a few dozen eyes on me. What the—?

And then I see the Ivies. What's left of us, anyway. Avery, Margot, and Sierra are holding court in front of the dining hall, arms folded over their chests. They're a human chain of grim disapproval. Avery breaks form, reaching to retrieve something from the table behind her. She whips it forward, pulling the pages of the *Claflin Ledger* taut so I can see the front-page spread. A story about Emma is above the fold. And below that is the college acceptances feature that throws to an inside page for the full list.

"Uh, hi?" I say, even though my every instinct is telling me to turn tail and run.

"So, Harvard. Congrats." Avery's words crackle with barely contained rage.

Shit, fuck, dammit. How?! I want to grab the paper from her, but my hands are shaking.

"It's complicated" is all I can manage.

"You lied." Avery's teeth are clenched tight. Margot and Sierra shift almost imperceptibly, but I see it. They angle in tighter to Avery. Margot's eyes go hard. Bear trap activated. Sierra bites her lip and avoids eye contact. It's them against me.

"I can explain." My voice is getting smaller. Quieter. I don't want everyone to see this, to hear it. It's lunchtime, and what's left of the student body seems to all be here, heading toward the dining hall. My shoulders itch under their stares. I know all eyes are on me. I'm gripping the straps of my backpack so hard that my knuckles have gone white.

"Go ahead. Explain," Avery's challenge rings out.

And suddenly, years of frustration and not speaking my mind, kowtowing to Avery and the Claflin status quo and what everyone else wants and expects, rise up inside me. They lied straight to my fucking face. Excluded me at every turn. I burst.

"Harvard was my dream school, too, you know. You don't own it. I always wanted to go there, which I told you. But you made me pick another school. Because everything, always, is about you."

"You were totally fine with Penn," Avery says in defense. "You acted like you were okay with it. How was I supposed to know? I can't read your mind."

"You didn't notice because you didn't want to. You are myopically selfish."

"Ooh, SAT word," Avery snaps back. "Too bad that didn't help you get a higher score."

Sierra sucks in a breath, and Margot looks at the floor.

"Do you really want to be bringing up SAT scores with me, considering . . . ? Emma even gave you a discount." I let it hang. I'm vague enough that everyone here doesn't know the big secret, but Avery and Margot know I've got their number. Avery appears unshaken. She smirks.

"Jealous? But then again, you clearly didn't need a good SAT score to nab that spot at Harvard. I'm betting you gave them a sob story in your essay. How hard it is to go to school with so many rich kids. Break out the tiny violins."

I snort. A literal snort. "Like you wrote about all those inspirational Haitian children?" That has her bristling, cheeks going red. Sierra shifts beside her, just so. Away. "Maybe I got into Harvard because I'm good enough and you aren't." Cards are out on the table now. "And you don't get to be upset that I didn't tell you.

212

Look what happened to Emma when she told you. You acted like a psycho bitch. Are you really surprised I kept it a secret?"

"Fine." Avery's mouth is tight. Her eyes flash with heat. "I'm a bitch. Okay. But lying to my face about Penn, working on RD essays with me—that makes you the bad person." She jabs her finger in the direction of my chest. I rock back on my heels even though she's feet away from me. "I thought you were my friend."

"I *am* applying to other places RD," I shoot back. Avery can call me a lot of things, but not a liar. "Unlike all you rich assholes, I have to. There's no college fund for me. I need to compare scholarship offers. Harvard gapped me."

"Oh, boo-hoo, you're poor." She mimics drying her eyes. "God, you never stop complaining about that."

"Is that why I was left off the Rich Bitches group text, then? By the way, great job deleting that off a dead girl's phone. Evidence tampering is such a good look."

My words are a tsunami, knocking back every single Ivy a step.

It all comes to me in a rush, that Sierra must have grabbed Emma's phone and deleted the text. She was the only Ivy who had access to the body before the cops got there. Probably did it while I called 911. And the backup only gave me older messages. Who knows what texts she deleted? Evidence against one of them, or all of them.

"I knew it. You've been snooping around like some asshole Nancy Drew," Avery hisses. "Or what? You're trying to win a Pulitzer or something?" She rips the *Ledger* in half, as if to demonstrate how ridiculous the notion is.

"I knew you were pumping me for information." Margot bristles. Like I've really put her out.

"Liv, I told you to drop this." Sierra doesn't sound angry. More sad. Resigned.

And then Avery comes back in with venom. "What the fuck is your problem?"

"Me? Why are you such two-faced fucking liars? All the shit you've pulled over the years behind my back? Bomb threats, spiking protein shakes and coffee, sleeping with girls to blackmail them . . . And you're lying about what happened after the party! Exchanging covert texts and burning hoodies in secret back rooms? How are you shocked that I'm digging? Someone on campus murdered our friend, and frankly, you guys look guilty as fuck."

"You think it's one of us?!" Margot cries.

Avery shakes her head. "You've lost it."

Sierra's eyes flick behind me to the crowd. Now they've heard all of this. I've come this far only to blow it at the final hurdle. My rage high fades into the searing burn of humiliation. What have I done?

Then I feel a light touch on my arm. I wrench my arm away violently.

"Olivia . . ." Ethan's eyes flick from me, to Avery, to the crowd. He worries his lip. Guilt.

"You printed it," I practically whisper. "How could you? I told you!"

"I didn't think—" His voice comes out feeble. Good, let him feel bad.

"You didn't believe me. Didn't trust me. Thought I was, what, paranoid? Crazy?" I hold a beat, catch a flash in his expression. "You think I'm like them?"

"You *are* like us." Avery simply has to chime in. "Ethan, you know the only reason you got co-editor is that Vasquez threw a wrench in the works after I did what I had to do to get Olivia the job. And you should ask her about Ingrid. Or ask Seth. You're a hypocrite, Livvy."

That's all she has to say. Ethan goes from contrite to wounded. I want to scream, to explain that I didn't mean to, that I loved being co-editor with him. It worked out for the best! And the catfish thing . . . it was stupid, years ago. But it's enough. He sees me for what I am. As petty and ruthless as any Ivy. So I do everyone the courtesy of leaning into my reputation.

"Fuck you, Aves." I flip her the finger. Turn around slowly and share it with the crowd. "Fuck all of you!" All they're missing is popcorn to enjoy my life imploding as entertainment.

My feet can't carry me out of there fast enough. I get in my run, all right, flying back to Bay at a breakneck pace until I collapse onto my bed in sobs. Finally, after snotting up half a tissue box, I retrieve Emma's decoy Wheat Thins box and dine on stale crackers as I try to wrap my brain around what the hell I'm going to do next.

My phone buzzes from across the room. My heart leaps. Ethan? I betrayed him, ages ago, but he betrayed me, too. We're square.

But when I pick up my phone, I see it's not a text. Instagram DM. Kaila's response chills me through.

Bingo. Though Tyler got shitty scores, so no clue why Emma used him. He's pretty but kind of dumb. And don't forget she used your log-in for the IDs, so if the cops find out, you're on the hook. Watch your back.

She's right.
Emma gave me the perfect motive for her murder.

CHAPTER TWENTY

I do not want to go to the memorial.

Ghostly light flickers through the window in my room. I peer surreptitiously through the curtains to the path and lawn below. Tyler's picked the edge of the lake for his ghastly display, right in front of Bay, so there's no escaping it. But I want nothing more than to hide in my room.

Yet I bend over to retrieve my boots, slip my feet inside, and start to lace up. Emma's phone hangs heavy in my coat pocket. It doesn't matter that I'm all on my own now, that everyone hates me. Ethan hates me. I've come this far, and I'm running out of time. Someone from the atrium will tell Detective Cataldo about the things I said. She's going to ask questions. I have to come with solid evidence. There are still so many tangled threads.

I have to go to the memorial.

I'm pulling on my coat when a scratching sound stops me halfway across the room. Fear grips my insides. What if it's Avery here to exact her revenge? The scraping picks up again. A key in the lock? I barely manage to consider hiding when the door creaks open. Mrs. Russo's mouth forms an O of surprise.

"Olivia! I thought you'd be at the memorial already. Hello."

"Uh, hi," I say as we do an awkward dance at the door. I've only met Emma's mother a few times in passing on move-in days. Polite but cool. It's worse now.

"I caught you on your way out. I won't keep you."

It's the conclusion to a conversation we haven't had. "Oh, right, yes," I stammer. "I was heading down. For Emma. Are you going?"

Mrs. Russo shakes her head. Her chestnut hair is tucked into a perfect chignon. "Charles is bringing up a few boxes. For her things." She grimaces.

"You're packing tonight?" I can't help the panic in my tone. It's too soon. I don't even know who Emma *is* anymore. Was. They can't take her away.

Mrs. Russo nods. "We decided it didn't make sense to make another trip after the holidays. Better to get it all done now."

She's efficient. Type A. Like her daughter. I search her face, looking for Emma. Wondering how far the apple fell from the tree. Or did Emma rot off the branch all on her own?

Mrs. Russo surveys Emma's side of the room, takes a shuddering deep breath. Then, like an animatronic, she springs back to life with the typical strong-mom veneer. "The memorial is a lovely gesture; I'll have to send a card. You go on. I'll get to work here. We'll be gone once you're back." She steps away from the door and sweeps a hand out.

I have no choice anymore. She ushers me out the door with a sad smile, and I trip along the hall to my doom.

Or maybe it's my reckoning.

It's a pitch-dark New England winter evening lit only by two hundred glittering candles. Claflin has dimmed the harsh glow of the streetlights for effect. Lack of floodlights provides me better coverage as I make my way into the throng of students. No one's picked me out yet. I don't see the Ivies or Ethan.

I'm handed a plastic candle holder by a sophomore girl; she passes me off to an older boy, who supplies a slim candle. I stick the two parts together and move along the line to someone with a lighter. Outfitted for respectful mourning—or, I guess, celebration is the point here—I crawl the perimeter of the student assemblage. I need to find the best vantage point for my plan. I'll be alone, with no cover, but the key is to find a spot where I'm able to catch a view of most, if not all, of the other attendees. I spot some of the drama club possibilities toward the back. It helps that the FIRST Robotics team is all together, next to where the teachers and admin are corralled to the right side of the small dais Tyler has had erected. He stands with a cordless mic in hand, portable speaker off to the side.

"Everyone, make sure you grab a candle, and please gather around. We'll begin momentarily."

I finger Emma's phone in my left-hand pocket to check that it's there. My phone is in the right-side pocket. I float on the outskirts of one side of a horseshoe formation everyone is arranging themselves into. My heart leaps into my throat when I catch sight of Avery, Margot, and Sierra. They're perfectly centered in the front row, directly across from Tyler and the dais. I slink back a foot, letting the lumbering football player to my right provide cover. I don't think they see me.

I glance around for Ethan, but there are too many faces cast into spooky relief alternately by flickering candlelight and by their phones. No better moment than now to prepare the seminal text. I have to time things like a dance, send my missive at a point during the memorial when everyone else won't be on their phones, so Beau stands out. However, I can't let him catch me on my phone, either. I tap in what I want to say.

> Miss me, lover boy?

It's stupid but should shock well enough. Even though logically he knows she's dead—we're at her memorial service, after all—the quip, the implication, hangs. I'll just look for the guy who's seen a ghost.

I secure Emma's phone back in its pocket and retrieve mine as a force of habit. Have to check if I have any messages. There's an email from my secret stalker.

> **From:** Meddling, Quit <backoffclaflin@gmail.com>
> **To:** Winters, Olivia <owinters@claflin.edu>
>
> **Subject:** You should listen to me
>
> I know what you're doing. Back. Off. Bitch. Do you want to end up dead, too?

Cold pierces my ribs, radiates outward as white-hot panic. My eyes pinball around the circle, looking for them. Who is torturing me with these messages? This is a real threat now. *Do you want to end up dead, too?*

Fuck.

Screw Ethan hating me, I need help. I need *him*. He'll know what to do. I move to leave, but then Tyler clears his throat at the mic, holds his hands up to indicate we should quiet. Phones are put away. Candles are positioned solemnly in front of torsos.

"Thank you, everyone. Thank you for coming," Tyler begins.

"First, I want to thank Headmistress Fitzgerald and the board for allowing me to put this together on such short notice. I wanted to honor Emma's incredible memory and give all of us the opportunity to grieve her passing but also celebrate her life." His voice chokes, and I can't tell in the candlelight whether he is crying.

Tyler launches into a fine speech about all the things he loved about his girlfriend, and I can't help but feel jaded. The Emma he describes is perfect, but I now know my friend was far from it. If I'd come to know all of Emma's secrets before she died, would I still have liked her? Will she now forever be crystallized as a saint because she died young and tragically?

I lean forward, eyes drifting over my friends. Their faces are hard, all three of them, though maybe it's the light. Everyone looks a bit like a jack-o'-lantern.

"And now I'd like to take a moment of silence, to remember and honor my beloved girlfriend, Emma Russo."

This is it. Everyone bows their heads in respect; some even close their eyes. I edge Emma's phone out of my pocket, bring up my ready text. Hit send. I expect to hear a chime from the receiving phone, but Beau is smart enough to have it silenced. For a steady moment, no one reacts to anything. I'm rapid-fire scanning the crowd, jumping at any minute movement.

Then, finally, there. As the moment of silence is ending, Tyler drawing a deep breath and exhaling a "Thank you" into the microphone, Mr. Tipton pulls out his phone from his jacket pocket.

Joe. He always wanted us to call him Joe.

Well, right now Joe has the damnedest expression on his face.

As if the dead were talking.

CHAPTER TWENTY-ONE

Mr. Tipton is Beau. Emma was sleeping with the college counselor.

Shit. That's why Cataldo was asking about him. How Emma got him to write her recommendation letter. Though I didn't have to sleep with him to get him to help me.

Cataldo! I whip around, search the outskirts of the crowd for her lumbering figure. I have to tell her now, I have to—

An electronic jingle rips through the peaceful assembly. A phone ringing.

My phone is ringing.

I always silence my phone, always, don't even like it vibrating with incoming messages. It's nails on a chalkboard, pings my anxiety every time. But I didn't think to check the other phone. Emma's phone, buzzing and ringing in my left coat pocket. I fumble to pull it out, silence it, feeling heat in my cheeks and hundreds of eyes on me as I mumble apologies. When I finally look up, any relief at having conquered the noisy beast congeals into humiliation. Now the Ivies know I'm here. They're staring right at me, throwing daggers with their eyes. I take a few steps back.

There's sniggering all around me, whispers about how I lost my shit earlier.

"She probably killed her."

I whip around. Who said that?

The whispers multiply to an overwhelming din.

Get away, something inside me screams, but no. I have to stay. Find Cataldo. Tell her about Tipton. My eyes rake across the crowd to where he is.

Was. Tipton is gone.

I stumble backward and trip over my own feet, landing hard on my ass. No one helps me up. Indeed, Tyler has wrested back his control of the proceedings, announcing a song in Emma's honor. Again on my feet, I push through the throng of bodies, make my way to the edge of the horseshoe, scanning for the detective's T.J. Maxx suit and tight ponytail, but everyone is a shadowed shape. I don't see her. Or *him.* Shit.

I leave the discordant sounds of half a crowd singing off-key behind me. I sprint toward Bay because it is home and it feels safe. I shove Emma's phone into my pocket and fumble for my own. I'll call Cataldo. I pull up the phone app, scroll through my contacts, but there's no Cataldo. I'm sure she gave me her number! Fuck, was it on a card? I'll have to go up to my room and get it. I'm almost to Bay. Twenty feet. Fifteen. Ten. I keep scrolling my contacts. There's Ethan's name, floating under the *D*s. I tap and hold, open our text chain, start swiping.

> Tipton is B—

A force like a sack of bricks barrels into my back, sending my phone flying to the grass. I pitch forward onto the cold, wet ground. My fingers scramble for the screen, and I tap haphazardly over and over and over until an arm wraps around my front, pinning my arms to my chest. I'm hauled upright, and a hand slithers over my mouth. My screams die into the cold, clammy skin. I try to kick, to force my elbows back into Tipton's chest, but he's stronger than I am. The flame in my chest, a stupid bravado I've always clung to, flickers and dies inside me. I thought because I was tall and bigger than all the other girls, because I row crew and keep myself in shape, that I could protect myself. But Tipton drags me back, back, back, behind the towering shadow of Bay Hall so quickly, so easily.

He hisses in my ear, "You blackmailing bitch." Perhaps I overestimated his strength, because he stops dragging and instead starts to pull, so I am forced to trip along after him. He's left my mouth free, and I let out a plaintive cry for help, but we're too far behind the building. The singing is too loud.

Tipton leads me behind Bay and then surprises me, stopping short and hauling me against the brick wall.

"Give me the phone."

"What?" I sputter.

"Don't play dumb."

"I don't know what you're talking about."

He knows I'm lying. I know I'm lying. But I have to buy myself time. Have to pray that somehow my text went through to Ethan. That someone is looking for me. Tipton squares off in front of me, flexes his jaw and fingers.

"I don't want to do this, but you've left me no choice."

Fuck, fuck, fuck.

I squint my eyes shut, because screw facing death bravely. I don't want to see this. I do scream, though, a raw shriek ripping from my throat as his assault lands. . . . But there is no pain. Only the flush of discomfort as his hands go everywhere. The space between my breasts and hips, up and down my legs. He's frisk-searching me. I open my eyes. He really just wants the phone?

But that's your only evidence, a voice niggles. Not dying, however, is higher on my priority list than proving their affair.

"Aha!" Finally he reaches my jacket pocket and retrieves Emma's phone. "Why'd you have to make that so hard? I'm not a creep. I don't want to touch you."

"Not a creep?" I bite back. "You raped Emma."

He recoils as if I've thrown boiling water in his face. "I am not a rapist. You've got the age of consent wrong. It's sixteen in Massachusetts."

"Men who memorize age-of-consent laws are big fucking creeps," I hiss. "You're our counselor. You're supposed to be the adult. Is that why you killed her? Because she was going to get you caught? Fired and arrested?"

"I loved Emma."

Tipton lunges for my throat, closing his fingers around my windpipe and squeezing. He comes at me so fast that my head slams back against the brick wall, bright stars bursting across my vision as he chokes my breath away. My hands scrabble against his chest; I try to push him away, but he's leaned all his weight against me, pinned my arms.

"TIPTON, FREEZE!"

Cataldo's bellow cuts through the oxygen-deprived fog in my head. I hear the click of a safety being disengaged. Tipton releases pressure, and I gulp thick lungfuls of air before doubling over with a cough that scrapes my raw throat like a rake.

"Against the wall, with your hands raised and behind your

head!" she orders Tipton, who complies, though not before dropping Emma's phone to the ground.

"The phone," I manage to croak as Cataldo approaches.

"What?"

She doesn't get it. Panic in Tipton's eyes crystallizes with intent, his foot coming up as he moves into position. Tipton stomps down hard, and a strangled, animal sound tears from my throat as I charge him, knock him on his ass.

"Stand down, Olivia!" Cataldo screams, retraining her gun onto me.

"The phone!" I repeat, pointing to the ground. Emma's lavender case is shattered. I can only hope the phone itself didn't take too much damage.

And then I'm spent, wrung out. I roll back, leaning heavily against Bay Hall as my head throbs and my throat burns with fire. Cataldo hauls Tipton up, reads him his Miranda rights as she handcuffs him, then grabs and pockets the phone. And a blurry figure comes into view.

"Olivia, oh my god, are you okay?" I try to focus as hands fuss around me, finally pulling me to my feet. Once I'm up, I see her.

"You're bleeding," Avery offers.

I touch my cheek. Indeed, I have a dripping scrape from one of the many times Tipton flung me on my face. I also reach careful fingers behind my head, expecting warm, wet blood, but it seems I merely have a really nasty bump.

"What are you doing here?" I sound as if I swallowed a toad.

"I saw you head this way," Avery says. She shifts uncomfortably, looks away. "I know you hate me, and I kind of hate you right now, too, but I don't want you dead."

"I don't hate you." I hesitate. There is so much to say, that needs to be said, but my throat hurts like a mofo, and I've watched enough procedurals on TV to know that Cataldo's going to need to take my statement. I should probably have my head checked out. "Can we talk later? Really talk?"

Avery nods.

"You two! Follow me," Cataldo barks, and we obey. With one hand on Tipton's cuffed arms, she frog-marches him around Bay as she makes a call on her cell phone with the other. We hear her inform the station she's bringing someone in.

Headmistress Fitzgerald rushes up to us as we round the corner, reach the main path. "What is going on here?"

"Ms. Fitzgerald, hello, good to see you." The detective injects false cheer into her tone. "Please see that these two report to the station after Miss Winters sees a medical professional."

"You can't just arrest my employees, Ms. Cataldo," Fitzgerald sputters. "Where is your warrant?"

"Mr. Tipton slept with a seventeen-year-old student, who is now dead, and assaulted Miss Winters. I'd say that's cause."

"Well . . . goddamn."

Cataldo might now be my favorite person for making Fitzgerald lose her cool.

Next up in the gawping parade is Tyler, who comes at us practically at a run. "Oh my god, did he do it? Did he kill my Emma? You monster!" Fitzgerald has to hold him back to stop him from launching himself at Tipton. I use the opportunity to retrieve my phone from the grass in front of Bay.

"I didn't do anything. You've got the wrong person," Tipton whines as he trips along behind Cataldo. I'm satisfied to see he's now the one being dragged against his will. The detective makes no effort to increase his comfort, though I suspect it's more a matter of damage control than cruelty. Everyone from the memorial is crowded around us now, people pointing at Cataldo and Tipton, their whispers raging like a wildfire. I hear "Emma" and "killer" and "Olivia wasn't crazy" behind my back. I bristle at the word. And then I groan. The adrenaline of Tipton's attack is fading, ebbing to leave an ache all over my body, a sudden exhaustion.

Avery puts an arm around my shoulders and steers me in the direction of the parking lot. "I'll drive you to the hospital. If that's okay with you, Headmistress?"

"Yes, yes, good thinking, Miss Montfort," she says. "I have to confer with the board and compose a message to the parents."

"Can I go, too?" Tyler asks, though he's already pushed forward to walk alongside us, making the request moot.

"Yes, I'm sure your sister will appreciate the company."

"Stepsister," Avery mumbles under her breath, so only I can hear. But I catch her sniffling, too, as we slowly make our way to her car. We've caught Emma's killer, and the grief of her death bubbles up anew. Even though this means closure, I don't think we will ever truly recover.

CHAPTER TWENTY-TWO

I do not have a concussion, or any other serious damage, so the ER doctor gives me a painkiller for my throat and head and sends me on my way. Unfortunately, instead of going back to school, we drive to the police station in town for questioning, as ordered. I'm there until after midnight, unraveling the past few days and all the threads of my amateur investigation for Cataldo. When I get to the secret room in the boathouse and Avery's burned Harvard hoodie, the veins in the detective's neck start popping.

"You kept all of this from me?" she says.

"Well, technically, I told you about the room in the boathouse," I offer feebly.

"I should charge you with obstruction, but I'm feeling generous."

"If you'd been straight with me about your line of questioning, about Tipton, I would have told you about the cheating and the phone," I say, though I don't know if that statement is true. Would I have trusted her if she'd told me where her investigation was leading? Or might I have suspected a trap and continued on stubbornly?

Either way, I am thankful to avoid a charge. I don't tell her about Kaila, or Emma and the SAT scam, because it doesn't seem relevant, and why blow up everything now?

It's 12:30 a.m. when I emerge from the interrogation room. I pull my phone from my pocket and hope it still has a charge so I can call a Lyft, but there's a surprise waiting for me in the lobby.

"You waited for me?" I ask Avery, unable to hide my shock.

"Again, not an asshole. You shouldn't ride with some stranger after all this. Tyler went back a few hours ago, though."

We walk silently to Avery's silver Audi. She beeps the locks open, and I groan as I sink into the leather seats. I could fall asleep right here. Avery powers on and steers us onto the silent, nearly pitch-black road back to Claflin.

"I know you're flying home tomorrow, and we might not have time to see each other before you go," she says. Her eyes remain glued on the road ahead, not because she must remain vigilant at this time of night but because it's easier not to look at me when she speaks. I find it easier, too. "I know I can be a bitch. We all can be. We kept . . . certain things from you, for your sake. I'm not sorry about that. But you still did plenty. You're not some innocent victim here, Liv. I asked you to join the Ivies because I saw it in you. You're ambitious and competitive. Having less money than we do doesn't make you a saint."

I know she's right, yet I suck in a breath, ready to go on the defensive. She doesn't understand what it's like to be me. But Avery doesn't skip a beat.

"I don't have many friends. I know that. Real friends, people who like me for me. I thought, Did you just want to hang around me for my money? Because I could do things for you? Free wine on Avery? Hand-me-down clothes?" This time she pauses to wait for my reply.

"No," I answer emphatically. "I can't fit into your clothes."

It wasn't meant as a joke, but she laughs anyway. "Good point. Emma was always happy to take a hand-me-down, though."

We both stall on Emma.

"I didn't think you were the type to cheat on the SAT," I say. "You take school so seriously."

"That was my mom." Her voice sparks with venom. "Arranged everything with Emma, paid her, and then informed me. But I refused, Liv. You have to believe me. Emma didn't take the test for me. I told Emma if she went through with it, I'd burn her ass on . . . well, take your pick from the laundry list of things you've been sticking your nose in all sorts of places to find out."

"Your name was still on her spreadsheet, though," I say, and before it's even out, I remember Avery's name highlighted in yellow. An exception.

"Emma did a credit swap. Got Tyler a better score instead. Mom adores him. And Emma would do anything the great Katherine Montfort wanted. She was angling for a cushy summer internship at Harker Pharma. I've tried to piece together at what point our friendship became purely transactional." It's like Avery is wounded and bleeding before me. But I'm stuck on Tyler.

"Kaila said Tyler was the guy who took the test for Emma's male clients. So how could she improve his score?"

"Oh, Emma replaced him ages ago." Avery makes a dismissive gesture with one hand, and the car drifts slightly off center. I grip the door handle. "She wouldn't tell us with who, though. Said he could crack fifteen hundred with his eyes closed, so she could charge a higher premium for the boys now. Tyler lost her thousands."

Rejection stabs through me. "You guys really knew everything. You say it was for my sake, keeping me out of the worst things, but I think that's bullshit, Aves. You're crying that you don't have any real friends, but you say that to me, who you kept at arm's length. You lied to me for three years. It's obvious Emma only got close to me so she could steal my key and get access to the ID maker. What did you use me for?"

Avery's jaw flexes. Back to a sure, two-handed grip, her fingers wrap tighter around the steering wheel. "Emma . . ." She blows out a heavy breath through her nose. "Yes, she used you for your office access. I didn't approve. I thought it was low as shit to angle for you as her roommate to keep tabs on you. And I kept things from you, but I never used you. No more than you used me."

"You didn't trust me. With anything real."

Avery looks at me sidelong. "Given the way you've reacted with your little investigation, I'd say I was right not to trust you. Again, Liv, the wounded act will only go so far. You accused me of murder."

"Yeah, well, you kind of lost your shit over Emma getting into Harvard. And you said some fucked-up stuff afterward, about Harvard reconsidering you."

"Maybe you were just projecting, since you were also hiding a Harvard acceptance. Congrats, by the way." There's a wryness to her tone. Almost like she means it.

"Thanks?" I answer tentatively. "And maybe I did jump to conclusions. But I was freaking out. Weren't you freaking out?"

"Uh, yeah, but unlike you, I didn't start pointing fingers at my only friends." Then Avery surprises me with a laugh, almost a bark. "Though probably because I knew Emma cast a pretty wide net with her secrets. It could've been . . . a lot of different people."

"I figured that out eventually," I mumble.

For a minute, there's just the steady hum of tires on asphalt, the rhythmic tick of the turn signal before we hang a right onto Claflin Boulevard. We're almost home.

"You really thought I murdered someone for getting into Harvard instead of me? You thought I'd kill you, too?" She's wounded again.

"I . . ." Is there any good way to explain this? All I can do is be honest. "After the fight at the party, yeah, I thought maybe. It's why I started investigating. I wanted to prove it wasn't true."

"And you wanted to direct the police away from you."

"You guys hacking the security cameras really didn't help with making me look guilty," I explain. "I couldn't prove my story to them." And now it's my turn to throw a wounded accusation. "How often did you guys hang out without me like that?"

We pull into the Claflin parking lot, into Avery's reserved spot close to the front gate. Avery turns off the engine but makes no move to exit. "It was easier that way sometimes. We could talk about all the stupid, frivolous bullshit we wanted without feeling bad. We did feel bad, Liv. Or at least I did. I don't like rubbing all my money in your face. You . . . never take it particularly well, even if you pretend about it. We all know."

She's got my number. "I know I shouldn't blame you. But it's hard, always comparing myself to you and coming up short. Everything seems easier for all of you. The money stuff, at least. I know everyone's got messy shit in their lives. No one wins the Oppression Olympics."

Avery bursts out laughing. "Where did you get that?"

"Oh, it's something my mom always says."

"I love your mom."

I turn to face her, craving that eye contact now. "You do? You acted like she was some freak whenever she came to campus. Our sad little life."

"Olivia, your mom is actually nice to you. No passive-aggressive put-downs about how much you eat or going behind your back because she doesn't think you're smart enough to get into her alma mater. She let you come hundreds of miles away to school to better yourself. My mom shipped me here so I wouldn't get in the way of her fabulous life. Big difference.

"And sometimes, it's not about you, Liv." Avery throws open her door, indicating that our heart-to-heart is over. "Now, let's go to bed. I have a nine a.m. breakfast scheduled with said hell beast of a mother, and I need my rest."

I raise my eyebrows as I move to get out, and Avery sighs.

"She texted while you were being interrogated. Fitzgerald emailed all the parents about the arrest, and she wants a play-by-play before we do some last-minute Christmas shopping in Boston. Aka: she lets me pick out my present because she hasn't figured anything out yet."

We tap in at the pedestrian security gate and walk mostly in silence back to Bay. Avery's room is closer to the elevators than mine is, so we say our farewells at her door. She pulls me into a hug, stiff at first, but then we both warm up.

"Message me over the holidays," she says as we pull apart. "I'll be desperate for a break from my supplements. Megan will be stopping by in person before the deadline to help us get it all done. I can ask her to proofread yours, too, if you want. We're paying her enough."

It's a peace offering, and I accept. I'll take as many steps to mend our friendship as she will. I can't help but wonder if I ever really *saw* Avery. How much of my perception was clouded by my closeness with Emma? The chip on my shoulder as a scholarship student?

I shuffle along to my room, pushing the heavy door open with my shoulder and flicking on the lights with my other hand. I shed my coat first, dumping it over the back of my desk chair, and collapse onto my mattress to unlace my boots. Then I look across the way at the stripped-bare mattress and blank walls. I pad barefoot to the closet. Empty. The desk drawers are littered with useless detritus—a mostly used Post-it pad, paper clips, stray pens. Emma's parents have taken everything of value, everything left of her. I knew they would, but it still hits me like a gut punch.

She's gone, and this is over.

CHAPTER TWENTY-THREE

My mother spends all of Christmas and the days after it fussing over me, which is pretty standard for her after long stretches without me. But on the heels of my roommate dying and my nearly meeting a messy end myself, she goes into overdrive. She brings me breakfast in bed. This woman taught me how to cook when I was six and hasn't made me breakfast in a decade. I'm weirded out but grateful. By day I marathon old TV shows on Netflix and subsist on PB and J and salty snacks, and at night my mom allows me to drink wine with her while we watch movies. We talk about anything but what happened to Emma. Love my mom.

I may not want to *talk* about it, but I'm not done with Emma's murder. I devour every article in the *Globe,* then the *New York Times,* the *Washington Post,* and *Vulture* once the story goes national. The story of the beautiful rich girl murdered by the pervy school counselor is too good not to go semi-viral. It helps that she's beautiful and white. Catnip for Nancy Grace and company.

I imagine Fitzgerald is losing her shit right now. Claflin's name is all over the place, and not in a good way. I read between the lines, analyzing the speech patterns in the anonymous quotes to try to figure out who leaked the story wider, and wish it had been me.

Avery thinks it was Seth Feldstein. His dad works for the Sox, so he knows tons of *Globe* people, according to her.

It's been strange, bonding with Avery over this. She doesn't shut me down like Sierra and Margot do. She's as hungry for answers as I am. We've been chatting, exchanging links and theories. "We should start a true crime podcast," she suggests over messenger. "College admissions love shit like that." I assume she's joking.

We don't talk about the Ivies, or the things we did, or the things I discovered they did behind my back. The blackmail, bomb threats, testing scam, sabotage. The blowup in the atrium, the halfway heart-to-heart in Avery's car will have to suffice for now. The way I see it, I only need to navigate these "friendships" for a few more months. I need my last semester at Claflin to pass smoothly. Get in and get out. Why not bond with Avery over Emma's murder in the meantime?

I haven't heard from Ethan.

I push down the swirl of emotions that kicks up every time I consider his silence. I've said my piece, and I'll have to live with that. Ethan left campus Monday before I could catch him, so I had to settle for a string of long texts in which I tried to explain. That I'm truly sorry to have hurt him, but I won't apologize for my ambition. Journalism is competitive; Ethan knows this better than anyone. I point out his hypocrisy. The boy who pursued Emma's murder investigation for a clip, who published my information in the *Ledger* after I begged him not to, hardly has a leg to stand on. I say it more nicely than that. Besides, it all worked out, with Vasquez splitting duties between print and digital editions. Catfishing Seth wasn't *that* bad. Bygones? To top it all off, I lay bare my yearslong crush, put myself out there.

And crickets.

Two days after Christmas, Cataldo calls.

"I need you to come up to Boston for further questioning."

"Okay, when?" I ask, expecting her to say, oh, in a few weeks, before Claflin starts up again. Instead, she says she wants me there on Thursday.

"You cannot be serious. You want me to fly up to Boston for New Year's?"

"The prosecutor wants to wrap this up ASAP. Unfortunately, Mr. Tipton destroyed the victim's phone, and I need your help to re-create the text chain between him and Emma."

When I tell my mom, she nearly blows a gasket. "Give me that woman's phone number. I want her to explain to me who's going to pay for you to fly up there, pay for a hotel!"

"Mom, it's fine. I'll take the train, which is much cheaper, or even a bus, and I'll ask Avery if I can stay with her."

She softens at the name. "That poor girl's parents are probably ringing in the New Year in Shanghai or somewhere equally ridiculous."

Actually, it's Barcelona, but I keep my mouth shut.

I promise to come back right after New Year's so we get the rest of our quality time together. Mom savors the three weeks of winter term break, and Cataldo is definitely throwing a wrench in the works. But secretly? I'm a bit glad. If Avery lets me stay with her, it means that for the first time, I'll be able to attend her blow-out New Year's Eve party, like one of the cool kids.

I've been to Avery's house more than once, but as the Lyft pulls up the winding driveway flanked by lush, crisp evergreens, and the country manor house—yes, that is what Avery calls it—comes into view, it is a revelation, like every time before. A glimpse into a life not lived, into a lifestyle I aspire to, if I can graduate from Claflin with my wits about me and matriculate at the most elite college I can afford. Strong foundations, networking, and a bit of luck will be the stepping-stones so maybe someday my children will know this kind of luxury. And they won't take it for granted.

The house sits on 1.8 acres and abuts a slim twist of the Charles River. I once heard Avery say to Emma that her house had the narrow span of the river but was a huge mansion, while Emma got the wide expanse of the Charles and a fraction of the living space. Emma lived in a four-story brownstone approximately six times the size of my house in Maryland. Or was it a shack? Stepping out of the car here and comparing the two, who could say.

But I'm happy to be on the receiving end of Avery's hospitality. Like staying in a hotel, but it's free. This is no vacation, however. Tomorrow, New Year's Eve, I'll take the train into Boston to meet with the detective. And tonight? Avery and I are working on our RD supplements. A bunch of apps are due January 1, though some colleges are generous enough to give us until Monday. Megan, the admissions consultant, is coming over tomorrow afternoon for last-minute help at prime prices. It's a tightly scheduled day, with the party. Work hard, play hard.

"You're in here," Avery says, opening the third door at the end of a long hallway. I wheel my suitcase in and practically have to shield my eyes for all the white that reflects the buttery light from the broad bay windows. "There are towels in the en suite, plus all the requisite toiletries. See you downstairs."

She leaves me to take a turn of the room, which I do. The bed is king-size, with crisp white sheets and fluffy pillows three rows deep. I check to ensure she's gone before swan-diving backward onto the down. Heaven. Better than the best hotel. And it's a guest room that's larger than my mom's master.

Next, I avail myself of the shower, which is a ten-foot-wide marble walk-in with a waterfall spray and programmable horizontal pulse features. The shampoos, conditioners, and body soaps have French names and smell incredible. Finally, freshly outfitted in clothing I haven't spent ten hours sweating in, I make my way downstairs for dinner, taking in the house with less travel-frenzied eyes.

The theme throughout the house is white: white-painted wood, white marble floors in the foyer, blindingly white kitchen and bathroom fixtures. The kind of white only the rich can afford, with a daily housekeeping staff to maintain it. The house is bright and fresh, open plan, and both effortlessly chic and completely lacking in personality. It doesn't feel like people really live here. Nine months out of the year, Avery and Tyler don't.

Avery ordered some artisan pizza, reminding me that even pizza delivery is highbrow here. We sit at a dining table in the windowed alcove off the open-plan kitchen, with plates of pizza and glasses of soda and our laptops open in front of us at angles as we work on our essays between eating and gossiping. She doesn't miss a beat.

"So, have you heard from Ethan? There's something going on there, right?"

"He hasn't responded since I texted him about putting him on the Ivies' List." There's a hard edge to my voice that's impossible to filter.

Avery knows this is her fault. She winces. "I'm sorry I told him. You know I was just really angry in the moment, right? And doesn't he get that it didn't even matter, since Vasquez overrode Stina, anyway?"

I shrug. "Guess it's all the same to him."

"Well, then he's an idiot who doesn't deserve you."

"Thanks," I say, and mean it. It's exactly the right thing to say, something only a good girlfriend would say. We don't hash it out any further; we both said and did things we regret, hurting each other. Plus, the pretending-to-be-queer-for-blackmail thing is too horrific to broach.

Pizza polished off and an hour gone by, we've done very little actual work, so we agree to a writing sprint—fifteen minutes and then we'll check in. Avery gives up after eight.

"This is impossible." She groans. "I want to write about Emma. I'm trying to. But a part of me thinks it's a dick move, and nothing is coming out right. It's this huge, life-changing thing, and every word I write sounds like trite bullshit." She turns to me. "What are you writing about? Are you . . . ?"

I grimace. I am. I nod. "Every time I give up and try to write about something else, it comes out sounding stupid. Like who cares about ECs and achievements when two weeks ago I found my friend dead in the rowing pool?"

"Right?"

We exhale twin huffs of frustration. Then Avery gets a glint in her eye.

"How much you want to bet every student at Claflin who's applying RD is gonna write about Emma?" Avery gnaws absently on an uncharacteristically ragged fingernail. "They'll steal our thunder if they apply to the same schools that we do."

I stare agog at my friend and her Machiavellian musings. Is

this really only about competitive advantage for college? I'm too shocked to say anything, and besides, before I can, Avery moves on.

"I'll text Megan and ask her for tips." She makes for the fridge to grab us a fresh batch of snacks.

I return to my Google Doc and delete every word I've written. Start fresh on something that has nothing to do with Emma. I am more than my friend's murder.

CHAPTER TWENTY-FOUR

Avery sees me off the next morning like a mom, making sure I get up on time, driving me to the station, even stopping for coffee along the way so I am caffeinated. It is eight o'clock and I'm expected at the FBI office in Chelsea by ten.

"Party starts by eight!" Avery calls out the car window as she drops me off at the Wellesley Square station. "Don't be late."

I wave her off. Thanks to the holiday, the train isn't packed, so I manage to get a seat. I get off at South Station to switch trains up to Chelsea, where I alight into the frigid cold. The FBI building is a few blocks away.

I'm too hot in my peacoat after a brisk walk, but I make it. The building looms above me, eight stories of sleek black steel and white concrete with hundreds of windows that reflect a gray, cloudless sky. I have to check in first at the security gate and then again inside in the wide, high-ceilinged lobby. The room is staid, corporate, with shallow, square leather seating and surprisingly dated honey-stained wood wall panels. I lower myself onto a vacant couch and wait for Cataldo to collect me.

She appears not even five minutes later, perfectly prompt and looking distinctly uncomfortable. Her mouth is turned down at the corners, and she tugs at the edge of her persimmon boatneck blouse, as if it's a bad fit. It's strange to see her in a black pencil skirt. She wore black trousers, sometimes khaki, and a rotation of sweaters and turtlenecks on campus. This must be her guest-at-the-FBI-field-office look.

Suddenly I feel underdressed in jeans.

"Olivia, good morning." She flashes me a tight smile and leads me to a bank of elevators, where she uses a key card to get us up to the fifth floor. We pass a sea of cubicles and wind our way to the back of the floor, past the bathrooms and into a clearly disused cluster of offices. She makes small talk as we go, asking how my Christmas was, remarking on the windchill. I'm perfunctory with my answers. I'll be doing more than enough talking over the next few hours, I know.

She leads me to a small office devoid of personality. Standard-issue furniture, no photographs or personal items other than a purple lattice-patterned Kleenex box.

"My temporary home," Cataldo says with a grand gesture as she takes a seat behind the desk. I settle down in a cushioned black metal chair across from her. I'm slightly disappointed it's not an interrogation room.

"Thank you for coming all the way up here to talk with me again." She starts an ancient-looking digital recorder and rattles off the details of the interview. "As I mentioned on the phone, our techs have been unable to recover data on Emma's iPhone, and seeing as it was her burner, we don't have information on whatever second Apple account she created for it. If Tipton helped her set it up, he's not saying, for obvious reasons."

"It's the only proof they were together, isn't it?" I say. My stomach turns over. This means he could walk. Cataldo hums.

"Absent any forensics on the body—which, having been sub-merged in water, is not looking great—indeed we'll be needing to corroborate his relationship with Emma via witness statements."

"Do you know how he killed her?"

I remember that last time I asked the detective how Emma died, she wouldn't tell me. This time, she considers me. I'm no longer a suspect. She turns off the recorder.

"Emma was strangled. That is confidential information, and you mustn't repeat it." She starts the recording again.

"Mr. Tipton does concede to being in the boathouse that night," Cataldo continues. "However, he swears he did not see Emma. He would have had no reason to go into the rowing room, and so he didn't find the body."

"He's lying," I say. "He has to be. He did it."

Cataldo inclines her head. "We are pressing him on that point. Your tip about Emma's earring ended up bearing fruit. We found the other stud in Tipton's office."

I barely suppress a whoop of triumph. "Then that's it. You have him!"

"Not quite. That's why you're here. Let's dive right in."

We spend the better part of the next hour going over all of "Beau's" texts with Emma. I try to remember as many of them ver-batim as I can. Cataldo writes everything down. Then she pulls out a cream-colored folder, flips it open, taps her pen on the pa-pers inside. It's upside down, but I can see it's a timeline. "What I'm stuck on is Emma's sweater in your room. How heavy of a sleeper are you usually?"

"Uh, it usually takes me a while to fall asleep, but once I'm really under, I sleep like the dead. And I was, uh . . ."

"You were drinking that night," she finishes. "So it stands to reason that from eleven-thirty to midnight or shortly thereafter, you probably would have woken up if Emma had returned."

I think about it. "Yeah, that makes sense."

"But if someone were in your room closer to two? Could that have woken you up?"

"I had a nightmare," I say. "That's what woke me up." Wasn't it?

"It's just . . ." Cataldo taps her pen some more. "According to Miss Montfort, they met in that secret room in the boathouse at midnight and were there until approximately one-thirty. Things were tense, and Emma left before they did, alive, according to them."

Avery explained this to me, too. She and the other girls had invited Emma to party with them in the boathouse, to air their grievances. They fought again, and Emma stormed out, and then Avery burned her hoodie as a sort of personal cleansing ritual— her words. I suspected this was partly glossy hindsight, the way Avery told it. Burning her Harvard paraphernalia was surely also Avery's own fuck-you to the school, to her mom.

"According to our last conversation, Emma texted her secret boyfriend from her second phone, asking him to meet her at their usual spot at two a.m. And we know their spot was the boathouse. Now, I suppose Emma might have gone back to Bay, but it's about an eight-minute walk each way, plus getting in and out of that window, going upstairs . . . It's a lot to simply drop off a sweater. She'd barely have made it back by two to meet her boyfriend. And Tipton claims he got there on time and didn't see her."

"Tyler's her boyfriend," I say. "Tipton was . . . something else. And he must be lying. Again. And it's not just the sweater. She had to have dropped off her phone, too."

"Because you found it in the Wheat Thins box," Cataldo

245

says matter-of-factly. She did remember the phone, but was she leading me to it? This is the first time I've pieced it together. The illogic of how the phone ended up back in my room. How could I be such an idiot?

"So either Emma sprinted back to our dorm to drop them off, or her killer planted them." My stomach does a flip. Is that what woke me up? Emma's murderer creeping around my room?

Cataldo doesn't say anything. She waits for me.

"Wait, do you think *I* did something with the sweater and the phone? That I—"

Cataldo stops the recording. "Let's break for lunch," she says.

We're back in the office after our meal in the second-floor cafeteria—a sandwich combo, her treat—when she properly pounces.

"Were you blackmailing Mr. Tipton, Olivia? About his affair with Emma?"

The accusation pushes me back in my chair. "What? No! I didn't even know it was him until the memorial."

"He claims you did." Cataldo pulls another folder, this one seafoam green, out of her bag, places it on the table in front of us, then makes a show of extracting several sheets of paper and laying them out in a row in front of me. She sits back, gives me time to scan the pages. It's a series of screenshots of text exchanges. I scan through them.

> You're pathetic. What kind of grown man has to get his rocks off with an underage girl?

What if they knew that she died so close to where you used to screw her? Maybe she was going to turn you in. Motive.

There were emails as well.

From: Claflin, Perv Joe <claflinpervjoe@gmail.com>
To: Tipton, Joe <jtipton@claflin.edu>

Subject: I have you two on video.

This message has no content.

From: Joe, Tipton <jtipton@claflin.edu>
To: Claflin, Perv Joe <claflinpervjoe@gmail.com>

Subject: Re: I have you two on video.

What do you want?

From: Claflin, Perv Joe <claflinpervjoe@gmail.com>
To: Tipton, Joe <jtipton@claflin.edu>

Subject: Re: re: I have you two on video.

You should confess.

"I—I didn't send these," I stammer. Push the sheets back across the table to her. The things Tipton said when he attacked me finally make sense. Called me a blackmailing bitch, mentioned Emma's phone as a trump card. "You have to believe me. And, wait—what was the blackmail? These are threats. Taunts."

The detective's mouth quirks into a smile. She produces

another sheet with a flourish. Another email, with a new subject that delivers a punch to the stomach.

> **From:** Claflin, Perv Joe <claflinpervjoe@gmail.com>
> **To:** Tipton, Joe <jtipton@claflin.edu>
>
> **Subject:** Murderers do better in prison than rapists

The message itself is a kick to the shins.

> If you don't confess to Emma's murder, I'll turn over
> your sex tape. Either way you're done, but it's far
> easier to just be a murderer. No one likes a pedo.

"He wasn't a pedo." I don't know why it's the first thing that springs to mind, why I say it. Cataldo snorts. "Sorry. I think he's a huge fucking creep, but she was seventeen."

"Indeed. Mr. Tipton was quite fixated on that distinction as well. And he reminded me that the age of consent in Massachusetts is sixteen."

"So the blackmail didn't even matter?"

Cataldo arches a brow. "Whoever sent the messages was clearly hoping Tipton wasn't well versed in the law, or they themselves were ignorant."

"So you know it wasn't me."

"It doesn't seem like your style," she says, sitting back in her chair, crossing her arms over her chest. "And I noticed your stunt at the memorial. It was smart. Not a move to make if you already had him pegged."

"So why ask? Why let me piece together the bit about the phone?"

Cataldo taps her index finger against her forearm. Considers me. "You're mixed up in this somehow. You may not know it, or understand it, but things keep leading back to you. Might be because of your meddling in my case, but the sweater and the phone . . . it's never fit for me. Why Tipton would run those back to your room."

"Do you not think he did it?" Something icy grips my heart. This can't be happening.

"No, I think he's perfect for it. An adult, a teacher figure, sleeping with a student. He met with her regularly in the very spot where she was murdered. Was there that night. Attacked you. It'll make a good case. Circumstantial, but solid."

"But?"

"The phone. If I were him, I would have destroyed it. As he tried to do when he attacked you. Would have been as simple as dropping it into the rowing pool. But it got from the boathouse to your dorm room. And the sweater. There to make you, us, assume she'd gone back to the room."

"So then someone else returned the phone. Not Tipton. One of the Ivies, maybe. Margot? She knew about the affair. Maybe she was protecting Emma." With the earring still on my mind, I remember the boot print. "Margot definitely came through the window that night. She's the only Ivy with a foot about the size of Emma's. The boot print I mentioned."

"You really think your friend would do that and still not have fessed up?"

"I don't know."

The detective taps her finger again, rapidly. A thinking tic. "You were running your own shadow investigation all along— you're lucky I didn't take you to task on obstruction, I'll remind you. Is there anything you uncovered that you haven't told me? Every bit of information is critical. Either to nail Tipton, or . . ." She trails off.

Or find the real killer. The case may be strong, but she's not sold on Tipton.

"Right now, after his attack on you, we have him on assault for sure," Cataldo says. "Emma's murder . . . ? He proclaims his innocence, and we don't have the texts anymore. It'll be your word against his. And there's the blackmail attempt to muddy the waters, help him claim reasonable doubt. So I called you back in. I need all the cards on the table. Everything you found out with your poking around. Anything that might undermine your testimony."

"What if he faked the bad blackmail to cover his ass? Look, I received threats, too." I pull up the emails from Quit Meddling on my phone, show them to her. "Both anonymous Gmail addresses. They could be connected, right?"

Cataldo lets out a slow breath as she reads the three increasingly hostile messages. "Possibly. Our techs are trying to chase the origin of the other email address. The texts were sent by a burner. I'll need you to forward these to me. We'll add them to the file."

I digest all this new information. Tipton might be innocent. Which means something else got Emma killed, not the affair with the teacher. I swallow hard. Check my phone for the time. It's 1:30 p.m. Let's hope I make it back in time for the party. I have a lot to tell the detective. About the Ivies. About the SATs.

"Coffee," I say. "I'm going to need coffee." And then I start from the top.

*   *   *

250

"Can I offer you some advice?" Cataldo slows her long strides, delaying our arrival back in the lobby after our marathon interview. It's nearly 4:00 p.m. I tap my fingers nervously against my thigh, thinking of the 4:36 train from South Station I have to make if I want to get back in time to catch Megan. When I checked my phone a few minutes ago, I had three testy messages from Avery, reminding me that her essay tutor was staying late to help me, too. I might have to take a Lyft to the station, and that'll cost a fortune—

"Olivia?"

I snap back to focus on the detective. "Yeah, sure, shoot."

"You should find some new friends. The Ivies . . . They eat girls like us alive."

"I'm almost free," I say. "Plus . . ." I hesitate. Think about how kind Avery has been to me these last couple of weeks. Shown her vulnerable side. "When you get some of them away from the bullshit of school, they're not so different from us. Just girls."

Cataldo frowns. "Watch yourself until the case is fully resolved." The lines around her mouth deepen. "If that's possible."

"What do you mean?"

We stop outside the elevator, and she drops her voice. "Your friends really screwed us, turning off those security feeds. Everything we have is circumstantial at this point. Be careful, and you call me if anything occurs to you, or happens."

This time I remember to put her number in my phone.

"Your classmates know you were playing amateur detective," she goes on, "so I need you to play dumb. As far as any of them are concerned, you are one hundred percent confident in Tipton's guilt. Don't make yourself a target." She gives my shoulder a squeeze.

"Olivia?" a familiar voice says. I look over and my heart stutters.

"Ethan," I say in a rush of breath.

"I apologize for the delay, Mr. Kendall," Cataldo says, either ignoring or missing our awkward reunion. "My conversation with Miss Winters ran unexpectedly long."

"Can we, uh, have a moment?" I'm already pulling Ethan by the arm over to the corner. The detective doesn't protest. "I told her everything." I keep my voice low. "So you don't have to lie for me or cover."

"Okay, good, um . . ." Ethan's eyes flick to the floor. He ducks his head, fusses with his hair. Then finally meets my eyes. He winces. "I'm sorry I didn't text you back. We went to Toronto for Christmas, and it was busy, and international texting plans are a real pain, and . . ." Then he sighs. "And I had to think everything over, honestly."

"Yeah, I get it." I play it cool, like his radio silence didn't hurt my feelings. I poured my heart out to him.

"Do you really, uh, have a crush on me?" His cheeks go red, and I am sure mine are the same.

"I thought it was totally obvious."

"Uh, you used to basically ignore me outside of newspaper. You ran a bit hot and cold. Before. But I'm glad. To know. I like you, too."

It's painfully kindergarten of us, but I don't care. My grin nearly breaks my face. "Are you staying in Boston?"

"Yeah, until Sunday. Then I'm taking the train back to Connecticut."

I tilt my head in confusion.

"Extended fam is in Canada. American residence is in the well-to-do suburbs of New York. Which Connecticut counts as."

"Well, you should come to Avery's New Year's Eve party. Tonight. I mean, of course it's tonight. Since it's New Year's Eve." I'm rambling like an idiot, but Ethan doesn't seem to mind. He smiles at me funnily, leans closer, cups my cheek with his hand.

"Is it all right if I kiss you?"

"Uh—uh . . . ," I stammer, but then I nod, and he closes the distance between us, lips soft and gentle. My internal organs shimmy up into my chest as Ethan deepens the kiss, but then Cataldo clears her throat noisily behind us, and it's over too soon. I can't say I envisioned my first kiss happening in the sweltering lobby of an FBI field office, but I wouldn't have it any other way. We break apart.

"So, where is this party?"

As if on cue, my phone buzzes with an incoming group text from Tyler, who I didn't even know had my number.

> Hey Liv and Avery, don't forget it's a costume party tonight. Theme is celebrities who died before their time. Like Janis Joplin and shit.

I can't help but gasp.

"What?" Ethan asks, but words escape me entirely. I hand him my phone.

"Oh, wow. I officially hate him," Ethan says. "And that cannot be serious. What are they gonna do? Not let us in if we're not dressed up?"

"Uh, last year's theme was 'make an unsexy thing sexy,' and Avery strictly enforced the costume dress code. I've been hearing about these New Year's parties for years. Avery delights in turning people away."

Hesitation creeps over Ethan's features, shows in the hunch of his shoulders.

"Don't leave me alone with the vultures, please," I plead. "I want you there."

"You want me, huh?" Ethan grins. "All right, I'll be there. Text me the deets." And with that he walks over to Cataldo.

I practically pirouette onto my train.

Avery can't contain her annoyance when I arrive hours later than we thought I would. She's huffy when she picks me up from the station, but I know all the Avery-refocusing tools in the book. Though I would prefer to keep it private, I spill my Ethan news, which immediately turns her mood around. I even get her to suggest that I invite him to the party, so I don't have to admit that I already took the liberty. But then I walk right into the good-mood trap when she says, "Sorry about the party theme. I wanted Gatsby glam but Tyler insisted it was his turn and, well. Anyway, I have something for you back at the house. You'll love it, trust me."

I'm sure I won't, and though I itch to ask her why she didn't tell Tyler to fuck off, I don't. There's no questioning Avery. I think about Cataldo's parting words: her warning not to trust the Ivies. Someone from Claflin murdered Emma. If Tipton didn't do it, I can't trust anyone. Cataldo's right—I have to watch my back. Play the part.

I'll test my acting chops tonight, pretend to enjoy the party. Pretend I might not be ringing in the New Year with a killer.

CHAPTER TWENTY-FIVE

As soon as we get to her house, Avery disappears upstairs. Her costume requires some intense makeup, she says, and she needs every second to get ready, since I've pushed things so late. She points me in the direction of the kitchen, where I find a thirty-something woman with magenta hair working on a laptop at the dining table.

"Oh, hi! I'm Megan." She pops up to shake my hand. Her grip is firm, and she makes steady eye contact. There's something open about her that I like. She's not what I expected, and it must show on my face. "Let me guess: I'm younger than you thought I'd be, and far less square."

"I suppose I thought you'd be a mom type in a suit," I admit.

"The woman who owns the company is indeed a mom type in a suit, but I'm the hired hand."

I like her immediately. "And they make you do house calls?"

Megan grins. "I'm charging them extra for this."

"They can certainly afford it," I concede. Then I apologize. "You shouldn't have to waste your time on me. I'm sorry I made you wait."

"Oh, please, don't worry. You're precisely the kind of student

I enjoy helping. Someone who can't afford my services. I still do pro bono work when I can, as a balm to my soul." Her buoyant expression falls. "But please tell me you didn't also write your essay about that girl's death. I'm two for two, and, uh, well, I couldn't talk either of the Blossom twins out of it, but if you have . . . I'd resort to begging."

Even though I didn't write the essay about Emma, the mere act of having tried brings heat to my cheeks. "Uh, no, I wrote about crew. It has metaphor, and it's more of a framing device for talking about my family and interests? I'm not describing it well."

"No, that's great! I can work with that."

"Yeah, my SCEA essay was specifically tailored to Harvard, so I had to write a new one."

"Good, good." Megan takes a seat at the table and pats the seat next to her. "Come on. Share your Google Docs with me, and I'll dive in."

I do as she says, sharing my Common App essay and a few supplements with her. While she reads, I pad over to the refrigerator. I haven't eaten since the sad FBI cafeteria sandwich, and I could drink a gallon of water, too. I settle for a glass and snag an avocado from the fruit basket on the kitchen island. As I slice it, discard the pit, I call over to Megan.

"Hey, who is the other person who wrote the essay about Emma?" I know Avery did, but I'm puzzled by Megan's reference to the Blossom twins. Guess she's a *Riverdale* fan.

"Tyler," she says. "I suppose I should be grateful it's less tone-deaf and narcissistic than his ED essay on productivity during quarantine. How coronavirus allowed him to explore his Wellesley mansion estate, start a viral TikTok account, and discover the good within himself by tipping his food-delivery drivers with toilet paper and spare face masks. It was . . . something." Megan hisses through her teeth. "I'm not surprised Cornell rejected him. But a grief-essay strategy for RD is such a bad idea. Death-inspiration stories really don't play as well with admissions as people think they do. They have to be immaculately written with enough emotional distance to work."

"Wow."

Megan twists around in her seat, eyes wide with panic. "Shit, that's unprofessional. Uh, pretend you didn't hear any of that?"

"Sure," I say, even though now I'm burning with a million questions. Since when was Tyler rejected from Cornell? I swear it was printed in the *Ledger* that he was going. I add some olive oil, salt, and pepper to my avocado halves, grab a spoon, and make my way back to the table. "So I'm guessing you didn't approve Avery's Haiti trip essay, then?"

Megan snorts. "Definitely not."

"That makes two of us."

"You hardly need my help at all." She points at her screen. "This is great. Creative enough, but not too much, personal, specific, covers a lot of ground. Minor notes so far."

It's a relief, because I'm definitely not editing tonight, not with the party starting in less than two hours, and without Coach breathing down my neck, I plan on drinking. The less I have to do on deadline day, the better. Megan finishes up with my main essay while I eat my avocado, then excuses herself to use the restroom, promising to look at my supplements upon her return. I take the opportunity, scooting over into her chair, jiggling her wireless mouse to ensure the screen doesn't fall asleep. I have three minutes, tops. It costs me nearly a minute to open Megan's main Google Docs directory, check the shared section. Avery's essays are neatly labeled with her full name, topic, and version number, but Tyler's is simply titled **New Essay.** I'm curious about both and aware that spying is super unethical. Oh well, can't ever shake being an Ivy entirely. I double-click on both documents, and they pop open in new tabs.

Avery's essay is a bit maudlin, but not terrible. She talks about knowing Emma for practically her whole life, that familiarity, taking her friend's presence for granted, and exploring her emotions and new perspective on life. I agree with Megan that "What I've Learned from My Friend's Death" likely won't play well with admissions, but I still don't fault Avery for trying. I understand the impulse.

Tyler's essay is something else. Several lines are lifted straight from the obituary he submitted to the school paper. I hear a toilet flush and resort to skimming. It's eerie, reading his account of the memorial, his staid version of Mr. Tipton's arrest. Things feel very different, very much not like fodder for college admissions essays, when you're the one being dragged behind a building and thrown up against a wall by a possible killer.

I rush to close out the tabs I've opened and get back into my chair with seconds to spare before Megan rounds the corner.

"If it's okay with you, I'm going upstairs to check in with Avery," I say to her. "Unless you need me down here?"

"Oh yeah, that's fine. Actually . . ." She checks the time. "I'll finish these at home. You'll have notes by the time you wake up tomorrow morning."

It's fine by me, so I thank her for her help and head upstairs. Avery is in her bathroom, and she looks like someone punched her in the face. When I walk in, she's leaning close to the mirror, applying black liner liberally, extending the lines far beyond her eyes, creating a smudged mask look. She's ratted and curled her hair, twisted sections into braids, and is only half-dressed, but I can already tell who she is.

"Lexa, huh?"

Avery grins at her reflection, making eye contact with me in the mirror. "Like it? It's the best I can do with this morbid-ass party theme. Plus, I get to wear a leather corset. Win-win. I put your costume on your bed. No wussing out."

"That makes me think I'm going to hate it."

"You'll love it, but you'll protest. Go."

With a groan, I head down the hall to discover my fate for the evening. There it is, laid across the crisp white bedspread, an equally white and crisp dress. Next to it, a short and carefully curled blond wig and a strapless bra. Oh no.

I take a deep breath and remember what I told Cataldo. I've got to play the game.

It takes some tugging, to be sure, but I manage to secure the strapless bra, somehow shoving into the cups with minimal spillage, and shimmy into the dress. Though the real test is whether the dress will zip up. I hear a shuffle at the door, turn around, expecting Avery. But it's Tyler. My hands fly up to the front of the dress to hold it in place so he doesn't get a show. His hair is immaculately coiffed, and he's wearing jeans, a white T-shirt, and a leather jacket.

"What are you doing here?"

"Sorry." He waves off my state of partial dress, eyes not even lingering. Perfect gentleman. Or I'm not hot enough for his tastes. Either way. "I wanted to ask how it went with the detective. What did she ask you?"

I take a deep breath, exhale into the most casual posture and tone I can manage. "Oh, nothing major. She needed to corroborate all the sexts Tipton sent Emma that I found on her second phone. Needs it all on the record for when it goes to court. You know."

Tyler's face falls at mention of the sexts, and immediately I feel like an asshole for being so casual about it. An apology doesn't seem like enough, so instead I deflect, change the subject.

"James Dean, right?"

"What? Oh, uh, yeah. It's my dad's. Some old Halloween costume."

"Quite the theme you picked for the party." I can't help ribbing him gently. Tyler's shoulders go stiff, and his mouth hardens into a straight line.

"It's to help everyone process their grief. My grief. I thought you, of all people, would understand."

He reminds me of one of those fire-and-brimstone preachers who used to be on television, firm and fervent in his conviction. I sense it's best not to argue, so I simply offer a tight smile. Avery appears behind him, nostrils flaring.

"Tyler, you perv, get out of here!" She boots him from the doorway and rushes in, shutting the door behind her. When she motions for me to turn around, I obey, and she zips me up. "See, totally fits."

Immediately I spring for the bathroom to check for myself. It feels really tight on top. My eyes practically bug out of my head. "Avery, my boobs are falling out of this!"

"Yes, it looks great." She appears behind me, hairnet and wig in hand. "Now for this."

I have no choice. Tonight, I will be Marilyn Monroe.

CHAPTER TWENTY-SIX

People start trickling in at eight, and lucky me, one of the first guests to arrive is my least-favorite Ivy. Margot makes clear from her just-sniffed-poo-under-my-nose expression that the feeling is mutual. Unlike Avery, she has not forgiven me for my sleuthing. Which sucks, because I really want to grill her about Tipton. She had to know that Emma was hooking up with him, which makes her the prime suspect as his blackmailer, or she might be aware of who else knew. I've had one drink, and already my blood is thrumming with that old drive. I know I'm supposed to be playing it cool, but the party is the perfect opportunity to gather more information. Everyone will be getting ass drunk and will be off their guard.

"You came all the way from New York?" I ask Margot, who is dressed in a tightly cinched trench coat and has artful smudges across her cheek and brow. I guess she's Éponine from *Les Mis*, which is so on brand for the musical diva that I nearly laugh. I try to make friendly conversation as she scoops herself some special punch. Because, yes, at Avery's party there is punch, and other classy drinks like gin fizzes and champagne.

"I'm staying at an Airbnb in town," she replies breezily, like that should have been obvious. "New York is overcrowded and so passé. You know people have to wear adult diapers to Times Square? It's gross. Of course, my parents always have a reservation at the Crowne Plaza, but I've done that so many times."

Typically, I spend New Year's Eve in my living room with my mother, wearing our pajamas and goofy hats, sipping sparkling apple cider and stuffing ourselves with cookies. Approximately half the time, Mom falls asleep before the ball drops, and I ring in the New Year to the dulcet sounds of her snoring.

"I invited Sierra to stay with me, but she says Los Angeles is perfect this time of year, and she just got back," Margot says. "And why are you here?"

"Had an appointment with the police," I answer matter-of-factly. It wipes the derision off Margot's face.

"Shit. Is everything okay?" She bites her lip. Is this my window? No. She's too sober. The bear trap is on a hair trigger. I say the same thing I said to Tyler earlier, and she visibly relaxes.

"Good. I'm glad they got that bastard." She hands me the glass of punch. "You probably need this." I'm too surprised not to accept. She pours herself another. Then we clink our glasses in solidarity and drink. We make small talk for a good five minutes, mostly about Princeton, though Margot is distracted, disengaged. Milo McNamara walks in dressed as Heath Ledger's Joker, and she makes a quick excuse to go say hi.

More people arrive over the next hour as I nurse a drink in the kitchen by the cheese plate. There are a Janis Joplin, a Selena, two other Marilyn Monroes (but my wig is the best), a Tupac, a Kurt Cobain, rather impressively a Lord Byron, and then, horrifyingly, a JonBenét Ramsey. There are plenty of generically good-looking guys in bog-standard shirts and tops, and I can't tell whether they are Paul Walkers, Corey Monteiths, or regular Heath Ledgers. I'm reminded at constant intervals that this party theme is the worst.

But then karaoke starts in the living room, and I am too weak for my own good. I'm two more drinks and four songs deep when Ethan arrives. Or should I say David Bowie. Like *Labyrinth*-era Bowie. I feel things that are not polite to talk about.

I approach him with a stupid grin splitting my face. I'm tipsy enough to pull him into a hug, shriek that I'm so glad he came! Taking in my outfit, he blinks slowly and stammers a hello, and then I lead him into the kitchen for a drink, so he can catch up. "I'm very confused by your costume," I say as I make him a gin fizz.

"He should have lived forever, so I say it fits. And, uh, yours is . . ."

"It's Avery's, so it doesn't exactly fit."

"It's good." Ethan's voice takes on a high pitch.

"Cheers!" I'm a bit too loud and enthusiastic, but the crowd has swelled to at least a hundred people, so the volume is needed. I don't even recognize half of them; they're not from Claflin, but they look our age—Dana Hall students? And a bunch of them haven't even bothered with the costume theme, which sends steaming-hot annoyance streaking through me. But then Ethan's goofy smile pulls me back. It's a party! I should have fun.

But then, oh no, Ethan does not look like he wants to have fun. His face has gone all serious, and I realize he's not drinking.

"We need to talk." He takes in the crowd, then eyes the out-door patio beyond the kitchen, but I'm already shaking my head. This dress is skimpy, and I will freeze.

"We can go upstairs." I lead the way, a wolf whistle or two following us, people's minds in the gutter. Even though I closed the guest room door, I hesitate in front of it, nervous we'll find a couple availing themselves of the bed, but when I open it, the room is empty, thankfully. My laptop is where I left it on the bedside table, a move I suddenly second-guess. I slip it into a dresser drawer, just in case. I turn to find Ethan sitting on the edge of the bed, kneading his fingers nervously.

"You told Cataldo about the SAT scheme," he says. No, *accuses.*

"Yeah. I told you I told her everything."

"Why would you tell her that? It had nothing to do with Emma's murder, and now you'll burn and piss off a lot of people."

"I had to. Tipton might not be guilty, and she had to know the full scope of things. It was time for cards on the table, especially anything that would make me look guilty." I hate the way Ethan is looking at me, jaw tight, eyes steely and guarded. He's upset with me, and I don't know why. Unease swishes around my stomach. I clench my teeth because he's clenching his. *Psychosomatic.* SAT word. But, no, I've used it wrong. I'm off my game.

"I wish you hadn't done that," he says finally.

"Why?" It's a demand. I approach, sit next to him on the bed. Nudge his shoulder when he won't turn to look at me. "Ethan, what's the problem?"

He heaves a deep sigh. Curses a string that knocks me back. Canadian Ken has a potty mouth. No, I shouldn't call him that. Emma called him that, to make fun of him.

"I'm the other test-taker," he says in one straight release of breath.

"Ex-fucking-cuse me?"

"I worked with Emma. Took the SAT and ACT for the boys."

My mind reels. "You replaced Tyler."

"I didn't know who did it before me, but if that's who it was, then yeah. I took it from fall of junior year until, well, now. I did the December sitting, right before . . ."

"Before Emma was murdered? Oh god." I taste the bitter acid of one of my drinks rising into my mouth. Could be gin or punch. Either way, I retch, stopping short of vomiting onto my shoes. I scoot away from Ethan, because what if he—

"Olivia, I didn't kill her!" He reads me too well. Though it doesn't take a genius to figure my reaction, I guess. And, wait—

"But you're Canadian. You're not even applying to American schools. Why would you need to take the SATs? Did you need the money?" Because no way Emma didn't pay him a cut. Otherwise, why do it?

"Canadians can take the SAT, too, Liv. I broke fifteen hundred on my first try. Emma heard, approached me . . . said her current guy struggled to touch fourteen hundred but had been the best she could do. She offered eighty percent on each test I took, although . . ." Ethan frowns. "When you sent me the screenshot of her tracking document, it became obvious she was bullshitting me on the actual fees. I got closer to sixty percent. How generous of her to break fifty." He's cold there. Killer cold. But I think I believe him when he says he didn't know until after . . . But, really, what can I believe?

"You lied to me," I state the obvious. "All that time. There I was feeling guilty about being an Ivy, and you're a goddamn cheat."

Ethan squirms. I've hit a nerve.

"I'm not proud of myself. But I needed—" He inhales deeply, as if to steady himself. "Listen, ambassadors don't make that much money, not enough for a pricey US education. I'm here on a partial scholarship, but at Harvard I'm an international student. No federal aid there. I owe full tuition."

He trips along casually, as if he didn't just discuss how he's going to pay for Harvard. My Harvard. Emma's Harvard.

"Ethan, did you apply to Harvard?" I ask through gritted teeth. He ducks his head, refuses to look at me again.

"Yeah. I, uh, kind of got in."

And I slap him.

CHAPTER TWENTY-SEVEN

"You asshole," I hiss. "All of that with Avery and Emma, and printing my admission news in the fucking paper, and you're sitting on a secret admission yourself? You're the third spot! The one who took it from Avery."

At that he rolls his eyes—at least the one I can see. He has a hand pressed to the cheek I slapped. "Pot, kettle. We all took her spot. God, this is insane. It's not even *her* spot. We don't know which one of us is the reason Avery didn't get in. Or even *if* it was because of us. This whole quota system you guys talk about isn't a hard-and-fast rule. Anyway, what does it matter? She didn't kill Emma over it."

"Didn't she?" I say, even though I don't believe it. Not really. I don't think. "I'm sure Cataldo also let you know that Tipton probably didn't do it? That someone was blackmailing him, trying to get him to turn himself in for her murder. That means the actual killer is still out there."

"Fuck. Seriously?"

"She didn't tell you. What did you two talk about?"

"Tipton's text string with Emma. All the stuff you and I

investigated. Then softball questions about the SAT thing. She didn't say anything about blackmail."

"Well, it's true. She showed me texts and emails between Tipton and someone who knew about him and Emma and wanted him to confess to the murder. They threatened to out him as a perv." I catch myself falling into our regular pattern. Investigation, facts, trading theories. "We are not done with the fact that you're a liar. All that time we were looking into Emma's secrets and you were sitting on a major one. What if she wanted to come clean about things, and one of the people she helped cheat found out?"

Ethan snorts. "You're delusional if you honestly believe that. Emma protected her own ass first and foremost. Why would she take down her enterprise?" And then he has the gall to appear wounded. "Hey, you lied to me, too, about my name being on the Ivies' List. You tried to screw me over."

"Apples and oranges. Except mine is like a baby orange. A mandarin. Tiny compared to your big-ass apple. I did mild scheming to get a résumé booster, which failed anyway. You published my Harvard acceptance in the paper, knowing I'd take shit from Avery. You hurt me on purpose."

"I'm sorry, I . . . I thought it would take the heat off me a bit longer. If there were two Harvard acceptances she knew about, she wouldn't find out about mine. While it's pretty clear she's not a murderer, Avery is vindictive. She'd make me pay for it in a way she'd never do to you. It was a dick move, I know."

The apology is sincere enough, but the words slide off me. I am slick with disappointment, reeling from his betrayal. He's a suspect now, I realize.

"I have to go." I bolt up, wobble on my feet, and curse. Screw period-accurate footwear. I peel off my heels and lace up my Keds. I grab my favorite black cardigan off the back of the chair and slip it on. Inside the double pockets I find tissues. I'm about to need them.

I storm past Ethan, who isn't even bothering to protest. He's back to his respectful self, the perfect, passive little liar, who simply watches me go. I slam the door behind me and cut farther into the house. The kitchen is a zoo, and I can't bear being on display. Instead I duck under the tasteless but effective *police line do not cross* tape strung across the basement stairs. It's a rich person's basement in their mansion in the woods, though, so it's all high ceilings, sleek wood paneling, and functional living space instead of dank retreat. It's cool and blissfully empty, the motion-sensor lights sultry and low.

The stairs spill out into a high-tech entertainment space, with a wall-size flat-screen TV and duplicate gaming system to the one upstairs. I fall back onto the leather couch and exhale deeply. I'll just stay here for the rest of the party. I grab for my phone but realize I don't have it. I left it upstairs in the guest room. With Ethan.

Ethan. He knew Emma far better than he ever let on. How close were they, really?

I think about everything else Ethan knew. Every way in which he inserted himself into the investigation. How convenient. *He* was the one who interviewed most people from the party. He created the suspects board. I trusted what he told me.

Ethan was the one who suggested Emma might have a second phone. Did he slip it into my room for me to find? He pushed me toward the supposition that Emma was hooking up with an older guy. Tipton.

But she was. That part was true. Everything with the phone that night at the memorial, that was me. My idea. That was real. Tipton was Beau.

Yes, but what if Ethan and Emma were hooking up, too? I think about how he helped himself to the whiskey at the bar in the secret room. He could have been pretending not to know about it, how to navigate the boathouse. Not to know about the code.

The blackmailer seems young. He didn't know the age of consent in Massachusetts. Maybe because he's Canadian?

No, no. I shake my head, shake away these toxic thoughts. Not Ethan. Just because he lied about that one thing doesn't mean . . .

He lied about two things, I remind myself. Huge things.

I hop up and begin to pace. Loud music thunders down the stairwell, throbs through the ceiling. I can't concentrate here. I wander down the dim hallway, past the gym on the left, and find a bedroom. Tyler's room.

The bed looks tempting, but that would be weird. The entire experience of being in Tyler's space is strange. To me, he is Emma's cocky boyfriend, Avery's model-hot stepbrother. And this is where he sleeps.

I walk the perimeter, getting a feel for it. It's huge. Fancy-hotel-presidential-suite huge. The California king in the center of the room would fill my Maryland bedroom with only a couple of feet on either side to spare. But in here, the behemoth seems like dollhouse furniture. I cross to a set of patio doors where cold fogs the glass. Press my ear to the gap in the doors, the burble of the Charles River echoing in my ear. Out of curiosity, I pop into the bathroom and find a walk-in shower and a spa tub. Swank. The padded chair in front of Tyler's Mac setup looks comfy, so I pull it out and plop down. The movement jostles his computer awake.

I'm not trying to snoop, not intentionally, but Tyler's Mac isn't password protected, so when it wakes, I get the entire desktop, which is littered with icons. I'm the kind of person who keeps her home screen maniacally clean—limited icons arranged in neat columns—so I can't help but lean in to peruse the clutter. An icon in the lower right-hand corner catches my eye.

EMMA MURDER SUSPECTS

Why does Tyler have a murder board on his computer?

CHAPTER TWENTY-EIGHT

The urge to know overpowers any good sense I have not to sneak around someone else's private files. I click on the program icon. What balloons up onto the screen is indeed a murder board. It resembles the one Ethan and I made, but digital. Tyler has used some program that digitally re-creates a corkboard with little index cards on it. There's one at the top for each of Tyler's suspects, and then cards below it list key facts. Something sour shoots through me at the thought of Ethan and our investigation. All the lies. And all my doubts. I push it down. But there's no way to escape Ethan now. Because he is *on* Tyler's murder board.

My finger traces from the top of the screen down along the cards that list corroborating evidence.

Suspect he replaced me in SAT scheme	
Wanted greater cut?	
Cameras down from Bay to boathouse—snuck out of	
Whitley?	
Strong enough to strangle Emma	

I gasp, because suddenly I can see it. Ethan is part of the movie in my mind, stalking toward Emma in the rowing room, holding her down in the water, choking the life out of her. I shiver involuntarily.

But Ethan isn't the only person who has a note card with their name in bold. My eyes flick back up to the top. Avery. Tipton. Paul, the night security guard at Claflin. *Me.* I gulp. Paul's card is the sparsest. *Strong enough to strangle Emma* is repeated, and there's a note about the cameras, but the only supporting motive is *Secretly obsessed with Emma???*

I'm drawn with morbid fascination to my own column. Half of the notations are lazy suppositions more than concrete evidence.

Jealous of her rich roommate?
Wanted her boyfriend?

A snort escapes before I can help it. Tyler's dreaming if he thinks I have the hots for him. Pretty boys aren't my style. I feel another pang over Ethan.

Then Tyler gets closer to good motives than I am comfortable with.

Found out about ID/SAT scam?
Outside Whitley on camera in the middle of the
night—no alibi

To quell the itch that makes its way up my spine, I turn to the last two suspects. Avery and Tipton have a *ton* of supporting-evidence cards. I'm blown away that Tyler was also investigating this whole time. That he got way closer than I did. It's all there. Tipton and Emma's make-out spot. That Emma had to have a second phone—there's a footnote that says *Find?* There's even an index card that says, *Dismissed from last job for being inappropriately casual with students,* and one that reads, *Earring?*

Then there's Avery's column. It's the longest.

Said she'd kill Emma for getting into Harvard
Fistfight at party
Reputation for being vindictive
Spoiled rich girl
Jealous of Emma and me?
Met Emma at the boathouse after the party
Last person to see her alive

It echoes, like an old-fashioned record skip. *Last person to see her alive.* Really, that pegs all the Ivies, doesn't it? And how does Tyler know?

The sound of footsteps on the antique walnut flooring in the hallway makes me jump half a foot. Shit. Hastily I push back from the chair. I close the suspects document and run to the first and closest place I can think of—the bathroom.

Once inside, however, I curse my stupidity. There is nowhere to hide in this ridiculous rich-person bathroom suite. The walk-in shower is all glass. The spa tub is at an angle—cowering in the bottom of it won't work. There are no closets or deep cupboards. I'm a large human; hiding is a challenge.

The best I can do is duck next to the toilet. It's a shit plan, but it's all I've got.

I strain to hear as someone enters the bedroom. I know they're in there—I heard the door open and close—but then comes a stillness. Hope soars in my chest. No drunken giggles or the sound of bodies hitting the bed. And I don't hear anyone moving about the room, inspecting. They might not even come into the bathroom—

The door opens, and then Tyler is heading straight for me, one hand tugging down his zipper, and I shriek something about not showing me his penis, please, as I squint my eyes shut.

"Olivia, what are you doing in my bathroom?"

"Peeing?"

"You're fully clothed."

"Thankfully, right?" I ease one eye open, then the other. Tyler's zipped up his pants to preclude any nudity. "I know it's weird. I'm sorry. I came down here to get away from the noise, but I know it's a huge invasion of privacy to go into your room, and then I heard someone coming, and so I came in here to hide, but there's really nowhere to hide, is there?" I ramble. Tyler has a should-I-call-someone? face on. My entire body goes hot, and I'm itchy. I don't like him looking at me like I'm unhinged. I'm not. "Sorry, I'll go." I slip past him, out into the coolness of his bedroom. Too cool. I look to the patio doors, which are now open. Then I feel movement behind me. Whip around. Tyler's left the bathroom.

"Aren't you cold?" I ask, shivering in my thin sweater and halter dress. Tyler shrugs.

"Not really." He looks over at his computer. Frowns. "Did you . . . ?" Tyler leans closer, sees an icon in the recent programs bar at the bottom of the screen. The suspects file. Fuck. Fucking Macs!

"I'm so sorry. I didn't mean to. It came awake on its own, and then I saw that, and I was curious." I bite my lip. "You did a better job than I did at investigating everyone. Except you were way off on me. Sorry, not interested." It's my attempt to introduce a little levity. A tepid joke. Tyler laughs, but there's an edge to it.

"But you're the one who found Emma's second phone and nailed Tipton. Thank you for that."

I must flinch or otherwise react, because then Tyler frowns. "Do you know something I don't?"

I fold like a house of cards. "He might not have done it. Or at least they can't prove it. In court."

"You mean he might walk?" Tyler's nostrils flare.

"I know it's awful. But what you have here . . . Maybe we share it with Cataldo? You can tell her what you discovered. I've told her everything I know already. Maybe you'll hold the missing piece to nail Tipton or . . ."

"Someone else?"

I think about the top suspects again. Excluding me, it's Avery or Ethan.

"Are you thinking about your boyfriend or Avery?"

"He's not my boyfriend," I snap.

He throws up his hands as if I've aimed a gun. "Touchy!" Then he turns serious, lowers his voice even though we're alone. "You know, Avery kind of scares me. Yeah, she's my stepsister, but . . . she's cold. And she's become cagey since Emma died." His eyes dart to the door, as if Avery could burst in at any moment.

"I can't believe Avery could be a killer." I worry my bottom lip and think about what he wrote on one of the cards, about Avery being jealous. My gaze flicks to Tyler, assessing, trying to picture them together. Avery swore up and down there was no way, but of course she would, as cover.

"We tried to keep it a secret," Tyler says quietly. "We hooked up once or twice, long before our parents—" He cuts himself off, looking pained.

Holy shit. Avery was sleeping with her stepbrother.

CHAPTER TWENTY-NINE

I stumble back, as if the room has tilted on its axis. Maybe it has. I steady myself with a hand on Tyler's desk, feel for a swaying, in case it was some freak earthquake. But no, it's only me, my blood pumping so hard I'm shaking.

"Are you okay?" Tyler reaches for my arm, but I evade his grasp. I cast a weak smile, back up for the door.

"I'm fine! Drank too much. See you later."

On the contrary, I am suddenly feeling very sober. My feet push me up the stairs, back up into the kitchen, where I scan the immediate area for my quarry. When I don't see her, I push through the crowded great room, then into the front hallway. She's here somewhere.

And then I see her. Margot is in the living room, queuing for another turn at karaoke.

"I need to talk to you," I bark. It's an order, not a request. For good measure, I grab her by the arm and tug. Margot protests but nonetheless trips along after me. There's a line for the bathroom in the hallway. Emboldened by liquor and murder, I cut in front of a girl with wild auburn curls, offering a curt apology. There's shouting, some pounding at the door once we're inside, but then it stops.

"Have you lost your mind?" Margot retreats against the sink, putting as much space between us as possible. In here, that means three feet. Everything in this house is huge except for the ground-floor powder room, apparently.

"Did Avery know about Emma and Mr. Tipton?" I say with no preamble.

"Uh, what? Are you drunk?"

I can tell she is; her face is fully flushed, but she's still savvy enough to misdirect. I huff out my annoyance.

"Margot, come on, I need to know." The look she returns is full-on frost queen. "You don't get to pretend to be Switzerland in this whole thing. You knew and didn't tell anyone, which I'm pretty sure counts as obstruction. You don't want me to tell Cataldo about that, right?"

"Why does it matter who knew? Or is your plan to rat us all out? You're not one of us, Liv, and we know it. Why do you think we left you off the group text? You can't be trusted. Always playing the victim."

It's a slap across the face that burns all the more because it's true. I am a rat. Margot cheated on her SATs, and I told Cataldo about Emma's scheme, which means I did snitch on my friends. With a jolt, I realize they'll have their admissions rescinded. Margot's not going to Princeton. Avery's shot at any good RD school is scuttled because her name, highlighted or not, was on that list. I almost hope Avery is a murderer; there's no way I'll survive the wrath of the Ivies otherwise.

Suddenly I wonder if telling the truth was a mistake. Emma's secrets are like shrapnel slowly slicing their way to our internal organs. Some of us won't make it.

"Margot, please. Did you tell Avery? Or anyone else that night?"

"Fine. I told Aves. But I'm not an idiot. I didn't spread it around. Sleeping with a teacher is bad news. And, well, look what happened." She grimaces.

"What if he didn't do it?"

"Of course he did it," she snaps back, a little too fast. I catch a flicker of fear beneath her haughty sureness.

I have what I need. Avery knew it was him.

I fling open the bathroom door, storming out and nearly bowling over the girl from before. "Finally!" she exclaims as I pass, then just as defiantly but quieter: "Bitch."

I am a bitch. A bitch on a mission.

The party, the house, blurs around me as I stalk about, room after room. And then there, standing casually at the kitchen island, chatting and smiling with some brunette who looks like a Wellesley College cliché:

"Avery!" I shout a little too loudly. Adrenaline is driving me now. Confronting a killer, even if she's your friend, is a terrible idea, but I have to know. "I need to talk to you."

"Uh, okay?" She's mildly annoyed, I can tell, because I'm interrupting her conversation, but she approaches me at the far end of the kitchen island. I'm by the drinks. I take a bracing sip of someone's discarded gin fizz.

"Were you blackmailing Tipton?" I ask plainly. She tilts her head, squints.

"What? Why the hell would you ask me that?"

"You knew about him and Emma."

"So?"

"He didn't kill her. Someone was blackmailing him. The police showed me."

"Why didn't you tell me this before? You've been sitting on this all night?" Then Avery claps on my expression. My brows are raised precariously. It's all there on my face. "You think it was me?" she hisses.

"I know about Tyler," I say back. She blanches. The swatch of black eye makeup, now gone a bit runny at the edges, stands out in stark contrast to her pale cheeks, the firm set of her mouth. She's a warrior turned scared.

"Olivia, you have to be careful." Avery's gaze darts all around us. "Keep your voice down."

"Were you jealous? She got everything you wanted? Harvard, Tyler?"

Avery makes a choking sound deep in her throat. It comes out a second later, a strangled laugh. "Ew. No."

"He told me about you two hooking up. You were the last one to see her alive. Avery, I know."

"I'M NOT FUCKING MY BROTHER!" she screams, face now mottled red. A hush falls over the immediate area. The warbled wail of an Ariana Grande song glides down the front hall.

"Fuck." She huffs, does a dramatic turn for the crowd, clarifies. "Stepbrother. I am not having sex with my *step*brother." Then she grabs me hard by the arm, her manicured nails digging in painfully, and hauls me around the island, past the dining table, out onto the patio. I wrest free of her grip, tripping backward a few steps, the backs of my knees knocking into the edge of the unlit firepit. It's fucking freezing, but she is nonplussed.

"What the fuck. We talked about this already. Do you seriously believe that I killed our friend because of *Tyler*?" She shudders, as if disgusted by the mere idea. "You've got it all turned around."

"He told me, Aves. You're on his list of suspects."

She tosses me a look of derision. "He *lied* to you. Obviously. And sent you upstairs to fling psycho accusations at me, embarrass us both in front of everyone. Jesus Christ, Liv. Get a grip on yourself. Why can't you just stop digging? Leave it alone."

The combination of words, the puzzle pieces of Avery's resistance—it all comes together at once.

"You're Quit Meddling," I say. "You've been threatening me."

Now Avery squirms, bravado slipping. "Look, I was only trying to protect you. You have to understand."

"You threatened to kill me!"

"No, I didn't. I said you don't want to end up dead, like Emma. Big difference."

"Avery. What the fuck?"

Everything she's saying, the way she's saying it, confirms my worst fears. She wants me to stop investigating because she knows something. She *did* something. To Emma.

"Come on, let's calm the eff down and talk about all of this." She says it low and slow, like I'm a toddler. Trying to lull me into a false sense of security.

"Get away from me!" The firepit scrapes against my calves as I scuttle past it. I back away, out of the spray of outdoor lights, into the shadows of the woods behind the house. Avery doesn't follow. For once, she lets me go. A psycho playing the long game. Probably thinks the police won't believe me. She's rich as shit and inoculated against petty things like murder.

I walk along the side of the house, circling it, unsure where to go. My phone is inside, so I can't call Cataldo. Adrenaline warmth is fading now, and I hug my arms tight to my chest to try to stave off the bone chill. A whipping wind cuts through the trees and straight through me. I walk faster now; I have to come back flush with the side of the house, following a stone staircase to the lower level of the lawn.

I stumble down the paving-stone steps. The doors that open into Tyler's room on my left are lit by a soft glow. Inviting, but I keep going, rounding the side of the house. I run smack-dab into a broad chest.

"Oof," we both exclaim. Then I take a step back, squinting in the dark to make him out.

"Tyler!" I exhale with relief. "I figured it out. I know who killed Emma!"

"I don't think so," he says. My eyes snag on his smirk. Then I see the gun that is pointing at my chest.

CHAPTER THIRTY

Startled, I stagger back, heel catching on a clump of something behind me. I crumple, right onto my ass, and feel a freezing wetness soak through my dress. I skitter back like a crab, try to right myself, to run away, but Tyler simply grabs me by the arm and wrests me up.

"Come on." He walks me out into the blackness of the woods, his grip firmer and harder than Avery's ever was. It'll leave a bruise. I hear the gurgle of the river, louder with each step. What's his plan? Throw me in? After he shoots me, obviously.

I curse myself for being so stupid. It's always the boyfriend.

It's like Tyler can read my thoughts. We stop, round off. He gives me a shove and angles the gun at me again. "You just couldn't stop nosing around. At first, honestly, it was helpful. Made you look super guilty. Then you did me a huge solid with Tipton. But you're just like those fucking Ivies. You never quit until you get what you want, no matter the consequences."

"So you're going to kill me?"

I've seen this movie. I need to keep him talking. Give me time to think. To figure out how the fuck I'm going to get out of this.

My eyes have adjusted enough to see Tyler shrug, glib. "I'm

still deciding. It'll be pretty suspicious if two Ivies turn up dead. You might have to disappear. It's a spur-of-the-moment thing. You didn't give me much lead time." His mouth curls to the side, and he mutters something under his breath. I can't catch it over the burble of the river.

Then both of us snap to attention at the sound of a sharp crunch, as if someone's stepped on a branch.

"Tyler, what the fuck!"

It's Avery. Relief floods through me. I'm saved. But then Tyler's entire demeanor changes, shoulders deflating, gun hand shaking. He starts to sob.

"Avery, it's her! She killed Emma!"

"No!" I shout, wishing she could see my pleading expression in the dark. "He's lying!"

Avery takes tentative steps closer, then hesitates. Her eyes dart between us. Then with the firm set of her mouth and a nod, she decides.

"Stay here, Ty. I'll get my phone and call the cops. And find something to tie her up with. Don't move."

Fuck. There's no time to protest, to make my case. She whips around and takes off without another word, or even a look in my direction. Any hope I felt exits my body like air from a punctured balloon.

And Tyler, that colossal murdering asshole, smirks at me. "I should have applied to Yale drama."

"You think they would have taken you, even though Cornell didn't?" I decide to hit him where it hurts. Ivy rejections. His mouth purses into a sour pucker.

"Who told you?"

"Megan."

"God, I hate that bitch. She had one job! Write me a killer essay that gets me into school. It's not that hard."

"I thought she didn't write your essays for you?" The snippet I read from his essay about Emma didn't sound professional, by any stretch.

"Exactly."

"You're a real piece of work, killing someone and then writing about it in your essay like you're the victim."

Tyler's eyes glint wickedly. "Did you like it? I think it's a winner, no thanks to Megan. You think I'm kidding about Yale? After I catch you, all the Ivies will be clamoring to let me in."

"So you're turning me in now? How exactly is that going to work? I'll tell them what you did."

"What did I do? The cameras were down. I was asleep in my room, officers!" He holds up his hands as if under arrest. Then he laughs. "I'm the picture-perfect boyfriend, Liv. I was cleared as a suspect ages ago. Doting partner, didn't know about any cheating, so no motive. You, on the other hand, have an excellent one. The whole SAT thing would really fuck up your life, wouldn't it? As far as Claflin is concerned, you printed those fake IDs. Emma really fucked you over. You found out, and voilà."

I shake my head. "I didn't find out until after she died. Besides, Cataldo knows all about the SAT scam. I gave her screenshots of Emma's spreadsheet. She knows I had nothing to do with it. I had no motive."

"You mean you weren't seething with jealousy over her and Ethan?" He makes a crude motion, tongue pushing against his cheek, to drive home the insinuation.

"Bullshit," I snap. "They didn't hook up. And even if they did, I'm not psycho."

He shrugs a shoulder. "Cataldo sure has questioned you a lot. You meddled in the investigation. Withheld evidence. You found the body, too. And the phone."

"You planted it in my room. And her sweater. The earring in Tipton's office. Why?"

"Needed to throw off the timeline, make it look like she went back to your room. You finding the phone was absolutely perfect. Emma's friend, her beloved roommate, would totally hide her phone with evidence that Emma wasn't such a good girl. And it proved the whole thing with Tipton. Either one of you makes a good patsy. Works for me."

"Shut up!" I sound childish and shrill, but I don't care. Tyler refreshes his grip on the gun. Judders his finger over the trigger. But at least it gives me some time to think. I'll only have a small window when Avery comes back, to convince her he's lying. Because for all of Tyler's bravado, I'm not stupid. His plan works best if I'm dead.

At last, the crunching leaves beneath boots signals Avery's return.

"I called the police. They'll be here soon. And I found this." She holds up a line of bungee cord with her phone. Avery drops them both to the ground, partway between Tyler and me. Something in her gait seems off, her right arm shunted awkwardly behind her back.

Avery squares off in front of me, her warrior paint rendering her doubly menacing in the shadows. Then her expression turns feral. She bares her teeth, and with a belabored grunt, she swings the cast-iron skillet in her right hand directly at my face.

CHAPTER THIRTY-ONE

She misses, swinging full round in a practiced arc, until the iron pan connects with a sickening squelch with Tyler's hand. The gun goes flying into the dark.

"You hit me with a fucking frying pan! What the fuck!"

"Get the gun, Olivia," Avery directs, now wielding the heavy cooking tool with both hands. She wags it in Tyler's direction. He's clutching his hand to his chest, wailing like a big baby. I scramble to the ground, trying to guess where the gun might have gone. My hands shake as I run them over brush and leaves, searching.

"I could have hit you in the head," Avery addresses her stepbrother. "You're welcome. And it's a cast-iron skillet."

"Who picks a cast-iron skillet as a weapon?!"

Avery shrugs. "I didn't want to bring a knife to a gunfight. My mom's going to be pissed, by the way. You know her guns are off-limits. But, then again, you're a goddamn murderer!" Her scream cracks in the night air. I feel something cold, metal, brush my fingers. Yes! I pick up the gun, stumbling to my feet as I try to aim it with both hands at Tyler. Avery continues to grandstand. I think she's buying time, too, until the police arrive.

"I can't believe you tried to pin this on Olivia, like I don't even know you. I've got your number, Tyler St. Clair, and I want you out of my house."

"I don't know what you're talking about." Tyler sniffs. He flexes his hand carefully, testing it. "Maybe you did it together. Ivies conspiring."

"Now you just sound stupid," Avery drawls. I think she may be having too much fun with this. I'm still razor focused on the danger. If Tyler's hand is okay, he can overpower us. Without it, even. He's got several inches on me, and he's strong. He literally strangled the life out of Emma.

Wait.

"You motherfucker," I say. "You wrote how you killed her on your suspects list." Then I scoff. "No, it was your frame-up list. Looking for the best fall guy. You're sick."

"I've been trying to tell you that," Avery whines. "You are very bad at taking hints."

I round on her, but I'm careful to train the gun on Tyler, keeping him on the edge of my eyeline. "Did you know it was him? This whole time?"

Avery shifts awkwardly, won't quite look at me. "I didn't know. Suspected. But then they arrested Tipton, and I just wanted it to be over. You did, too, Liv."

"Hey, Aves?" Tyler calls over, casual as can be. "You might want to rethink your friend here. She told the cops about Emma's SAT scam and fucked you over good. Emma may have switched the test to me, but your name is on the accounting document. They'll void your scores, and you won't get in anywhere. It'd be easier if we killed her. Say she doctored that evidence to make you look guilty."

Avery's whole body goes stiff. Fuck. She narrows her eyes at me, takes a step back. Away.

"Liv, please tell me you didn't."

So this is my reckoning. Doing the right thing was wrong. I should have stayed a liar.

I don't even have to answer. She sees it on my face, and I see her eyes flash with panic. Then she turns to Tyler.

"How—how would that work?"

The wind seems to drop, and my entire body washes cold. I am going to die.

"I'll say it was Olivia all along, not Emma. Emma found out and decided to turn Olivia in. Olivia killed her and added you and Margot to the test list to fuck you over. Emma told me all about it, officers! They'll believe me. Then we say we shot her in self-defense, go our separate ways. You'll only have to see me at holidays, at least until the divorce. Which is inevitable. Your mom's a real bitch."

I expect Avery to snap back. Contradict him. Call him a psycho. But she doesn't. She chews on her bottom lip thoughtfully.

"Avery, what the fuck!"

"Why did you tell them about the SATs? I'll be totally screwed." Her tone walks the line between plaintive and pissed.

"I didn't mean to," I say feebly. "But killing me for it? Come on." I tighten my shaking hands on the gun. "Think it through. They won't believe it. My SAT scores were shitty. Who would pay me to take the test for them?"

That seems to get to Avery. "How low are we talking?"

"Lower than Tyler's, and Emma replaced him because he couldn't cut it." I hesitate to share, even though I've already proven I can get into Harvard with my score. "Fourteen twenty," I whisper, shame warming my core briefly. "Super score. Three tries."

Avery's eyes go wide. She knows I'm in the lowest quartile for

Harvard. Yes! Now they can't pin the SAT scheme on me, can't use that excuse to murder me, do a frame-up.

Tyler must realize it, too. A rough force barrels into me from the side. He wrests the gun from me, returns to his stance, and I'm looking at a gun pointed my way again. I am an idiot, letting my guard down, concentrating on Avery. Like she could save me. Tyler winces, giving the gun a squeeze.

"We'll say you purposely threw your own scores to hide your test-taking ability. They won't be able to prove otherwise." Tyler cocks the gun with his good hand.

"Fine!" I shout. "You assholes. If you're going to shoot me, then I deserve to know why. Why did you kill Emma, Tyler?" I'm half-desperate to buy time, half-serious about needing to know.

"I have to admit, I'm curious, too," Avery chimes in blithely. I really, really hate her.

Tyler's eyes narrow in consideration. Then he shrugs.

"I already told you. You're just not as smart as you think you are. Did all that investigating and couldn't put two and two together."

"Tipton?" I wager.

Tyler barks a cold laugh. "I didn't care who Emma slept with. We were open. I didn't own her. I'm a feminist, you know."

I can't tell whether he's serious or fucking with me. He's smug enough that he might think it's true.

"But." He stops to chuckle to himself. Waggles the gun at Avery and me. "You Ivies really made it difficult, you know. Taking everything for yourself. Do you know how hard it is to be a rich, above-average white guy in college admissions?"

Avery snorts, her expression cracking into one of amusement. Tyler whips an icy glare in her direction.

"Oh, wait, you're being serious? Sorry." The apology is

perfunctory. I can tell Avery is still rife with the bemusement I'm full of as well. But I'm hiding it better. I haven't become a master actor—I just know that Tyler is deadly serious. I'm too scared to play around.

"Emma and I should have been co-captains of the FIRST Robotics team, but she wanted it for herself. It's important to support women in engineering, plus she was my girlfriend, so I deferred. Besides, I did everything else right. Perfectly. Rowing captain, championship winner, created a nonprofit, launched an app, near-perfect GPA." He pauses, seeming to grind his teeth, then takes a steadying breath. "You know, my SAT score wasn't perfect, but fine. Emma dearest, or whatever asshole replaced me, fixed that for me. I'm smart, and capable, and fucking talented. But rejected from Cornell ED. Because I'm a white guy. And Emma, fucking Emma, gets into Harvard? Her GPA was barely higher than mine. And I carried her in FIRST. Drummed up half the business for her SAT scam, too. I'm the entrepreneur. The planner."

He's spitting fury, and Avery and I let him talk. And he does. He's comfortable now.

"You know Milo got in? He got a four on his AP Physics exam. I got a five. It's because he's a quarter Latinx, so he got to tick that box and had a leg up on me."

Oh, great, now comes the racist-tirade portion of his confession. We all know there's a racist undercurrent to college admissions hand-wringing anytime someone like Tyler doesn't get what they want. But hearing it spoken so plainly is . . . uncomfortable. He's not done.

"Your boy Ethan? Half-Black, so Harvard. Snooped that out on Tipton's computer when I planted the earring in his office. And, of course, Sierra. Yale."

I think that if Sierra were here, she'd have punched Tyler in the face already, and this would be over. Except, no, she wouldn't, because she's done everything in her power to fight ugly stereotypes, and here Tyler is, insinuating that everything is easier for her because of her race. She *earned* her spot at Yale. What a dick.

"If I got to tick one of those boxes, you know I'd get in. It's just not fair." Tyler pouts like a literal toddler throwing a tantrum.

"So, what? You get Emma's captain position? Revenge on her for taking what you wanted?" I'm still trying to understand.

"No, that's not it at all. It is what it is. My GPA, résumé, SAT score. It's all about the essay. That's what let me down. Let *us* down." He indicates Avery, who bristles.

Me, my insides are constricting, shriveling up as realization dawns. "You killed Emma so you could write a fucking college admissions essay?"

The psycho asshole smirks. "Megan is wrong about grief essays. You watch. Emma's death has showcased my sensitivity, my strength. Grit."

I'm stunned into silence. Avery makes a high-pitched noise in the back of her throat and then lets loose. "What the fuck! Are you hearing this?"

"What's the matter, sis? You wrote about the same thing. Not as well as me, though."

I dig my fingers into my palm to stop myself from correcting his grammar. He's a sociopath.

"Did you ever think that maybe you didn't get into Cornell because they saw right through you? That maybe you're just mediocre."

Avery's words spark a flash of white-hot anger. Tyler's mask slips, charm leaking from him, and all that's left is cold derision.

"I almost killed you, you know. I narrowed it down to the two of you. But I had to consider who would make for better essay fodder. Emma hid her sins better than you did. She made a better victim. Nobody mourns the mean girl."

"I'd rather be a bitch than a sociopathic murderer. You're done, Ty. We got you."

For a second I'm confused. What happened to Avery conspiring in my murder to save her from being SAT scam collateral damage? Then I see her draw a phone from the back pocket of her pants.

"Your passcode was easy to guess," she says, tossing me my phone. "Sorry for pretending to want to murder you." Then to Tyler: "Say hi to Detective Cataldo. She's been listening attentively to your confession."

"That won't hold up in court," Tyler scoffs, but his bravado is false. I can see the panic in his eyes.

"No, it won't. Recording people without their consent is illegal in the state of Massachusetts, so we didn't bother. But the point is, she knows. You don't get to lie anymore."

I am momentarily awestruck by the sheer unadulterated badass bitch that is Avery Montfort. I was right to never underestimate her.

But there is still the matter of Tyler and the gun. He raises it with his left hand, tries to anchor his grip with the other hand, but grimaces. I seize the opportunity, charging forward in my best impression of a football player. I hit his chest, and it's like barreling into a solid wall; Tyler grunts but doesn't fall. So I punch him between the legs and wrest the weapon from his hand as he winces in pain. Then both Avery and I stand over him, skillet and gun poised, until the police arrive.

CHAPTER THIRTY-TWO

In the movies, they cart away the killer in handcuffs, shoving him into a police car whose blinding lights throw swirls of blue and red onto the wan faces of the shocked partygoers. It's in slow motion, with a dramatic swell of music as the camera cuts to the heroine, who survived the fight, shaken and bloody but triumphant. Justice is served. Everything is going to be okay.

That's not how it goes in real life. Not when the rich and privileged kill and get caught.

Mr. St. Clair hires Tyler the best defense lawyer money can buy, the kind who has all sorts of connections with respected journalists and rags alike. The best defense is a good offense.

Stories smearing Emma's character begin to appear immediately.

She cheated and backstabbed her way to the top of the class.

She stole her best friend's spot at Harvard by sleeping with the college counselor.

She ran a test scam for years.

Emma Russo was a common criminal.

From there, it snowballs and explodes into an international media frenzy. The College Board and ACT void the scores of everyone involved in the scam and launch an investigation. Claflin's name is dragged through the mud, first for hiring a predator like Tipton and then for producing such students and allowing the scheme to take place on its grounds. And, you know, there's the murder and all that.

The school opens an inquiry before winter break is even over, and the administration comes to a conclusion swiftly. It was my name that was used over and over again to print the fake IDs. The files themselves are wiped, but the digital traces remain. I was her roommate, one of the notorious Ivies. There is no proof that I wasn't involved.

I am informed of my expulsion by telephone one day before I'm due to return to campus. My things will be packed up for me and shipped to my home in Maryland, at Claflin's expense. The expulsion isn't official, don't worry; it won't be on my transcripts. I'm simply not welcome to return. Claflin wouldn't want to invite a lawsuit. Not that Mom and I could afford the lawyer.

My only consolation is that none of this is public. When the SAT cheating story is published by *Slate,* I am spared by the truth. I had nothing to do with it. But tell that to Harvard, which rescinds my early-decision acceptance in February. Or to the rest of my RD schools, which in April regret to inform me they are unable to offer me admission to the class of 2025. I don't know what Claflin did or didn't tell any of them, but based on the slew of rejections, it can't be good. Claflin probably didn't have to say anything at all, truth be told. My sudden transfer to a public school in Maryland to finish out senior year spoke loudly enough.

I think Avery, Margot, and Sierra might have checked in on me had it not been for the *Atlantic* article that dropped in late January. **They'd Kill to Get In,** the headline read over a pixelated image of Tyler. And at the end of the third paragraph: **And then, there are the Ivies.**

It wasn't talking about the schools.

My friends and I are exposed in ten thousand scintillating words to an audience of millions. Along with Tyler, we are endemic of the sociopathy running through an entire generation, obsessed with elite college admissions. That article goes on to win a Peabody. Heiress Avery Montfort, media mogul's daughter Sierra Watson, budding Broadway hopeful Margot Kim, and, of course, villainous victim Emma Russo are described in painstaking detail. And me?

> **Russo's roommate, a scholarship student from the Mid-Atlantic states, discovered her body one pitch-dark, frosty morning in December.**

That was all I got. A footnote in Emma's murder. It was the double-edged sword of it all. Publicly, I am too insignificant for the Ivies to claim, but privately, I was Claflin's perfect scapegoat.

In the end, I take a gap year. I graduate from public high school on time and, to my credit, with barely a dip in my GPA. But I have to start all over again on college applications in the fall. There are no Claflin recommendations, no rowing achievements to bolster my chances. Every school I applied to before is burned, given my complete slate of "mysterious" rejections. I aim for schools where Claflin doesn't have board members, alumni, undue influence. It's a short list.

And then, one year and three months after I found Emma's lifeless body in a rowing pool, in between my shifts of serving up caramel macchiatos at Starbucks and sweeping stale popcorn at the local movie theater, the subpoena for Tyler's trial arrives. Which is how I find myself in courtroom number 204, back aching from the punishing wooden benches, once again feet away from Emma's killer. Tyler is smug as shit in a swank suit, with a bloated defense team straight out of a Hollywood drama. I spy multiple cameras throughout the courtroom, capturing everything for the HBO documentary. Because of course there will be a documentary. I've been fastidiously avoiding emails and calls to participate.

Right now both the cameras and I are laser focused on the current witness, a girl I used to consider one of my closest friends.

"I told Emma to pound sand when she asked me to join her little operation," Sierra answers calmly. Tyler's defense team is slick and cocksure, but they're dealing with an Ivy. "She wanted to double her business with the girls, since the SAT was easy for me. Sixteen hundred on my first try. Anyway, I didn't need the money, and I wasn't about to let a bunch of privileged white kids benefit from my success." Sierra pulls a cluster of braids over her shoulder, fiddles with them. The only sign she's nervous.

"Why were you friends with a group of girls whose sole goal was to sabotage others in order to get into the Ivy League? Surely you didn't need them, with your grades and that SAT score." The lawyer has asked the question I've been burning with for too long.

Sierra sniffs, gives a microshrug. "I knew their secrets, and they knew mine. It was mutually assured destruction. Avery, Emma, and Margot made that clear. Keep your enemies close."

I cringe at the line, Sierra's most memorable from the *Dateline* special on the Ivies. I wonder if the PR specialist she hired wrote it for her.

"Secrets like Miss Russo having an affair with Mr. Tipton?"

Sierra smarts. "I never held that against Emma."

"Did you hold it against Mr. Tipton?"

"I didn't blackmail Mr. Tipton, if that's what you're implying."

"Objection," opposing counsel calls out.

"I'll move on," Tyler's lawyer responds.

But I don't move on. I always assumed Sierra was blackmailing Tipton. She cut the video feeds. Who else would have had access? And then it hits me like a thunderclap. *Paul.* Security had access to the cameras, and he was on the night shift. He would've seen Tipton and Emma hook up all the time. Instead of reporting the abuse of power, he did nothing. *Boys will be boys.* But in doing so, he handed the defense a healthy dose of reasonable doubt.

"What about Olivia Winters? What was her role in the friend group?"

I perk up at my name, despite the fact that in the lawyer's mouth it's said like a damnation.

"Olivia was harmless," she responds. "She wasn't my competition." Sierra's eyes flick over to me, and she at least has the grace to flinch, ever so slightly, as we lock gazes.

I should be relieved, but instead I just feel . . . empty. Bottomed out. Sierra didn't ever see me as competition. None of them did. We were doomed long before Emma died.

I can tell it's not what the defense wants to hear, either. Harmless nonliars don't make good patsies in a murder trial. Lacking further questions, Tyler's lawyer dismisses Sierra from the stand, and I barely notice as the judge calls a recess for lunch.

The courtroom is nearly empty when I feel a tap on my shoulder.

"Olivia?"

I recognize him immediately.

"Ethan," I reply, voice tight. I tilt my head up to get a proper look. He's wearing a goddamn Harvard hoodie.

He sits without invitation. "How are you?"

I stare at him. "Really?"

"I guess you're still mad," he says, sheepish. "I did try apologizing. You never replied."

"My mom tells me not to waste my energy on bullshit," I volley back. "You want to absolve yourself? Fine, I get why you did it. But there's no more romance or friendship after that. You can't come back from getting me expelled."

"I didn't get you expelled!"

"It's not what you did, Ethan. It's what you *didn't* do. You're the only one other than Tyler who knew I wasn't involved in the SAT scam. The only person who could have saved me. But you chose yourself." I let out a heavy breath. "Look, I might have done the same thing. But I wouldn't expect that person to be all hunky-dory with me."

"You talk like a grandma sometimes, you know." He smiles. But when I fail to match his expression, he adds, "Sorry," with that little Canadian *o* thing that I used to find adorable. Now it grates. Or maybe it's that he keeps apologizing.

I move to grab my stuff. "We're good now, okay? If that'll make you go away, we can be good."

"So you won't mention me on the stand? My role in the SAT thing? The prosecution hasn't mentioned it, so I think I'm in the clear. . . ."

I freeze. I want to kick the eager puppy I used to love.

"Go back to Harvard, Ethan. Live your dream. I gotta go." I haul myself up to my feet and head to the nearest exit. Let him remember the back of me.

I fly, fuming, into the farthest bathroom I can find to splash water onto my face. The defense's questions make it clear. They're trying to pin it all on me again, I'm sure. Shit like this sticks. I will never escape it.

I hear the creak of the old wooden door, then heels clacking on the yellowing tile.

"Oh," Margot says as she and Sierra round the corner. Guess they're still friends, then.

"Uh, hi," Sierra says, but to the floor, not my face. "How's it going?" She brings her eyes up to sink level.

"Oh, great. Love being used as a pawn in the defense argument to try to get Tyler to walk free."

"Yeah . . ." Margot shuffles back and forth. "But no way the jury will believe it. Hopefully."

I turn my focus to Sierra, her words from the stand still echoing in my mind.

She wasn't my competition.

"How's Yale?"

"Aside from some serious white nonsense, it's good. I basically live at Hogwarts. I'm pulling mostly As, some B pluses. Normal stuff. How about you?"

It's a social nicety, but it still stings. I shrug. "I'm taking a gap year. Applied to a few places, and I should find out soon."

"Like where?"

"University of Maryland, University of Missouri, University of Georgia, University of Alabama . . ." I hold back one school. My secret wish. I'll be too embarrassed if I don't get in. A fool to hope.

"Oh" is all she says.

"It really sucks you had to take a gap year. I don't see why you couldn't have attended one of your other schools," Margot says.

"I wasn't accepted to any schools," I say, and boy does that drop their eyes to the floor fast.

A toilet flushes, followed by the bang of a stall door. And there is Avery, in all her pearl-necklace-wearing, yuppie chic glory. "Not all of us have parents who can donate a cool million to a school so they'll . . . overlook a scandal. Enjoying University of Michigan, Margot?"

Margot's nostrils flare, but it's Sierra who jumps in with barbs flying fast. "That's rich, coming from you. First, how's Stanford, and second, how's kowtowing to the defense going?"

"I got into Stanford on my own merits. No namesake wings required. And I'm just keeping my enemies close."

Guess Avery saw the *Dateline* special, too. And Sierra's not wrong. Avery's been sitting right behind Tyler, dressed to the nines like an angelic schoolgirl. Everyone knows that her mom is paying for Tyler's defense. For Avery's Stanford tuition, too, I imagine. I'm afraid of what Avery will say on the stand. Or what she won't say.

Margot hooks her arm with Sierra's. "Come on, let's go find another bathroom. It's not worth it."

They don't even wave goodbye to me. I'm the afterthought friend again. The bathroom door closes behind them. So much for our reunion. But then, some friendships aren't meant to last forever. They occupy a moment in time, and then you move on.

I'm left with Avery blocking the exit.

"*You're* not worth it," Avery mumbles under her breath, crossing to the sinks to reapply her lipstick. It's a gorgeous coral that brings out the blue in her eyes. Which I note look watery. Is she going to cry? "Can you believe her? I'm not the one who called my friend a heinous witch on national television. Anyway, how are you?"

"Avery, seriously?"

She pivots away from the mirror, leans back on the sink, and purses her lips.

"I got expelled from Claflin because none of you would stand up for me. I've been working two jobs to save for college, in my gap year, I might remind you. The one I was forced to take."

"Olivia—"

But I don't let her cut in. "Thank you for standing up for me there with Margot, but it's a little late. And frankly, I can't believe you, talking to me like everything is normal when you're playing happy family on the defense side. What the hell, Avery? I know you're a messy bitch, but this really plumbs the depths of ethical lapse."

Avery crosses her arms over her chest, a wall erected with a cocked hip and half sneer to fortify the ramparts. "Are you finished?"

I give a terse nod.

Her expression falters slightly, as though she hadn't really expected me to give her the chance to talk.

"I'm sorry about what happened with Claflin. Really, about everything. I was a shitty friend. And person, a good half of the time. I've mellowed a lot in California. I'm out, first of all. Got a fully public girlfriend and everything. College cliché." She smiles to herself. "You'd like her. Eva is kind of intense, really into doing the right thing. Simpatico."

I do a double take. "Wait, why would you threaten to out Stina for being gay if you're also gay?"

Avery snorts. "Never happened. Stina and I were dating. I asked her to do me a solid and recommend you for editor, and she did. When Autumn found out and got suspicious, Stina covered my ass."

"You call making you seem like a homophobic sociopath covering your ass?"

"I didn't say I was smart. I regret it *now*. I regret a lot of things, truth be told. My priorities have shifted. And I know it's important to make amends." She offers her hand, and I take it, too shocked by an Ivy—Avery, of all people—actually apologizing.

A phone trills, and Avery pulls back with a groan. "That'll be Mommy Dearest checking in. Look," Avery continues with surprising sincerity, "I've got your back. When I'm on the stand, I'll tell the truth. You didn't do anything. You earned your spot at Harvard. And I'm sorry about that, too. Being so shitty about it. To Emma, too." She grimaces.

I find myself comforting her. "We all have regrets. And Emma . . . was complicated. I'm the moron who didn't realize the extent of it until she was gone. I still wonder all the time if she ever even liked me."

"We all liked you, Liv. Enough to have you around. We just . . . didn't treat you as nicely as we could have. Never got really close. It sucks, and I'm sorry."

We push out of the bathroom door, and the phone chimes again. "You've got to be kidding me!" Avery yanks her phone from her bag but then looks confused as she sees there's no notification.

I pull my phone from my pocket and realize it was my phone going off.

"Aves, actually . . ." I trail off, eyes glued to my screen, raking over the new email icon. My notifications are cluttered, so there's no text preview. I hover my finger over my in-box. Suck in cool air through my nose, brace for impact. Then I tap in and read through squinted eyes.

I scan the email twice to ensure I'm not hallucinating. A shuddered breath escapes, and I make an undignified yelping sound.

"Olivia, are you okay?"

"I got in," I choke out. I'm crying, good tears.

"Where?"

"Smith," I say. "Full fucking ride."

Avery rushes forward, pulling me into a tight hug and shrieking congratulations into my ear. It's surreal, celebrating with her. Fitting, though. After all we went through in the name of college admissions. Naturally, it would end here.

I'm going to be a Smithie. I let the realization settle in. Because I'm going, aren't I? Nothing UMD can offer will match it, and that's if I get in. And Smith is twenty miles from Claflin, because the universe loves some irony.

"But how?" Avery asks. Even now I'm not sure if she sees me as her equal.

I shake my head. I owe it all to Emma, in the strangest way. And to the only person other than Ethan who knew unequivocally that I had nothing to do with the SAT scam: Kaila Montgomery.

"Kaila's mom is the dean of students at Smith College. Kaila and I kept up with each other, and she told me to apply to Smith and she'd take care of the rest." True to her word, here I am. Kaila's very last fuck-you to Emma Russo and Claflin Academy just might be the making of me.

Avery hugs me again, and I'm so stunned I let her.

"Avery!" a voice calls down the hall. I tense, expecting Katherine Montfort, but instead a dirty blonde in a jean jacket marches over, stops just short of us.

"Hey, Kim," Avery says. This Kim does not look at all like the sort Avery Montfort would deign to speak to. Maybe California truly has mellowed her.

"We have a conference room at the Marriott rented for tonight so we can do your postmortem on the trial so far. Good?"

"Yeah, just has to be after dinner with the Wicked Witch of the West." Summoned like said witch, Avery's phone finally does ring again, with the famous string riff from *The Wizard of Oz*. Avery huffs. "I have to go. See you later!"

I don't know if she means me or Kim.

Now alone, Kim sticks out her hand for a shake. "Olivia, right? Kim Swanson, Super Blue Pictures. I've been trying to reach you."

Shit. This is the documentary.

"Oh, hi." I hope I don't sound too strained.

"I understand your reluctance to participate, but I promise you I'm not a vulture. It's not about vilifying any of you, but about a system. I'm offering you a chance to tell your side of the story. The scholarship student who got screwed."

I can't help my surprise. "You know about that?"

"Avery told us everything. It was her idea to get in touch." Kim senses my hesitation. She fishes in her purse for something. "Here's my card. We're in the Quincy Room at the Marriott all week from five, doing one-on-ones. Stop by if you change your mind."

I take the card to appease her. Problem is, all documentaries have bias. Can I trust that this one will be biased in my favor? I'm doubtful. Avery must have lost her mind to have agreed to participate. Then, of course, she got the brunt of the *Atlantic* article fallout. They parodied her on *SNL*. The documentary is probably image resuscitation for her.

But after the trial, will I need some PR life support as well? Tyler's lawyer seems determined to dredge up all our dirty laundry.

I tuck the card into my bag, just in case. Now to call my mom and let her scream my ear off about Smith.

"You'll get used to the lights," Kim says, taking a seat across from me, not that I can really see her. She's haloed in light, a ghostly figure in the darkness.

The lights burn hot, but the hotel conference room is bone cold, AC blasting even in March.

"We'll backtrack in a later interview, go over basic biographical information. But tonight, let's focus on the trial. How are you feeling after the last few days? With questions leading back to you?"

Indeed, Tyler's lawyer has found a way to bring me up in nearly every cross-examination. More than once I've almost had to leave the courtroom. Before I respond, I think about how my answers will be used, chopped up as sound bites. "I'm an easy target. Not like the rest of them. The scholarship student. Emma used me so she could run her test-taking scam. I'll always have to live with that betrayal." I look down at my hands, think to chew my lip a bit. "The defense is scrambling to cast attention away from Tyler the sociopath. But the truth will out."

"Will it? In these cases, so often the wealthy, the privileged, get away with murder. Often literally. After Claflin expelled you without cause, you really believe in the system?"

We lock eyes. Hers dance between cocksureness and assessment. I work to project confidence. I'm a better actress than I used to be.

"Technically, I wasn't expelled," I say with a smirk.

"Right. You're on a forced gap year. A very different outcome from the actual cheaters."

"Oh, a bunch of them were forced to take gap years, too. To places like Rome, Seoul, London, Tokyo. Someone has to intern with the titans of industry, you know?"

That one makes Kim laugh. "It's good you have a sense of humor about it."

"Laugh so you don't cry." I shrug. "Anyway, I got my own good news the other day. I'm going to Smith." Saying it out loud to a stranger makes it feel even more real. I did it. This is what it was all for.

"Congratulations! I went to Amherst." I feel Kim seeing me with new eyes. I'm like her now, they say. A thrill of satisfaction runs through me. I've proven I belong. One more rung up the ladder.

"Was it all worth it?" Kim turns serious, her gaze a thousand-yard stare. Between her dark brown eyes and the black of the camera lens, I stare, losing myself to an abyss. A chasm of what-ifs.

What if Ethan had stood up for me.

What if Emma hadn't died.

What if she hadn't betrayed me, or anyone else, in the first place.

What if I'd never done anything underhanded in pursuit of college.

What if I'd never joined the Ivies.

But I know that if I went back, I would do it all over again. I would have accepted the Ivies' invitation in every possible scenario. I needed their approval like oxygen.

In the present, I take a deep breath. I smile for the camera. And I lie.

Because this is the game. The long game. Play the part, try to fit in. Earn their trust. Take their shit. Claw my way up, up, up.

The bright lights burn my eyes. I stare, straight ahead, and don't blink.

ACKNOWLEDGMENTS

Every book is a deeply personal endeavor that forever marks for the author a particular span of time, but *The Ivies* holds a particularly bittersweet significance for me. I can mark the stages of drafting and editing this book by *before my mother died* and *after my mother died*. It's quite a thing to write a "murder book" in the midst of real-life death and grieving; *The Ivies* was alternately a distraction when I needed it and an outlet to process my feelings after she was gone. Quite morbid to share with perfect strangers, I know, but necessary for context. Though my mother died before she could read *The Ivies*, I did get to tell her about it before she got sick, and know she believed in me and it so much. She was the first person I thought of when it sold. And she is the first person I must think of here. Two books in a row I thanked her last, when she should have been and always will be first. So, first of all and always, thank you to my mother, Dorothy.

To my agent, Elana Roth Parker, for being the best human, business partner, and friend. I couldn't do any of it without your immense support.

To my editor, Elizabeth Stranahan—thank you for your brilliant guidance, detailed and thoughtful edits, and helping me to make this book better than I could have ever imagined. To the entire team at Crown and Random House for your support in making *The Ivies* sharper and helping to get it out in the world: Phoebe Yeh, Melinda Ackell, Barbara Bakowski, Alexandra Hess, Caitlin Whalen, Jenn Inzetta, Emily DuVal, and many more I've yet to meet. And thank you so much to photographer Christine Blackburne and designer Casey Moses for a cover that blew me away and made all my dreams come true!

To my lovely, wonderful, amazing friends who listened to me blather and brainstorm this book, who read drafts (often multiple!) and encouraged me every step of the way: I love you. Basically anyone who ever talked to me about or read this book: Rosiee Thor, June Tan, Gretchen Schreibner, Dana Mele, Emmy Neal, Lainey Kress, Kat O'Keeffe, Heather Kaczynski, Rebecca Schaeffer, Adrienne Kisner, Mary Elizabeth Summer, Kristin Dwyer, Tabatha Duckworth, Courtney Gould, Lindsey Meredith, Austin Siegemund-Broka, Alyssa Colman, Emily Skrutskie, Farrah Penn, Emily Duncan, Rory Power, Christine Lynn Herman, and so many more I am sure I have missed.

To the CPs and friends who did targeted beta reads, sensitivity reads, and multiple reads: I owe you all the things. Particularly: Natalie Simpson, Kevin van Whye, Emily Lloyd Jones, Emily Wibberley, Elly Blake, Deeba Zargarpur, Casey Fiesler, Jessica van Allen, and J. Elle.

To Tillabook, already thanked above but thanked here again. You got me through act two and are the best! Also, CHEESE!

Thank you as always to my WriteGirls: Joy, Taya, Sophia, and especially Miranda for her Yale connects. To Kevin Z for sharing your experience of elite Northeastern boarding schools. To every student who let me share a bit of their college admissions experience. Brainstorming, guiding, editing, and helping you is a joy. I'm proud of every single one of you, you brilliant diamonds. Also at WriteGirl, thank you to Alison Deegan and Leslie Awender, who run the college program. You do incredible work, and thank you for making me a part of it.

Thank you, Stacey Brook at College Essay Advisors, for your generosity, wisdom, and top-notch organizational skills. You made my time in private consulting a delight.

To Boston University, thank you for accepting me even though I quoted a Fiona Apple lyric in my admissions essay. I was a teenager with a lot of Feelings.

To my California family who are basically my actual family at this point: the Hannas. Thank you for always opening your home, sharing your holidays, letting me draft during football, and taking me to Disneyland, and for the cheeseballs. Patty, especially: love you forever.

And finally, to my family, for being there: Aunts Mary, Bonnie, and Mary Ann and Uncles George, Paul, and John; plus my cousins Katie, Sarah, George, Tom, Athena, Jimmy, Jordan, George, Teig, Bill, Erika, Kayla, and Mary Theresa.

ABOUT THE AUTHOR

Alexa Donne is the author of *Brightly Burning* and *The Stars We Steal*, sci-fi romance retellings of classics set in space. A graduate of Boston University, she works in TV marketing and has done pro bono college admissions mentoring since 2014. A true INFJ, in her "free" time she mentors with WriteGirl, organizes the Author Mentor Match program, and runs one of the most popular writing advice channels on YouTube. She lives in Los Angeles with two fluffy ginger cats named after characters from YA literature.

alexadonne.com